NapPily faiThful

ALSO BY TRISHA R. THOMAS

Nappily Ever After

Would I Lie to You?

Roadrunner

Nappily Married

Nappily in Bloom

Un-Nappily in Love

NapPily faiThful

Trisha R. Thomas

St. Martin's Griffin
New York

Published in the United States by St. Martin's Griffin, an imprint of St. Martin's Publishing Group

NAPPILY FAITHFUL. Copyright © 2008 by Trisha R. Thomas. All rights reserved. Printed in the United States of America. For information, address St. Martin's Publishing Group, 120 Broadway, New York, NY 10271.

www.stmartins.com

The Library of Congress has cataloged the first
St. Martin's Griffin edition as follows:

Thomas, Trisha R., 1964–
    Nappily faithful / Trisha R. Thomas. — 1st ed.
        p. cm.
    ISBN-13: 978-0-312-36131-0
    ISBN-10: 0-312-36131-9
    1. African American women—Fiction.   2. Women judges—Fiction.
3. Divorced men—Fiction.   4. Atlanta (Ga.)—Fiction.   5. Marriage—
Fiction.   6. Domestic fiction.   I. Title.
    PS3570.H5917N374 2008
    813'. 54—dc22

                                                                2007039756

ISBN 978-1-250-62388-1 (trade paperback)
ISBN 978-1-4299-3153-3 (ebook)

Our books may be purchased in bulk for promotional, educational, or business use. Please contact your local bookseller or the Macmillan Corporate and Premium Sales Department at 1-800-221-7945, extension 5442, or by email at MacmillanSpecialMarkets@macmillan.com.

Second St. Martin's Griffin Edition: November 2019

10   9   8   7   6   5   4   3   2   1

You are loved
To the girlz:
Tiffany, Hailey, Tracee,
Shawn, Shannon, Monae, and Tahira

Acknowledgments

I thank God for family, friends, and fans, for without them none of this would be possible. A great deal of appreciation to Kelly Mason, for being patient with all my court and law questions. Any errors of course are mine. I'm grateful to my first readers, Cameron Thomas and Seraphine Kinlow. To Rena Logan, my mom, for letting me know it was the best thing I'd ever written.

NapPily faiThful

Glass Houses

Delma Hawkins took in a deep breath and counted to ten while she slowly exhaled. Twenty-two years presiding over the municipal family court bench, only twice could she admit to making a mistake. The first was Latisha Barrow; fourteen and pregnant; she'd run away claiming her parents hated her but Delma ignored the child's pleas. Didn't all teenagers make the same claim? Her own daughter had played the hate card every time she didn't get her way. If Delma refused to let her stay out past ten or wear too tight clothes, or listened in on a phone call or two, she was labeled the Evil Witch of the South. "You hate me, don't you?" her daughter would accuse.

Well, if parenting a child to a safe, happy life with a tough hand was considered hateful then Delma was guilty as charged. Her daughter had graduated cum laude with a degree in criminal psychology, following in her old mom's footsteps, so she must've done something right.

However, in Latisha Barrow's case, the hate may have been real. A week after Delma remanded the girl to the custody of her mother and preacher father she was found dead in a bathtub filled with water and the bloody remnants of giving birth. The parents claimed they helped Latisha with a natural childbirth and only stepped away for a few minutes to tend to the newborn. When they came back, Latisha had drowned.

Mrs. Barrow eventually told the truth. Latisha died fighting and struggling as her parents tried to force her baptism in the bloody bathwater. "The blood of the innocent would wash away the sins of the flesh. If she'd only given herself over to Jesus," she professed while being led out of the courtroom in handcuffs. The baby was eventually adopted by a good family; Delma made sure of that. Mr. and Mrs. Barrow went to jail; she made sure of that, too.

The second mistake was not quite as tragic. No one had died in the Higgins household. Mr. Higgins, a black lawyer, Mrs. Higgins, a white housewife, refused to share equal custody of their seven-year-old son, each determined to crush the other parent into oblivion. Four appeals came down to who was less vicious, a father who used the old southern discipline of a tree branch to beat his son, or a mother who refused to let her boy play sports or go outside for fear he'd get too dark and suffer harsh words like *nigger* or *monkey* from the other children in the all-white neighborhood in Suffix County.

"You did know Mr. Higgins was a black man when you married him, did you not?" Judge Delma had asked the woman, with as little disdain as possible.

"Well yes, but my ex-husband's so much lighter. I didn't know our son would get so . . ."

Ahuh, go ahead, say it. "So what, Mrs. Higgins?"

". . . so dark," Mrs. Higgins replied in between sniffs and wipes of her tissue.

"Judgment for Mr. Higgins, full legal and physical custody." The gavel slammed down hard and final. "Mrs. Higgins will have visitation two weekends a month," Delma said through gritted teeth as she signed the order and nearly scratched a hole in the paper.

"That's not fair at all," Mrs. Higgins whimpered. "He's my son. Mine. I gave birth to him. This is so unfair."

A sly smile rose on Delma's face. "Unfortunately, you've taught your son a sad misconception that the darkness of his skin would limit his happiness. That, Mrs. Higgins, is not fair. Court dismissed." Delma considered herself an impartial judge, ignoring race, class, or pure ignorance, but that woman made her see red. Her decision in

Mr. Higgins's favor had nothing to do with facts, and all to do with personal fury. Judge Delma Hawkins took in another long deep breath. One, two, three . . .

Now there was this case, two sets of parents, one child. The little girl had eyes as big and bright as black pearls with dark satin lashes surrounding them. She reminded Delma of a living doll. An overused metaphor, but this child really was. Her round face and soft cheeks made for kisses and cuddles were no match for her spindly long arms and legs—like a baby giraffe not yet grown into her bones. Her hair was untamed curls in some parts and kinky tight in others, with a pretty bow across the center like a doll. Who wouldn't love her? Who wouldn't fight for a child so sweet?

The tap at the door shook Delma from her thoughts.

Hudson, her law clerk, stuck his head inside, then slipped his narrow chest past the door. "In here meditating or what?"

When she hired him, he claimed he was finishing up a law degree of his own. Turned out Hudson had barely finished high school, a con man who'd been in and out of jail on various misdemeanors. Being locked up in a juvenile facility for the better part of his young life gave him plenty of time to read. His favorite, *To Kill a Mockingbird*, made him want to be a lawyer. Real books were in lockup those days, not the hustling trash lining the library shelves *now*. These days a child released from a detention center knew more about how to pimp and sell drugs than when he went in . . . all courtesy of a *good* book.

"I'll be right out." Delma eyed him over her reading glasses. "How they doin' out there?"

"The natives are restless. Might be some chair-throwing, a little eye-gouging, and definitely some name-calling." He raised one brow. "Haven't seen a good fight lately."

"Well there better not be one today. Five minutes," she said with finality. "Keep an eye on them. I don't want to put anyone in lockup today for acting silly."

The door closed gently. When Hudson's footsteps disappeared

she got up and stretched. The back pain came and went, but mostly came on days like this one, throbbing around the meaty thickness where her waistline used to be. Her doctor warned her to lose some weight; strike that, a lot of weight. The daily stress of her job along with her dedication to M&M's Barbecue & Fried Fish on Berber and Fifteenth Street was a bad combination for her five-three frame.

She picked up the paper with her statement typed out. She read the first sentence out loud. "In the case of *Venus Johnston-Parson versus Airic P. Fisher* regarding minor child Mya Fisher, the court has entered a decision." Her voice cracked at the start of the next sentence. Delma balled up the paper, crushing it to its smallest form before throwing it in the trash. She walked to the wood-paneled wall and stared at nothing it seemed, until she slid aside a small circular disk. She pressed her face against the hole. There they were, both sets of parents. Poor Mya was somewhere else without a clue her life was about to be changed forever.

"Father Lord, Jesus, give me strength." Delma straightened her robe, picked up her gavel, and headed out to make what would be her third most regretful decision, the one that could end her career, her relationships, and all things as she knew them. People in glass houses should never throw stones, and here she was about to toss a boulder.

1

Venus

Two thousand miles across the country in a quest to make a new start, I lay awake listening to the sounds of the new house. Jake slept on his side with his back to me. He wasn't really sleeping. Wide awake, same as me. I took a chance and slid my thigh against his, scooting closer and curling myself around his body. I nuzzled against his ear. He stayed still. I slid my hand between his arm and waist until he clamped tighter, blocking entry.

I whispered, "Jake."

He said nothing, his body refusing to give way.

It was his idea to move, to get away. His choice was Atlanta, where a friend in the music industry had invited him to help produce a young unknown artist's first album, so why not take the opportunity to make a fresh start. I agreed. I thought the change would be good for us both. We sold our house on the California coast and moved where the acreage was big but the price was small.

Atlanta wasn't all that different from Los Angeles, something I noticed right away. Women had their fair share of enhanced breasts, Botoxed foreheads, and collagen-filled lips. Women of color proudly wore heavy weaves though it was too hot to be carrying around five packages of hair. Men had their equal share of symbolism, shiny high-end vehicles, expensive bling, and too much time on their hands. The real difference was on a piece of paper called "deed of ownership." It was probable that there were more home owners than renters in Atlanta even though the per capita incomes were the same. The guy idling in a nice Benzo most likely owned the garage to go with it. In L.A. the cost of home ownership equaled two limbs and one's firstborn, their brother's firstborn, and maybe sister's, too. Living at home with your mama wasn't a bad thing, just a reality like earthquakes, landslides, and smog.

Our new home looked like the White House, only it was beige. Endless trees surrounded the land. It took three little brown men on riding mowers to cut the grass. Within a couple of days the grass grew back even taller. I had a theory about why the grass and trees grew so bountiful: slaves. I was sure my ancestors were buried under the ground where I slept, only adding to the many reasons I spent most nights with my eyes wide open.

Jake told me to stop being ridiculous. Million-dollar homes were not built on cemeteries. Well, that would explain everything, seeing how our people were buried right next to the cotton they picked every day. No headstone. No markings.

I was tired of the insomnia. I was tired of the loneliness. Before I could go into full-throttle whining mode, my cell phone buzzed and shook until it landed on the floor. Had to be my mother. The three-hour California–Georgia time difference had yet to sink in, resulting in a lot of midnight phone calls. She made her late-night calls after watching reruns of *Magnum P.I.* Tom Selleck was the only man my mother threatened to leave my father for. Twenty years after the last episode and she still had faith Tom could fit those tight-ass khaki short shorts.

I crawled over Jake feeling for the phone where it'd fallen between a box labeled BATHROOM and another one that said KITCHEN. In fact boxes surrounded us wall to wall. Two months in the new house and unpacking seemed like a waste of time. Why bother, I thought every time I went to open a box, feeling I'd soon have to pack again.

I answered with fake grogginess so my mother would get the

hint it was late in our part of the country. The voice I heard in return was bad timing to say the least. "Venus."

"What?" I foolishly tried to whisper. Jake still lay unmoved, pretending to be asleep even after my elbow landed in his rib cage.

"I want to see Mya," the man's voice answered back.

"How nice of you." I tried not to sound full of hatred, but the whisper came out in a hissing sound. "Please, I mean, really. Can I call you back during daylight hours, how about that? Or will you be sleeping?" Because as far as I was concerned Airic Fisher was a vampire who'd been asleep for the last three years and was suddenly awakening with a thirst for blood. Long-lost blood, namely our daughter. He hadn't seen Mya since the day she was born but suddenly now he *needed* to see her. I'd briefly guessed, or hoped, he was dying and it was his one final wish. No such luck.

I slammed the phone closed then jumped when Jake's hand landed on my shoulder. "What's going on?"

My heart was racing. I was about to explain when I realized these were the most words Jake had spoken to me in months, causing my anger to swell. I shook my head. "Leave me alone."

His hand trailed down my back. "Tell me," he said, sounding like the voice of comfort.

"So now you want to be my friend?" I pulled my knees to my chest. "That was Airic. He wants to see Mya."

The comforting hand fell away.

Jake said nothing. Shocked. Confused. Stunned back into silence. I knew the feeling. Airic's messages, which I refused to answer, had started weeks before with a gentle *Hello, how are you, wishing you well.* Then shortly after, *How's Mya, I bet she's beautiful just like her mother.* Then came the real reason for the calls, *I think it's time I become a father to my daughter.*

But Mya already had the father position filled quite nicely. Didn't matter if Jake and I weren't getting along. Didn't matter that we regularly said no more than three words to each other in a full day. There was a method to our madness and being responsible parents was the one thing we took seriously.

I closed my eyes. "He wants to see Mya."

"What the hell does that nig—" He rethought his choice of noun. "Why out of the blue does he want to see Mya? Did you call him? Have you been talking to him?"

"Are you serious?" I attempted to get up. Jake's grip kept me from moving. "Excuse you." I eyeballed his hand. He kissed my shoulder instead.

"Look, I'm just saying, this makes no sense. Not one word, then all of a sudden he pops up out of thin air, calling here in the middle of the night like he's got a right to. It doesn't make sense."

Jake snatched the phone out of my hand.

"No . . . uh-uh." I snatched it right back. "You are not calling him."

"Then tell me something. A simple answer. I'll help you; you just fill in the blanks. Airic wants . . ." he sang out and waited for my answer.

"He started calling a few weeks ago. I ignored him and thought he'd go away. But I think he's serious. He wants to see her."

"This is bullshit." He leaned back against the pillows.

"Jake, I'm just as upset as you are."

"I'm not playing this game. I'm not. He needs to put it on the table. I need to know what I'm dealing with."

And there it was.

"What *you're* dealing with?" The words danced and sputtered against my ears. "What you're dealing with . . . is that what you just said?" By this time I was standing, pacing back and forth. If Airic's intrusion was what it took, the catalyst for the wall to come down, then so be it. "How is this all about you? Why is this only Jake's problem? I'll tell you—"

"Keep your voice down." That was Jake's tactic when he was being out-talked or out-debated, usually followed by, *Mya's in the next room*, only this time she wasn't. She was five doors down, courtesy of our new southern manor with its nine bedrooms and four baths. I hadn't thought about who was going to be scrubbing all those toilets when I signed on the dotted line. Space. Jake needed space. I needed space. Yet here we were with nothing between us but animosity.

"No . . . I will not keep my voice down. I've been walking on eggshells around you for months, and I'm sick of it. Now you want to know what's going on. Well guess what, so do I."

◯◯

Together four years, Jake and I had our share of ups and downs. The last half of the year registered as a definite downer. Back in Los Angeles, Jake had been charged and arrested for murdering a man. Byron Steeple had stolen millions and nearly bankrupted JP Wear right under Jake's nose. After finding out about the embezzlement Jake fired him, but the damage was already done. JP Wear was left in a miserable spot forcing Jake to sell off half his company or lose it all. He sold it and eventually lost the other half out of sheer bitterness.

The night Jake was taken away in handcuffs was the night a part of me died, a part of us both. Right then I knew what was meant by "hell on earth," summed up in one word, *fear.* Constant unnerving fear. Jake hired a very expensive lawyer, Georgina Michaels, famous for celebrity cases including Guy Richardson, better known as Big Pimpin', the music producer charged with racketeering, IRS fraud, and manslaughter, just to name a few. If she could get Big Pimpin' off, Jake would be a cakewalk, especially since he was innocent. She happily took his case, not because he was still a celebrity but because he could afford to pay and in the land of bling, money is the answer to everything.

The lawyer fees could have bought a midsize country, say, Paraguay.

There was no proof, no physical evidence. There was no *CSI* smoking gun or eyewitness. Had it not been for Byron Steeple's boyfriend, a prominent gay rights activist who accused the city of discrimination and threatened to bring a civil suit on behalf of his slain lover, charges would have never been filed against Jake at all.

The expensive lawyer got the case dismissed. A small price to pay; your money or your life. We still had our health, as my mother liked to say. We had each other and enough to buy a pretty southern mansion to pretend all was right in the world, though we both knew it wasn't. Nothing had been right for some time.

Was Jake really guilty? Had he beat a man senseless for stealing and bankrupting his company? The answer was simply no. I knew the truth and the answer was still no. I would never believe any different. Only thing I knew for sure was that our lives had been irrevocably changed. Adversity resulted in new strength, or so I'd been told. I'd yet to see the good come out of what we'd already been through. The drive beaten right out of me, I was tired of waiting. The distance between us was growing like weeds after a summer rain, out of control, no end in sight.

"*We*, do you understand? I'm not speaking French here. You and me, we've been together through thick and thin. I worried, I prayed, I jumped for joy when they finally dropped those charges against you. You didn't go through that alone. How can you disrespect me every single day by pretending you went through it alone?"

He was up on his feet holding me against his bare chest. His heart was beating twice as fast as mine.

"No." I pushed or at least attempted to move him but Jake was solid. True, he never saw one day inside a jail cell but he was as thick and muscular as a man who'd done the time. His prison was self-built in his head. He ran five miles a day, lifted weights and did sit-ups as if preparing for a heavyweight champion fight, always believing they were coming for him, that the madness wasn't over.

He rocked me back and forth. He kissed the top of my head. "I'm sorry," he whispered. "Please, okay." All the hurt, the pain, the fear he'd been holding spilled like a burst dam. I kissed the salty moistness off his chin. The kiss was light at first then ravenous. We both had been starved far too long.

His hand trailed to the center of my thigh. His fingers gently danced in the moistness then pushed inside. I grabbed his head and led his face to the center of my chest. His lips skimmed the tip of my nipple. The first tender bite made me gasp. He took a hold of each breast, barely a handful, taking his time suckling, licking, nibbling back and forth. His tongue was a powerful weapon made even more lethal with the workings of his smooth palms and steady fingertips.

The pulse had grown full and warm with no other place to go. Before I knew it, he slid into position and pushed every inch of himself deep inside, stretching the tightness he'd not entered for some time. I held on to his hips, still needing more but at the same time relishing the sweet pain. I inhaled the beauty of him, the warmth and safety. He pressed his face into my arched neck.

A wave of warmth swept across my entire body. I begged for what I'd been missing. He moved faster, harder, each pump of his hips getting me one step closer. He slowed, tasting my nipples to stay on task. His pushed his fingers between our moist bodies and mingled lightly with the uncontrollable wetness. He found the magical spot, the tender button, and rubbed it back and forth. He knew exactly how many flicks it would take to get to the center of this Tootsie Pop.

"Right there, baby," I whispered.

Throbbing jolts shook my body. He waited for my panting to subside until I calmed to a heated stir. He took full control of my hips, pushed my legs open wider and went after the best part. His shoulders flexed. I held on tight and kept up with his rhythmic strokes.

He scooped his arm around my body, pulling me up. He finished, letting out a hoarse moan. For the first time in our big Georgia house we made love. His weight fell against me and I took a hold of his hand, grateful we'd come to this place, regardless of how. Sometimes adversity was like glue for relationships, a formidable foe, a cause to unite and fight for. I didn't know it then, but this would be the biggest fight of our lives.

2

Trevelle

At forty-eight, Trevelle Doval hadn't planned on falling in love and getting married. Her plan was to simply live in abundance and joy. God's plan was entirely different, thank goodness. Trevelle and Airic met only two short years ago. She'd been invited to speak to the religious studies department on the college campus where Airic taught business ethics. Something he knew a great deal about, with the SEC closing him out of his company because of unethical behavior. Proof that God works in wondrous ways. How else would she and Airic have met?

He was her soul mate, delivered right to her feet. A smart, loving man who'd been put in her path by divine order. A plan she couldn't have devised or imagined if she'd tried.

She watched as her husband hung up the phone, once again making the same plea to the woman who'd birthed his child. The jade green St. John knit sweater made it easy for Trevelle to lift her arms open, ready to offer solace.

"You knew it wasn't going to be easy but God's way never is." She wrapped her arms around Airic's lean shoulders. They hugged gently, then released. Once, his watchband had snagged the delicate knit she liked to wear so he understood to keep the contact light.

"She's got a lot of anger." Airic used the white handkerchief from his top suit pocket to dab the nervous moisture from his forehead. His wide eyes stared out, blank and confused. "This isn't going to be easy."

Trevelle took both his hands. "Don't let it deter you from doing what's right." Trevelle batted her long dark lashes and continued to smile. But then the smile disappeared, replaced by stern compassion. "Every minute and every day you put this off, that child's life could be in danger. She's living with a man who committed murder, the first deadly sin. A mother who's been institutionalized, Lord bless her soul. Time may be what Venus needs, but it's not what that child needs. Anything could happen each moment you delay."

Airic contemplated Trevelle's words of caution. "I can't force her."

"You have absolutely every right. You most certainly can force her." Trevelle pushed her heavy mane of hair off her shoulders. She moved to the temperature control in the hotel room and pushed it to a cool sixty degrees. They'd checked into the Beverly Wilshire in Los Angeles the night before with separate but adjoining suites for that reason, among others. Trevelle liked it chilly, anything to obliterate the scent of the other guests who came before her.

Airic hated the idea of different rooms. It was one thing to have separate sleeping arrangements in the privacy of their home, but in the public domain he found it embarrassing. Mr. and Mrs. Fisher being handed two different room keys by the desk clerk. Trevelle would have it no other way. Separate beds allowed for more peaceful rest. If there was one thing she needed it was her sleep. She was the most celebrated gospel evangelist nationwide. Millions who loved and adored her watched her televised ministry. Last thing she needed were bags underneath her eyes from listening to a man's snoring all night. But her biggest, most important reason lay hidden like an ugly monster waiting for darkness to come alive.

She drew water at the bathroom sink to fill up the vase with fresh cut flowers. Bouquets in clear glass vases sat in various arrangements on any and every flat surface, a requirement of Trevelle's while traveling. They'd covered six cities in five days for her book promotion tour. The scent of nature replaced the stale odor of hotel rooms, giving vitality and energy.

"You have every right to be with your child, Airic. Why is that so hard to understand?" She wasn't through with the subject of little Ms. Venus and Airic's sudden cold feet. They'd agreed on the plan, a simple one, and now he was having second thoughts. After seeing pictures of the precious child, Trevelle was more determined than ever to give Mya a good home in a spiritual environment surrounded by God's love. The thought of that child living with an accused murderer made her sick to her stomach.

Her husband wasn't stupid. The man was downright brilliant when it came to the management of the Doval Ministry Foundation. He'd turned her money over six times her initial worth, giving her the true status of millionaire wealth. There was no denying how much he'd changed her life in the short time they'd known each other. The least she could do was help him be the man he should be.

"If she doesn't agree to meet with you in the next couple of days, we'll file the papers. All we have to do is say the word and the lawyer is ready to move." She picked up her clutch bag and tucked it under her arm. "Shall we go? Dinner reservations are near impossible to get at Table 8." Her patience was wearing thin of talking Airic into doing the right thing. They rode the elevator down in silence.

Before they could make it outside the large lobby doors, a woman's voice came from a few feet away. "It is her," the woman shrilled, making her way toward Trevelle and Airic. "Ms. Doval." Her tan shirt and burgundy skirt was the uniform the hotel maids wore. She came toward Trevelle with her arms and hands positioned for a hug.

Trevelle put on a face of grace and appreciation to greet her enamored fan but clutched her purse front and center to avoid full contact.

"Oh my goodness, you don't know how your words have helped me. God is good. God is so good."

"Yes, he is." Trevelle shook the woman's hand. "What is your name?"

"Wanda Jacobs. When you came to L.A. a couple of years back,

I drove two hours in traffic just to hear you speak. Ms. Doval, you are an inspiration. I was raped when I was twelve years old, same as you. Repeatedly molested and abused by a grown man, same as you." Wanda spoke hurriedly, fearing her time would be cut short. "Then I spent the next twenty years of my life blaming myself, until you showed me the way. Ohmigoodness, are you speaking tonight? How could I have missed knowing? You are such a blessing in my life, Ms. Doval."

Trevelle kept the woman's hands embraced in front of her. "Knowing God's love is the blessing and the power."

"It's been a struggle, but I'm making it."

"I will say a special prayer for you, Wanda, for all things are possible through Christ our Lord Savior." Trevelle touched the young woman's forehead. "Go with grace." Tears sprang from the young woman's clear eyes.

"Thank you, Jesus. Thank you," Wanda sang in a low hum.

When the woman opened her eyes, Trevelle would be nowhere in sight. She and Airic were in the car and headed to the gourmet restaurant. She watched from the tinted window as the woman raised her arms to the sky and did a small dance of appreciation and called out a prayer.

I was raped when I was twelve years old, same as you.

Trevelle doubted very seriously if anyone's life had been the same as hers.

She was nothing but a child when she'd learned how to please a man. She first saw Cain drive through her neighborhood in his bronze-colored Cadillac with shiny spoke wheels when she was a mere child. She watched the car go up and down her street like clockwork. She had no idea he'd been watching her grow the exact same way, like clockwork, as she grew into a pretty preteen.

One day he slowed, then stopped. When she realized he was backing up, she wanted to run into the house. She would have if

Kevin, her older brother and his friends weren't smoking herb parked on the living room floor and sofa like sprawled ivy. She hated being in the house when they were high, the way her brother and his friends stared at her, eyes low, lips wet, watching her every move. Hated the way her brother dissed her in front of his friends.

"What'd ya'll looking at my ugly sister for? She so ugly, she fugly. Look at her, flat-chested, big feet, she got a nose like an ostrich beak. Get the hell out of here," he'd yell at her, throwing whatever was at his reach. She'd scamper off like a punished puppy.

None of her brother's antics worked in dissuading them from being attracted to his baby sister. His friends had eyes. They could see the soft brown skin, her silky dark hair long and thick to match her cat eyelashes. They knew the young slim girl was budding into womanhood and each one of them hung around hoping they'd be first in line when it came time.

Though Kevin's friends ignored him, Trevelle heard and believed every word. She was fu-gly. She saw what her brother saw, a nothing, a nobody. Her low self-esteem made her ripe for the picking when Cain backed his car up that day and asked if she wanted a ride. She'd be the first girl to ever ride in it, he said. "Brand-new Cadillac with leather seats, all for you." Though she'd witnessed numerous women, lots of them, with glossy lips and Afro wigs of every shape and color pushed underneath his shoulder while he drove with one hand on the wheel. And the car was hardly new. The same car she'd been watching half her life go up and down her street.

She looked back at the small yellow house before getting into Cain's car. No one would miss her. Her mother worked all day at the elder care facility. After work, her mother's reward for cleaning up old people's puke and piss all day was to head straight to the Elk's Lodge where she drank and hung out till two in the morning. As for her father, Trevelle knew he lived in New York with two daughters with his blue-eyed soul girlfriend. He sent money by Western Union whenever their mother threatened to take him to court but not enough to pay for gymnastics like Trevelle wanted, or for Kevin's baseball uniform and cleats. Kevin would have to sit out the season and eventually join another team called "drug dealers and thieves." Though the two were not inclusive—dealers rarely boosted cars—Kevin was multitalented and did both.

She rode in Cain's smooth car, amazed how she couldn't feel the potholes or bumps in the street. The seats were soft, caressing the tender skin of her legs. Her cutoff jeans were too tight, precisely why she'd cut them in the first place. She'd noticed Cain's line of vision and wished she hadn't cut them *so* short. His hand landed on the thickest part of her thigh. "You sure is lookin' fine these days. How old're you now?"

Trevelle marveled at the fact he could look her dead in the face and still drive. "Twelve. I'll be thirteen next Saturday."

"Um. So I guess you never let somebody touch you down there before, huh?" His hand moved up her thigh. He pushed and struggled to wiggle his fingers past the frayed edge of her shorts. She was glad they were too tight. He kept trying, rubbing the inside of her thighs too roughly, pulling the skin until she thought it would rip.

"I haven't . . . never . . ." she stuttered, nervous at how much she wanted his hands to finally reach their goal.

"Look at you." He gave up and moved his hand under her shirt giving her soft formed nipple a pinch. "I bet you don't even wear a bra yet. Just a tenderoni, ain't cha? Umph, umh umh."

"Where we going?"

"Anywhere you want to go." Again, he faced her seemingly too long for driving safety. She averted her eyes, hoping he'd do the same and watch where he was going.

She thought about it. She hadn't been outside of the city limits. The farthest she'd gone was on a bus trip to Temple Baptist Church to join other choirs for a concert. On the way there she'd noticed a great big mall, bigger than five or six Kmarts put together.

"You ever been to that giant shopping mall?" She didn't know the name of it. She didn't even know what highway it was near.

Cain wasn't the church-going type so describing it as on the way to Temple Baptist would've been a waste.

"I know where it is," he said. "I'll take you there, buy you something special for your birthday."

He kept his promise. He bought her everything: outfits, shoes, vinyl belts, one red, one green, one white to match the boots he'd also paid for. He wanted her to try everything on together so he could see how hot she looked. They checked into a motel. She went into the bathroom to change. When she came out wearing the mini-skirt, halter top, hat, and boots she was shocked to see Cain sitting on the edge of the bed naked. "Come here, baby girl. Damn, look at you, umph." He licked his lips and squeezed the hardness of his erection.

Part of her wanted to run right out the door, the other part relieved for being wanted, desired by a grown man.

"You ever seen one of these?" He stroked himself up and down. The answer was no. She'd never seen a man's private parts before, at least not a real one. Only the silly pictures her classmates drew on notes and passed around for instant laughs. "Touch it. I swear it won't bite."

The razor-sharp energy shot up her hand. Soft. Hard. Hot. Vulnerable yet powerful at the same time. He grabbed her hand when she tried to pull away. "Squeeze it right here," he moaned. "Why you so beautiful, huh? I'ma get into trouble messing around with some little girl. A virgin, too." His hand slid up her skirt, one finger flicked the panties out of the way while the other tested. "I don't want to take that from you." He kissed her lightly then stuck his full tongue into her mouth. Her head swayed and warmth overtook her.

"There's something else you can do, so I don't have to take that from you." The lilt in his voice grew deep. "Do this for me, right here." He pulled her to her knees, grabbing hold of the back of her neck as she strained to pull away.

The head of his thing barely touched her parted lips and she already felt dirty. "I don't know how." She struggled against his grip.

"I'ma show you. Relax. Easiest thing you ever done. Keep you from having babies, too. You don't wanta be one of them girls having babies before high school."

Her mouth opened to the width of him. She tasted and cringed, ready to be sick. But to her surprise, Cain tasted rich and thick as cocoa, the real kind her grandmother used for baking. His hand guided her head lower, to take more of him into her mouth. Love at first bite one could say. She choked, pulling back, then tried again.

"That a girl," he said, holding her shoulders steady.

"We're here," Airic said, touching her shoulder. The driver stood outside the car holding the door open in front of the restaurant. "Sometimes you scare me, drifting off like that," he said.

Yes, she had to agree. Her memory was a scary place. "Just daydreaming of the new life we have planned." She smiled behind her dark sunglasses. "You're going to make an amazing father," she said. "And I'm going to make a great mother."

3

Jake

Jake had nothing against Airic Fisher. Every now and then he came across Mya's birth certificate, always surprised to see someone else's name under *father* instead of his own, as if it would magically change itself. He knew being a father meant more than the name typed in the rectangular box. Jake knew better. He'd seen his father try to strangle his mother before walking out on them forever. His father did everybody a favor by walking away. Jake discovered biology was only one-tenth of the law. The other nine-tenths went to possession, dedication, and full out love and support. Edgar Laws and his mother were only together a few years, but in that short time, he learned what a real father was supposed to be. Even after they broke up, Edgar showed up to every talent show, basketball game, open house, parent-teacher meeting. Nothing could keep that man away except the cancer that eventually took his life. Jake was fifteen when Edgar died, but the seeds of virtue and honesty had been sown. "Do what you say you're gonna do and never turn your back on the people who love you." At least he'd followed most of Edgar's philosophies.

Jake had turned his back on his wife, but it was time to heal, to make everything right again.

"You're up. I got some bagels." She crouched, then crawled onto the king-size bed holding the bag. Her tank top was cut low, showing a healthy amount of smooth brown skin. Her hair was pulled

back with a headband and the rest stood high and wide like a cres-
cent moon. She was all natural, had been since the day he met her.
So different from the video vixens he'd been used to dealing with.
The very thing that captured his heart and mind was her unique-
ness, her wish to stand strong with independent thoughts and actions. Even if sometimes they coarsely went against his own needs
and demands.

He rolled over and leaned on one elbow to spy into the bag. Asi-
ago cheese and onion, his favorite. "Where'd you find these?"

"There's an Einstein Bros. right around the corner. I'm liking
this neighborhood more and more."

Jake didn't respond. He sometimes felt guilty for making her
move so far away from her family. They'd left California fast and in a
hurry. He missed it, too. His mother was there. His brother who
played for the Golden Warriors in the NBA. He missed the beach
where he ran almost every morning. He missed his company and
the one friend he could still trust, Legend, who was now running
said company. *When you're ready it'll be here, man.*

He reached into the bag and gave her the first bite and then took
one. Toasted to perfection with warm cream cheese. "Hmmmph."

"I'm going to meet Airic this morning," she announced, chewing then swallowing with some difficulty. She took a swig from the
take-out coffee she held in both hands.

He stopped chewing and dropped the bagel back in the bag.

"I just want to get this over with," she said. "He's been calling
nonstop and I can't stand it anymore. He's here in town for business.
Two days and then he's gone."

"Fine. I'm going with you."

"Oh, come on. I don't need the drama."

He pointed his finger, knowing exactly what she was referring
to. "Ah, that wasn't my fault with you and your boy. If you'd been
honest and just told me your old boyfriend was going to be in the
same hotel with you I wouldn't've had to kick his ass." He stood up
and pulled the drawstring closed on his pants. "I'm going with you."

She leaned over and touched his arm. "Forget it. I'm just not going to take her. He wants to see her, he's going to have to sue me. I can't deal with this."

He rose up and walked around to the other side of the bed. He kicked a few things out of the way before picking up some loose clothing. There was shit everywhere. The room was a mess. The whole house was in disarray. After four months, he was ready to make the house a home. He wasn't used to living with his bags packed, one foot in and one foot out the door. But he felt it, too, like it was all temporary.

He paced back and forth. "No. You're right. I don't even know why I'm tripping. Get it over with. Take Mya with you. He's not going to stick around. He's going to run like a little punk just like he did three years ago."

Jake swallowed twice in succession, trying to keep the overriding fear at bay. She came and stood in front of him, her head coming only to his chest. With that he let out the air he was holding and took a much-needed inhale. Living with asthma all his life, he knew not to play when it came to breathing. Out, in, out, in, like measured strokes when learning how to swim. Worry and fear had consumed them both for the last year and a half. This was one more hurdle they'd have to get past before the waters settled.

"Just promise me . . . promise you won't let him introduce himself as her father."

She hesitated, knowing it was a promise she couldn't keep. "I already told him he's got twenty minutes. We're meeting in the lobby at the InterContinental where he's staying. In and out, that quick." She snapped her finger.

Jake paced awkwardly, feeling his knees getting weaker by the second. He cautiously moved to the only clear spot in the room not filled with boxes and stuff he didn't even know he owned. He'd lost everything else, his company, his good name, and his dignity. Waking up every day to the same reality made him want to hide. But then he'd hear Mya call his name, "Daddeee." The sweetest sound known to mankind, he was sure. So he forged ahead, did his best to swallow the raw ball of bitterness in the back of his throat.

"Hey, Mya." Jake saw her first as she pushed her baby doll stroller into their bedroom, oblivious to the stress level of her parents.

She took her little doll, wrapped in one of her old baby blankets, and handed it to Jake. "Give her a kiss, Daddeee."

He scooped her up right along with the doll and hugged her harder than she was used to. Mya hugged him right back, then remembered her task at hand. "I'm going shopping, want ta come?" Mya pointed to the toy stroller.

"No, Daddy has some work to do, but you and Mommy go shopping, okay?" He put her down, her long legs touching the floor and taking off before he was ready to let go. Mya pushed off with her baby in the stroller singing a song that only made sense in her head. The child had talent.

"It's going to be okay," Venus assured him again. "I love you," she said before walking out the door, leaving him alone.

4

Venus

I called Airic and let him know we were waiting in the lobby.

Mya stood only a few feet away, spinning, arms out, eyes closed, singing at the top of her voice, making guests look her way and smile. The beauty and strength of a child was that they didn't care who approved and who didn't. The problems started when they got older and hit the wall of self-evaluation.

I sat still and focused on the checklist of reasons I shouldn't get up and walk right out of there. Three years ago, Airic had made it clear that if he couldn't be a full participant in Mya's life, he didn't want to be there at all. He didn't want to be a paycheck daddy who sent child support and only got to see his kid on the weekend. He'd already lived that life with his first wife and two daughters and refused to play the game again. All or nothing, he'd said in his ultimatum, which would include me being his wife. I said, *No thank you.* I didn't love Airic, not in the way I should have.

Still, I believed he would come to his senses. At the time I believed a biological father should always be a part of his child's life, so I kept my fingers crossed through year one, prayed for his heart to soften through year two, and gave up completely by year three. But why now? After all this time why had it suddenly hit him to change his course?

Airic approached, impeccably dressed in a light gray suit, holding a woman's hand. She was also exceptionally well dressed. She was nearly as tall as him with her four-inch heels, and slender, with elbow-length hair draped like a superhero's cape over her shoulders.

"Venus, how are you?" He hugged me with a superficial pat on the back. He leaned to the side. "This is my wife, Trevelle."

The word *wife* struck me deaf and speechless. My mouth was moving. I thought I said how nice it was to meet her. My hand guided itself out to her.

Trevelle graciously took the offer, caressing my hand between hers. "It's so good to finally meet you." Her elegant neckline framed by a frilly white blouse stared me in the face. She searched around. "And Mya?"

"I see her," Airic said with profound joy. "She's adorable," he whispered.

I followed their eyes to Mya. I couldn't help but smile. Mya stood gathering herself after spinning around. Her wild dark hair shot up in spirals with a pretty fabric-covered headband holding it away from her face. After a few moments' rest she began to spin again. She was smart, funny, sweet, and quick-tempered. I could go on watching her for hours without a care in the world but I shook off the mama proud face and got right down to business. "So what's going on?" My eyes searched his, looking for an ulterior motive.

Airic swallowed out of nervousness. "I already told you what this is about. It's not complicated. We can start out slow, but I want visitation with Mya. We're in the process of moving here. This is actually Trevelle's hometown." He turned and gave an approving nod to his wife.

I coughed when I'd meant to laugh. "So out of convenience, since we're all in the same city, that's your reasoning?"

"Of course not. We're buying a house here specifically to be closer to Mya."

"Well, that's not necessary. She doesn't know you, at all. I mean . . . it would be like leaving her with a perfect stranger. I can't do that."

Trevelle spun around. The soft so-happy-to meet-you purring was replaced by a formal enunciation of every vowel and syllable. "Airic has already lost three years and it's regrettable, but there is no time like the present to start anew." Her shiny pink lips parted in a smile to show a full set of equally shiny white teeth. "God has a plan for all of us. Sometimes it takes longer than we'd like but it always falls into place."

My eyes fluttered from the pure audacity of what she'd just said. I turned to Airic, putting my back to *wifey*. Before I could say a word I felt her shiny acrylic nail tap my shoulder. I turned around, more audacity slapping me across, upward, and sideways.

"Venus, I already know what you're feeling and you're right, this is none of my business. It's just that Airic was so afraid and I'm the one who convinced him time heals all wounds. Please don't be upset. We've all come so far. Please." She began backing away. "I'll wait over there. You two talk." She slowly turned to leave, her glare lingering on my child for a few seconds too long.

Airic remained behind like a reprimanded child. "It really is good to see you."

I rolled my eyes. "Cut the crap. She's gone. You don't have to pretend to be some man-done-wrong by his ex. We both know the real deal." Airic wasn't a nice person. At least not the Airic I knew. He looked harmless enough but then he'd always worn that same clueless expression even when he was milking his investors for millions of dollars.

"Venus, I've changed. My life is in the hands of Christ now." His temples creased along the biting movement of his square jaw line. "I'm surprised you didn't recognize her. Trevelle Doval, she's famous worldwide."

The name clicked. Trevelle Doval. It *was* her. I clasped a hand over my mouth. "You're married to Trevelle Doval?" Who didn't know the name Trevelle Doval? Books, tapes, CDs. How could I not

have recognized her? She donned the long lashes, big hair, and elegant stilettos and strutted on stage better than Tina Turner in concert only she wasn't singing "Proud Mary," she was spreading the
holy gospel.

After I was finished being impressed I landed back on my feet.
"So when you said your life is now in the hands of Christ, you
meant our lady Doval, the second coming. She's obviously pulling
the strings of this little reunion."

"She encouraged me, of course. But this is something I've wanted
to do for a while now, long before Trevelle came into my life."

A child's scream echoed through the lobby. We stopped glaring
at each other long enough to turn our attention to Mya, who was
on the ground and already surrounded by helping hands. Her soft
cry echoed against the tall gold embossed ceilings. "Mommy."

"Sweetie, it's okay." I rushed to pick her up. Her long legs
scraped the sides of my knees. Tall for her age, other parents and
preschool teachers would say. Then they'd look at my short stature
in full wonder and say, "Her father must be tall," followed by a
preening smile. *No,* I wanted to shout, her father's *only five eleven.*
But the man who'd planted the biological seed was well over six
feet, slender, and a distant memory. *Until now.*

Mya buried her head in my shoulder. Airic reached out for a
consoling touch. I swung her around before his hand landed. For
now he was still a stranger and strangers weren't allowed to touch.
I'd also taught Mya that friends and family weren't allowed to touch,
in certain ways. The message could never be emphasized enough.

"Why don't we sit?" Airic said, indicating a place off to the side.

I followed him a short distance to the stucco planter surrounding a huge palm tree.

"You okay, baby?" I kissed Mya's forehead. She nodded yes.
"This is Airic Fisher, an old friend of Mommy's."

Airic gave off a tight smile. "Hey there." Two words and he already lost his mojo. He folded his hands in his lap and tried to think
of something else to say.

"She needs ice."

"I can get ice. Hold on." He stood up, happy for an excuse to be needed. I watched him move through the lobby to the concierge desk.

"Mommy, I want Daddeee." Mya pouted, as if my kisses weren't good enough.

I gave it a moment of thought. "I want Daddy, too," I said, then slid Mya off my lap onto her feet. I took her hand and walked casually toward the double glass doors.

I turned around to see Airic coming toward me with a Ziplock bag full of crushed ice.

"Leaving?"

"No. Um, just thought she needed some fresh air." I was grateful he didn't remind me that it was ninety degrees outside topped off with 70 percent humidity. I led Mya back to the stucco planter and put the ice on her head. We sat on opposite sides of Mya. I noticed his expensive watch and platinum wedding band. The tie, shirt, and suit cost well into the thousands. His sandy-colored hair was cut short to his scalp, camouflaging the gray hair at his temples. Airic was almost eleven years older than me. I thought an older man was what I needed at the time. Smart, mature, no-nonsense, all the characteristics that really had no bearing on one's ability to love.

"So, I guess you're not teaching anymore?"

"No. I manage the Doval Ministry Foundation."

"Nice." I tried to clear the nagging tickle in my throat.

"I earn a living. Same as I always have." His voice lowered. "I tried paying you child support. You didn't want it." He looked past me to Mya. "She deserved at least that much."

"We don't need your money. Not now, not then, not ever. I mean the last time I saw you, you were working as an associate professor. Not a very lucrative position."

"And the last time I saw you, you were in Virginia. Then you're in L.A. Now here, in Atlanta. That's a lot of change in only a few years. One would think you were in a witness protection program the way you and your rapper husband move around."

"I'm surprised you claim to know where I was, or where I wasn't. You've never given a damn—"

"Let's not go off on tangents. Let's stay focused on the here and now. We need to figure out how we're going to handle this situation. I realize it's delicate." Airic leaned closer to keep his voice low.

He smelled of ChapStick and alcohol-laden cologne. When I was pregnant with Mya the morning sickness was made worse anytime he leaned near me. I suddenly felt queasy with the memory and wondered why he hadn't upgraded his scent along with everything else.

"When do you plan to tell her?" he asked.

I turned slightly, so my words wouldn't carry. "I need time."

"Listen. This is an unfortunate situation. I wish things were different, but it is what it is. She needs to know. We need to work out arrangements, decide on dates, times for planned visitation."

"Okay . . . um. I was looking for an easy way to say it, but over my dead body."

"What?"

"No." I swung my purse around my shoulder, grabbed my keys, and took Mya's hand. "No. I'm sorry."

Airic was quick behind me. "Wait a minute. Venus. Wait."

The hotel entrance was lined with cars as guests unloaded their luggage. My car was still at the curb. I hadn't planned to be there long.

I turned around. "Airic, really. I'm just not ready. I've had a lot happen and I just need some time."

"Fine." He looked over his shoulder, sensing the presence of his wife. I saw her, too. She stepped back inside the sliding doors. "I'm here until Friday," he said. "We're going to have to agree on something."

"Say good-bye, Mya." I said with little validation.

◯◯

The air-conditioning wasn't working fast enough. I adjusted the vents to blow directly on my face and heat shot out instead. There was no way to prepare for the hot humidity of the south. No getting around the dull thickness of the air the same way there was no getting around the fact that Airic was Mya's biological father. It was the nature of things and nothing could ever change it. I sat at the light wondering how to stop the sweat from dripping out of every pore of my body. Was the air conditioner broken? I pressed the up arrow to the limit.

"Mya, you all right back there, sweetie?" I tilted the rearview mirror to see her fast asleep. The shiny bulb on her forehead glistened with a sheen of perspiration. What pain had she endured on the inside along with the obvious knot on the outside?

Jake would be furious.

Speak of the man himself. I answered the vibrating cell phone in a false happy tone. "Hey, baby. Everything went great. We're on our way home," I answered before he could ask.

Didn't work. Jake had X-ray vision and superpowers of sniffing out dishonesty. "What happened?" he asked in a knowing tone.

"Fine. Everything's fine. Mya's slee—" The phone cut off. Cell phone reception was terrible in certain spots of the city, even worse near our home. We had yet to have the landline turned on. I waited at the light and tried to think of how I was going to tell Jake about Airic's lofty plans. The phone didn't ring, thank goodness. I needed time to think.

It wasn't that Airic was the worst person in the world. Hell, I'd been engaged to the man for two long blurry years. His only fault was not loving me enough. Not feeling what I wanted him to feel. There was no crime or sin in that. When Airic and I met he had no relationship with his ex-wife or the two daughters they'd shared. I let the mystery go unsolved, thinking that was their problem. Airic's aloof and emotional unavailability toward them had nothing to do with me. I was special, after all. Soon I learned I wasn't so special. By the time I found out it was too late. I was pregnant with Mya.

Admittedly I'd fallen out of love with Airic long before the day he was exposed for cooking his company's profit-and-loss statements so the stock price would soar. It was during my mother's illness, a bout with cancer that woke me up to the pitiful mess I'd become. I wanted to be married so badly, I didn't care to whom, even if he was incapable of loving me the way I needed to be loved. Shame on the desperate woman who believes any man is better than no man at all. Shame on me.

Last I'd heard, Airic was teaching at a small private university in Boston. Not a word, not a peep out of him until the calls started coming. I had kept the same cell number all these years, taking advantage of the new law that you could keep your phone number even if you changed carriers. In all that time, he never called, not once.

I didn't buy the excuse of a changed heart. As far as I was concerned Airic's heart was missing right along with his good common sense if he thought I would just hand Mya over without a fight. I tried to stop the ranting going on in my head like mini land mines, so much that I hadn't paid attention to the beeping in my ear. The Bluetooth was signaling a call. I answered expecting to hear Jake; thankfully it was my mother. Relief replaced anxiety. "Mom."

"Oh sweetie . . ." She waited until I was through sniffing back tears. "It's going to be okay."

"No . . . no it's not. He's serious, Mom."

Pauletta had a knack for breaking things down to their simplest form. "You knew this day was coming. He's her father."

"No. He doesn't deserve to be in Mya's life, not now, not anymore. He had his chance."

"Has nothing to do with deserving. That's her father."

"Well, he's in for a fight, I swear."

"What kind of fight?" Pauletta asked with an air of annoyance. "Unless he's done something that would jeopardize the health and welfare of that child, he has every right to see her."

"He abandoned her. Not to mention he was found guilty by the SEC, they even sentenced him to community service."

Pauletta scoffed, "Could someone have told him about you being in the hospital?"

"What . . . no. How would he know?" I'd spent seven days in the loony bin, or the mental rehabilitation ward to be politically correct. Mandated to seven days of psychiatric evaluation after having my stomach pumped to remove half a bottle of antidepressants. The small print written on my file said "attempted suicide" regardless of how many times I corrected them. It was an accident plain and simple but no one believed me.

Yet it all made perfect sense. Airic's sudden reincarnation, all confident and filled with self-righteous determination, could only mean he knew about the brief mix-up.

Another call signaled in my ear. "Mom, I have to go. I think that's Jake calling back." I pushed the button, finally ready to face his questions.

This time it was a woman's voice, soft and lazy. Wendy was smiling through the phone. "Girrrrl, I don't know what you were thinking. How you liking that heat, huh? I heard it was ninety-one degrees down there and it's humid. You could've just moved back here to the D.C. The mosquitoes are half the size and we have public transportation," she laughed.

"Wendy, Airic is here."

"Here, where?"

"Here, here. Atlanta. He's married. Found God and wants to be a father to Mya." I spoke fast knowing I was running a hotline. A new call could trump the current one at any second.

"Okay," she said, missing the urgency.

I wiped away a droplet of sweat before it fell into my eye. "He has no right."

"You're her mother. He's her—"

"Wendy, is that the best you can do? He walked out of her life the day she was born."

"I know, girl. I was there. I witnessed the whole ugly scene, but you knew this day was coming." Not her, too. Did everyone know this day was coming except for me? Of course I knew Mya would have to be told. I wasn't planning on lying to Mya ever, but timing was everything, as they say, and this was not the time.

"I hate him," I said before I could stop myself. I peeked in the rearview to make sure Mya was still asleep. Words like *hate* and *stupid* were stricken from my vocabulary for the very purpose of saving Mya from ever feeling either one.

"Oh, sweetie. You don't mean that."

"He's the one who abandoned Mya. He walked away. Now he's trying to step in like he hasn't missed a beat, like he was up all night with her when her fever hit a hundred and two, as if he changed a single diaper or made a bottle at three in the morning." I took a few seconds to get a grip. "Worst of all, Wendy, he knows. He knows I was hospitalized for trying to— He's going to try and use it against me."

"You lost your baby and anyone can understand that, Venus. He would understand that. I don't think that's why he's there. Maybe he just wants to do the right thing, finally."

"He's married now."

Wendy's silence was all too telling.

"Ohmigod . . . you knew."

"Well, it was in the paper out here. You and Jake were going through so much with his case, I wasn't about to add any more drama, you know."

"So you knew he was married to Trevelle Doval and you never thought to tell me?"

"Honestly I figured they'd be married and divorced before the conversation came up. Maybe it was for the best. There's power in the spoken word. So between you and me thinking out loud, wishing poor Airic to hell, he might've met his maker and it would've been all my fault."

"I've never wished him any ill will . . . until now." Before I knew it I was home and pulling into the driveway. "Wendy, I'll keep you posted. I have to go inside and talk to Jake." I eased into the garage. I swallowed the lump in my throat and helped Mya out of the car. She was staggering from her nap.

"If you need me, call. I can be there lickety-split. Jamal is doing summer camp at Georgetown and Tia's staying with Sidney till August."

"Thanks. I might take you up on the offer. I love you, even if you didn't tell me about Airic."

"I know," she whispered. "I got some making up to do."

Jake was waiting at the entrance to the house. He wasted no time picking Mya up, kissing her gently on the bump. "What happened to her head?"

"She was spinning and fell, hit her head."

"You all right, baby?" He faced me. "You weren't watching her? What happened?"

Mya wrapped her arms tight around his neck and nuzzled him.

"She was spinning, you know how she does, and got dizzy. I need a shower. I'm dripping with sweat."

"Wait a minute. Aren't you going to tell me what happened?"

"I will, later." My eyes pleaded for understanding. I moved past him and took the winding stairs two at a time. I could still hear the echoes of daddy talk when I reached the bedroom. It was the one connection that hadn't been broken. The one line not crossed. Though Jake and I had been at odds over the past year, the father-daughter tie remained intact. He always made Mya smile. He always made her feel safe. I closed the door behind me and turned the shower to a light mist. I wanted it to be cool, barely any heat. I undressed slowly, trying not to look at myself in the mirror. The smiley scar right below my pelvis line had healed perfectly, but I could still see it. Proof that it wasn't a bad dream no matter how hard I tried to forget.

So sorry, the obstetrician and the nurses kept repeating. The baby didn't survive after the emergency cesarean. A boy. Five pounds, two ounces. *So sorry*. The words played in my head like a tom-tom beat.

Who was to blame?

I took my prenatal vitamins. No alcohol. Never smoked. No coffee. Ate only fresh organic vegetables and skirted the table salt. I did everything right.

So sorry.

I wouldn't survive losing another child. Not this way. Not to Airic and his new wife. I didn't care what kind of celebrity she was or who had the better relationship with God. Mya was my child, plain and simple, and no one was going to take her from me.

I pushed my face upward to the shower and let the tears stream down my face.

5

Here Comes the Judge

Delma listened to the cases one after the other with her usual conflict, of both compassion and disdain for the craziness pouring through her courtroom doors every day. One plus one still equaled two no matter what year, what part of the country, what race or culture, and yet these people couldn't add up the truth. There was no such thing as a good fight, especially when it involved children.

"So you're saying . . . ," Delma prepared herself to reiterate the broken language of the young woman with pink embroidery twined into her black hair and a shockingly low red halter top, "you asked the father of your three children if you could borrow his car to take them to their grandmother's house. When he said no, you got a ride to the man's house and took the car, so when he woke up the next day, he had no transportation to go to work?"

"Yes." She answered as innocently as one could with all her cleavage spread out. "And then he called the cops on me. Then me and my babies was pulled over. The kids saw me get pulled out of the car like some criminal. Then he had the nerve to press charges. Now I gotta pay bail money, and he still haven't paid me nothing for child support. He the one should've been thrown in jail, not me."

"Mr. Crawford, when's the last time you paid child support for your three children?"

The man put his head up as if to search his memory somewhere in the wood-paneled ceiling. "Maybe four or five months ago."

"Mr. Crawford you think these children can live on air?"

"Well, I can't pay if I can't get to work. She stole my car."

"She took the car one time." Delma refrained from saying the rest of what was on her mind, *She took the car one time, Negro, now go on and act stupider than you look so I can throw your butt in jail.* "That's no excuse for not having paid all those months before. When were you planning to pay?"

"Nevah evah." The cleavage said out loud.

"Is your name Mr. Crawford?"

The young woman rolled her eyes.

"Mr. Crawford, when were you planning to pay?"

"I can pay now. I got the money, I just don't know where to send it. She be all over the place. Can't find her. One week she living with her mama, the next she staying with her cousin, a crazy crackhead threatening to shoot me every time I call."

Delma took a moment to count to ten. It wasn't working. "You can pay me, Mr. Crawford. From now on the money will be deposited to an account managed by the state of Georgia. Every month the check will be dispersed to Miss Bingham. Garnishment will begin in two weeks." Delma surveyed the perplexed faces. "Garnishment," she explained, "is when the money is taken directly from your check, Mr. Crawford. If you leave your place of employment, if you're fired or laid off, you report this immediately to my clerk. Wave at the man, Hudson, so there's no confusion."

Hudson peered over his reading glasses and shifted the toothpick in his mouth. He lifted an uninterested hand and waved before Delma continued. "If you do not report changes of this kind, an immediate warrant will be issued for your arrest. Are we clear?"

"I have a question," the cleavage interrupted with a hand up, "do I have to wait two more weeks 'cause my babies and me can't wait that long."

"Good question. Mr. Crawford, you are ordered to pay Miss Bingham five hundred dollars today. I do believe you said you had a nice fresh paycheck in your pocket."

"I only got five hundred, what am I suppose to live on?"

"Same thing you expected your babies to live on . . . air." The gavel went down. "Have a nice day."

Hudson snickered as Delma moved past him. "Glad I can entertain you," she said, before kicking off her shoes and plopping onto the leather sofa in her chambers. "These people are going to drive me to the nut house. I should be on the superior level by now. Here I am stuck with all the crazies."

Delma watched with grace and humble patience as her colleagues magically got recommendations one by one while she stayed put. She had more years of experience and the best record of them all. No taking days off to golf or fish. She was present and accounted for every single docket. Yet she was being stepped over and ignored.

"I may as well face it, I'm going to be stuck here till I give up and go home. I should've been out there golfing and rubbing elbows instead of doing my job like the good ole boys."

"Over here," Hudson ordered. "Come on." He motioned her to the chair. Delma couldn't refuse. The tightness in her back and shoulders felt like a vice grip. The pain only seemed to subside after one of Hudson's tender massages. The man could work the kinks out like nobody's business.

"What I tell you about stressing over these fools?" He slid his thumbs to the center of her neck and stair-stepped them down before sliding them up to start again. "You should be proud of your accomplishments. You have the least appeals on record. No absences. And . . ." He paused for a minute as if this was the biggest one. "And you smell good." Hudson grinned at his own joke.

Delma sucked her teeth and tsked, "Well thanks for telling me, I'll change my perfume 'cause all I'm attracting is niggas and flies." She slapped at his hands. "Unhand me."

"I should be charging. I don't put these hands on just anybody." Hudson let go and not a moment too soon.

"Knock, knock." The heavy voice of Judge Lewis sounded at the open door before he peeked inside. The weight of age creased heavily around his gray eyes.

"Hey there," Delma said lightly, pulling herself out of her chair since Hudson wasn't moving fast enough to get out of her way. "How was that fishing trip?" She always enjoyed seeing Judge Lewis, even though he was another example of the injustice. How he'd professionally surpassed her over the past twenty years could only be answered with one word. *Woman.* Forget about her two degrees in psychology and one in law. Forget about her ten-year stint in the district attorney's office. He'd started out as a patrol officer who earned his degree at night from the local state college and hadn't earned a full law degree until he was damn near forty years old, yet he was her superior. Made perfect sense.

"I caught a twenty-pound sea bass. Got the picture in my office. You should stop by and see it."

"I will do that," Delma said with extreme ladylike manners. "But more importantly, when's the fish fry?"

"I'll be sure to have you over." He winked before getting to the reason he'd stopped by. So many years ago she'd fantasized about him, back when he was fine for a white boy. Even with the pocket of healed burns on his left cheek, he had the mandatory chiseled chin, with a rugged seriousness about him. Hard on the outside but a soft heart on the inside. Now all she saw was a receding hairline and enough crow's-feet to start a bird ranch. "You up for taking a few of Judge Benjamin's cases?" he asked.

"Oh, sure. No problem."

"Good. I knew I could depend on you."

"See you around." Delma waved him off before letting her hand slide back on her hip. She closed the door and faced Hudson. "Like I need more pitiful cases on my docket?"

" 'Oh, sure, no problem,' " Hudson mimicked, not really sounding all that different from his usual voice. "You should've said no."

"Judge Lewis is on the committee of judicial assignments. He might be my only ticket out of here."

"Right," Hudson sarcastically agreed. "I can see how highly he thinks of you."

"What's that supposed to mean?"

"He was eyeballing your goodies." He strutted toward the door, convinced he was bringing sexy back with his too-tight polyester pants.

"What goodies?" Delma caught herself laughing. "Out, you're not doing nothing but messing with my mind. I don't have time to-day, Hudson."

Hudson went to the door but as he passed he made it a point to look only straight ahead. "You see, I respect you. Your goodies are off limits."

"Out, Negro. Now."

She fell into her chair and took a sneak down her flowered blouse where one button was opened lower than usual, by accident of course. What would Judge Lewis be doing looking down her blouse? The man was a saint. She rolled her eyes and took a moment to lay her head back against her high-boy leather chair, grateful for the day's end.

6

Venus

Trevelle Doval could be the one reason Airic was interested in being a doting father. I couldn't resist doing a bit of Internet research on the woman. I typed in her name and information poured, jumped, and beat across the computer screen. I was suddenly immersed in her tumultuous childhood of poverty and prostitution followed conveniently by being rescued by a good Christian family who took her in and taught her about faith and God. She then went on to the seminary and led a celibate life until meeting the man of her dreams, Airic Fisher. *Ha!*

I landed on a fantasy story of how they met at a college in Boston where the lecture turned ugly after students began to heckle and verbally attack Ms. Doval for speaking against fornication on campuses; deeming the entire coed population to eternal hell if they didn't change their ways. One of the professors stepped in to rescue her by offering his agreement on the matter. That professor was one Airic Fisher. They lost me at the rescuing part. Airic had never stood up for anything in his life, least of all for the sanctity of virgins.

The rest was history, as they say. Within six months, Trevelle and Airic had the biggest wedding ceremony the black elite had seen in decades. Horse-drawn carriage, hundreds of white doves, a dress beaded with Austrian crystals, over five hundred guests. Trevelle had spared no expense, "knowing there was no greater blessing than the union of a husband and wife."

Spare me.

I ignored my own bitterness for a second and scrolled down to see pictures. Courtesy of Who's Who Online, I saw photos of hundreds of guests, including government officials along with a few celebrities sprinkled about. Airic looked happier than I'd ever seen him. Handsome in sepia-toned images with a bright smile and sparkling eyes. So happy.

Money could do that, at least temporarily.

I clicked on the next Web page and found Trevelle Doval's book tour schedule. She was speaking at Spelman College *tonight*. My heart raced. Surely there would be a huge crowd, too large to notice me. It was a public place, a free world. I could go if I wanted.

After buffing and polishing myself I told Jake I was attending a seminar on positive change. After all, I desperately wanted insight on this woman who might one day become a part of my daughter's life. I wanted to find peace and change my evil thoughts, so it wasn't like I was lying.

The evening started out pretty standard. Hundreds of students listened respectfully to Trevelle Doval's carefully constructed lecture on Christianity in business. Ethics had lost all meaning in a world of gorging consumers and stock market fraud. I looked around for Airic, seeing how he'd known a thing or two about the concept, since he defrauded his stockholders of millions only a few short years ago. No sign of him. Didn't matter. Trevelle was far more interesting.

She strutted on the stage after being introduced and met with moderate applause. She wasted not a second once she was centered and in position. Her microphone was attached to the shiny gold lapel of her suit that matched her gold five-inch pointed heels.

"How many times in our lives have we been told, this isn't about you, it's not personal?" Her voice flowed effortlessly through the auditorium. "When I was growing up, my mother use to tell me daily, 'Everything's not about you, this world will continue on long after you're gone and no one will have known your name.'" She threw back her head, tossing her hair, gently laughing. "I'm here to tell you, it's always personal, and it's always about you. You," she pointed, "are the one who God speaks through. Your words, your actions, your decisions are measured and weighed each and every day. Trust me, it's always about *you*."

The woman had skills. I listened intently for a solid hour before I remembered I wasn't supposed to be impressed. I was supposed to dislike Trevelle Doval, not sit there nodding to her sermon. When question time came the line stretched from the front to the exit. The first young woman wearing a black scarf draped over her head in traditional Muslim attire adjusted her thick square glasses before asking her question in a highbrow tone. "Ms. Doval, you speak about the woman's place to stand submissive behind a man. How can you condemn the Muslims' treatment of women when you as a Christian believe women are second-class citizens?"

The audience sat in silence, waiting for her response. Trevelle seemed relaxed and unfettered by the fact the question had nothing to do with the topic she'd just spoken about for the last hour. Ethics. Decision-making in business. Was I the only one paying attention in class?

Trevelle strolled to the left side of the stage. Her heels clicked lightly on the wooden stage. The wireless microphone attached to her lapel gave her free range to move as she chose. A sly smile rose on her perfect glossy lips, as if she'd been waiting for the opportunity to talk about something a little more interesting. "I am a woman. Does anyone have any doubt of that?" She pivoted with the agility of a runway model, getting a few claps and whistles from the audience. "As a woman, a Christian woman, I stand before you but I am always behind my father God in Christ. He leads. I follow. I believe in supporting a strong man in his endeavors. A strong woman will make a strong partner but she is not to be the dominant personality in the male and female relationship. Now women in the Muslim religion are not only relegated to second-class citizenship, but they must physically be assigned that position. A perfect example, the wearing of the scarves around the hair, and in some sects, I believe they must be shrouded from head to toe in black sheaths."

The young woman leaned into the microphone. "That is not true. We wear the scarf out of respect for our self to not be defined by superficial physical aspects, like hair, to attract a man. In fact, it is American women who purchase the shorn hair of Muslim women to adorn themselves due to their preoccupation with attracting the opposite sex."

A few groans of "no she didn't," were heard through the audience.

"I can respect the modesty aspect of wearing the scarf over the hair. However, God made the woman different from the man and there is no sin in embracing those differences with a modest sense of fashion. Women were put on this earth to serve as helpmates, doesn't matter what country or continent from which you hail."

Another set of disapproving groans.

Trevelle continued. "At one point the Islamic religion was very progressive, fourteen hundred years ago during the days of Prophet Muhammad. He encouraged a more liberal view of the woman's place in society, for example he believed that women should be able to own property, which was a revolutionary stance back then. However, I believe over the years, teachings that came after Prophet Muhammad had more fear of women and their position in life and began to remove many of the progressive ideas and maintain the oppressive garb. I do not condemn your religion so don't you dare condemn mine." Trevelle turned her attention away to show she'd spoke her peace on the subject and was moving on.

Next. The person behind scooted forward, a matronly dressed student with a handbag too small for her big body. She stepped to the standing microphone. "Ms. Doval . . ." From the lilt of her voice, one expected a good southern Christian defense. Instead the young woman's voice deepened. "You are just covering up your backwards ideas about women. I have heard you say that a woman's place is in the home and that she should give up her career to raise children. You have your own business. I don't see you sitting at home."

"My dear, listen to yourself. Should we retrofit men with a uterus, shoot him up with estrogen, and make him have the baby, as well? What you women are not seeing is that God has divinely made the sexes different so that they can perform different tasks and one of those tasks is to serve her husband."

"Where is your husband? Where are your children? You were in *Ebony* magazine sitting on top of a brand-new Mercedes parked in front of a giant mansion. I didn't see no man in that picture."

The crowd was now keeping score. Trevelle was losing, but only by a small margin.

"I was not married when that photo was taken. God is the man in that picture and he shall show no one his image until he has chosen to do so. I had taken a vow of celibacy until I met and married the man God chose to send me. Some of you could take a lesson in prayer and wait." She could hear a couple of ladies sucking their teeth and moving their way to the aisle to get to the microphone. Trevelle remained calm and cool.

Another young black woman made her way to the microphone but this one was dressed to the nines. Her orange Todd handbag matched her orange shoes. Trevelle looked hopeful; the woman had as much sense as she did style.

"Welcome, Ms. Doval. My name is Denise Burrows. I'm a PhD candidate here at the college and I have a comment. Wouldn't you agree, in today's dangerous times of HIV, that it's better to leave men alone and focus on your own goals? Being single is not a death sentence but chasing dick will get a sista killed."

The audience fell out laughing. Trevelle acted unfazed. "I definitely agree with you, in spite of your chosen use of words. You shouldn't be chasing a man. He should be chasing you. But the young women out here are so busy giving themselves away, the men have what ya'll majoring in business call a 'surplus.'" She strutted to the other side and let her hand fall on her hip. "Supply and demand, ladies. If there's too much of anything stored in the warehouse, it drives down the price. Suddenly it has no value." Nearly half the audience stood up and began clapping. The other half were naysayers giving grunts of disapproval. Trevelle let both sides subside before continuing.

"Women are giving it away, putting hardworking whores out of business. Our young women don't know how to say *no*. Then we have all the magazines telling you to move on and let it go. You don't need a man. You can do bad all by yourself. Step over any man who doesn't pay the bills. *You do right by him*, he's going to pay the bills." The crowd got louder, some in agreement, some not. Trevelle's words seemed to incite the women to their feet. A few even pushed each other trying to get to the microphone. "If you can just hear the truth of what I am saying you'd understand that you can be a strong female in heart, mind, and spirit, without sleeping next to your man with your fist balled up looking for a fight." It seemed to be the last straw. A few of the women started to move their way to the stage with pointed fingers and angry voices.

"What I'm trying to say is that if you find someone that you love and respect there is nothing wrong with honoring your role. Everyone has a place in a relationship as individuals. Both partners can lead in their specific roles as the man, as the woman, to build up each other spiritually as well as financially."

"You're a hypocrite," one student lashed out. "You're setting women back fifty years with your submissive role talk."

Trevelle breathed a sigh of defeat. "Did anyone hear me say 'submissive'? I said, helpmate."

Before things got any more out of control, the woman who'd originally introduced her stepped in. "Let's give Ms. Doval a round of applause to let her know how grateful we are for her coming this evening."

I clapped along with most of the audience. Only a handful booed and refused to join in the applause. I watched her masked smile as she was escorted over to the table with an overabundant

stack of her latest book ready to be signed. A large black man in a
suit and dark sunglasses stood only an arm grip away, obviously her
bodyguard. One look at him and the dissenters probably figured it
was best to leave.

A line formed quickly of chattering women, full of smiles and
goodness. Where were these women during the speaking turmoil?

I stood in line for close to an hour listening to Trevelle's voice
sing out blessings and praise to each and every young woman as she
signed their book. I wondered what I was going to say when I got to
the front.

"I'm Venus, Mya's mother." I was standing before the great
Trevelle Doval, feeling awkward for having stood in line just to say
what I'd said.

"I saw you in the audience." She beamed. "Nice to see you."
The tone in her voice must've alerted Igor. He took a slight step
closer.

"I enjoyed your talk. Can't wait to read the book," I said, as if I
had never wished for her and Airic to be run over by a bus some few
hours earlier. "I also wanted to apologize for the way I acted when
we first met. You didn't deserve that." I extended my hand, holding
the book I'd purchased with the price of admission.

She took ahold of my hand. "I know this is difficult. You're
probably trying to figure out why we've stepped into your life. Fear
is the devil's playground. I want you to know you have no reason to
fear our intentions. We simply want the best for Mya."

Something in the way she said it made me snatch my hand back.
"What is it that you think is for the best?"

"A stable Christian home." Her eyes danced with a private secret. "There is no healing without God. Do you have Jesus Christ in
your heart?" She handed me the book. The title *Armed with Faith*
was in the form of a knight's shield. I stared at the cover waiting for
the answer to come to me. Of course I had Jesus in my heart. I was
a Christian by birthright. I didn't have to do all the dirty work of going to church and donating boatloads of tithes and offerings. My

mother already did it for me. That was my running joke for the religion-mongers who liked to throw stones at the less blessed souls such as myself. I knew my place in God's heart just like I knew his place in mine. I didn't need a full house of worship and Holy Rollers screaming from the pulpit to make me know where my bread was buttered. I believed wholly and fully and prayed every day.

"Mya needs to have God in her life." She spoke in a gentle, matronly whisper.

"I know," I said with a disconcerting effort. The heat of the woman behind me, impatient from waiting too long, and the sudden panic surrounding me made my words shake. "I'm sorry," I said to the woman in back of me. "This'll take just a minute more." I leaned close to Trevelle so no one would hear what I was about to say. The bodyguard stepped forward putting a hand nearly over my face.

"It's all right, Stuart," Trevelle said gracefully.

Any closer and he would've had my teeth marks in his arm. He dropped his hand and I continued. "Whatever you may think . . . you've got it all wrong. Whatever you may be planning . . . it's not going to be that easy, don't even bet on it." I turned and walked away seething. I dropped the book in the large trash can near the exit and peered around for the rest of the Trevelle haters. Luckily they'd already gone or I would've become the new ringleader.

I stared out the kitchen window taking in the green grass and grove of endless trees, wondering how I was going to get through the day after another sleepless night. All night I'd tossed and turned thinking of all the different ways I should've responded to Trevelle Doval and her threat. *Hey, I'm going to take your child and there's nothing you can do about it. I've got God on my side and he don't like ugly.*

Well, I've got God on my side, too.

I stirred water into the instant oatmeal for Mya's breakfast. All the while I continued staring out the window in a half-zombie state.

Only Mya's voice while she played with her doll and miniature doll-house at the table kept me in the here and now. I stuck the bowl in the microwave and stood in front of it while the glass plate spun in a slow circle.

The doorbell rang at the precise moment the microwave beeped. It took the insistent knocking to capture my attention; it was far more fun to see the muddy mess I'd made on the glass plate. I pulled the hot bowl out with a towel and sat it on the table. I'd just ruined Mya's breakfast. Oatmeal wasn't her favorite food by a long shot anyway. Eggs. Now that was a complete breakfast.

I briefly looked through the peephole. Having only lived in the new house for a few months, there was always someone coming over for one service or another. We had gas, electricity, water, cable—*what had we missed*? I was thinking *phone,* when I unlocked the door and swung it open to the overheated man with red splotches all over his neck and face. The suffocating heat rushed into our air-conditioned house. His blue shirt and gray slacks were not the uniform of any utility company. He pushed a package-size envelope toward me.

"Mrs. Venus Johnston-Parson?"

"Yes."

He handed me his electronic clipboard. "Sign on the line, please."

The clipboard had a stylus pen attached. The pen was moist courtesy of his sweaty hands. I signed as he'd ordered. We exchanged quickly, me handing back his slimey box, and him giving me the red, white, and blue envelope. The printout on the front was smudged. I could faintly make out "Law Offices of . . ."

I tore the envelope open and took the contents out, hurrying the envelope to the trash like it was contagious. I sat at the kitchen table across from Mya, except she wasn't there.

"Mya," I called out nervously, "where are you? Come back and eat, right now."

"I'm here, Mommy. Find me," she called out, angry that I wasn't willing to play along.

I tried not to say another word. *"Damn* you."

"Mommy," Mya said quietly, this time from my side. Her small hand reached out, rubbing against my cheek. "I sorry."

I pushed the papers across the table and picked Mya up onto my lap. I squeezed her tight. "Oh, no, I wasn't talking to you, sweetie. You didn't do anything wrong." I kissed her again and again. Mya grabbed the spoon and played in the oatmeal clumped in the bowl. Still no breakfast for the child. That's the kind of mother who is unfit, a mother who doesn't feed her child, or keep her safe.

"I'll make some more." My movements were robotic. I scooted Mya into the next chair, rose up to dump the contents down the sink. The oatmeal wouldn't budge. I slammed it against the metal sink, the oatmeal still there. I slammed it again. The ceramic bowl broke down the middle and across the sides. Some things were no good once they were split down the middle, a child for instance.

"Mommy, you broke it."

I flipped the ceramic pieces into the trash can. "It's okay. We've got plenty of bowls." But there was only one Mya. One child. A tingling sensation rose through my fingers and up my arms against my chest. Were these the first signs of a heart attack? The pain shuddered then moved to the top of my rib cage. Anger was mounting, waging a war, causing me to get light-headed. I had to sit back down.

By this time Jake came into the kitchen. "Who was at the door?" He was prepared to go straight to the refrigerator until he took a second look in my direction.

"Babe, you all right?" He leaned directly into my face, searching my eyes. The court summons drew his attention. The papers shook in his hands. "What's this?"

"They had this planned all along." The top of the sheet said "Legitimization." Airic was making his rightful claim as the father to Mya. The second page read like a ransom note with a list of demands, including joint physical custody.

Jake was standing over me, the veins popping from his neck, his eyes squinting with rage. "He's suing . . . for custody?"

Mya's large eyes were fixed on the two of us. She was used to our strained communication. Mommy and Daddy seemed to only talk in hushed whispers of concern. Everything was a new fire to put out. This one was a full scale blaze. We'd need help.

Jake had me by the elbow. I was up on my feet. Mya started to follow. "Can you sit here for a minute, Mya? Daddy needs to talk to Mommy. Okay? Just a few minutes."

"She hasn't eaten. We can talk later," I said out of pure delirium. I had no answers. I wasn't in a hurry to be asked, how, why, or what. *Who was to blame?*

Jake pulled out a box of too sweet cereal that he liked to eat in the middle of the night. He grabbed a bowl, then the milk from the refrigerator. He poured the cereal. Poured the milk. Got a spoon and handed it to Mya. "She can feed herself."

"She's not eating this sweety fruity crap." I snatched the bowl and dumped it down the sink.

"Fine. Then she doesn't eat." Jake leaned into me. "Let's go."

"What are you doing?" I moved out of his grasp. "Just calm down." I was one to give advice. My heart flipped out of rhythm; standing there I didn't know how much longer I could stay upright.

"Hey sweetie, let's all go upstairs. Can you play in your room for a little while I talk to Mommy? Then we'll go out and have a big breakfast at Cocoa's."

"Happy pancakes," she said excitedly, slapping her small hands to her cheeks.

"Yep. My favorite, too," Jake said with a genuine smile. He scooped Mya up for a shoulder ride while I followed behind.

Inside our bedroom, with the doors closed, Jake and I sat side by side on the edge of the bed holding the court summons in our hand.

"Listen, this thing has got me thrown off. I'm sorry I just didn't think he was serious. This is crazy. This man abandoned you and Mya. He walked and didn't look back. Now all of a sudden he wants to be Bill Cosby? When you saw him, you said everything was going to be fine. Now this? The man actually wants joint custody?"

"It's his wife. She's pushing him to do this. She's behind his new-found need to be a loving daddy. Trevelle Doval wants her fairy-tale marriage to be complete with a child: Mya."

"Trevelle Doval, praise the Lord and dial 1-800-Cash-or-Credit-Card?" Jake's head fell into his hands. "Why didn't you tell me?"

"I knew you'd be even more worried. I knew . . . how serious it was, how much trouble we were in up against her and her holy name." I reached out and rubbed his shoulder. Only seconds ago it was me on the brink of a collapse. I surmised Jake was the more fragile of the two of us. Only because I'd already been broken and had somehow learned to live with the pain. I feared Jake would fall apart like Humpty Dumpty, unable to put himself back together again.

He took my hand. "You know, you and Mya mean everything to me."

"I know, baby. I wish—"

"He spent ten minutes with her. Ten." He shook his head. "We need to call Georgina."

"She's a criminal lawyer." The last person I wanted to see on our doorstep was Georgina Michaels. Not that she wasn't a wonderful person, an upstanding human being and all who'd fixed our legal woes with one fell swoop of her manicured nails. She was soft spoken and unassuming in her tailored suits that showed off a lean Pilates body. She never said more than what was necessary, believing someone speaking too long will eventually speak wrong. Polite. Trustworthy at the right price. But she still scared me.

"She's a California lawyer. She's probably not certified to practice law here."

Jake gave me a look that begged the question: what choice did we have? Who else would understand our dilemma? She already knew what we'd been through, my hospitalization combined with Jake's murder charges. We were not likely to make model clients in anybody's law books.

"I'm calling her," Jake said. "We don't have a choice."

7

In the Interest of the Child

Sitting on Delma Hawkins's desk were stacks of petitions, complaints, and responses that nine times out of ten involved children. Hudson separated them by ease. The ones requiring only a signature—final divorce papers, child support orders, liens, and wage garnishments—sat directly in front of her chair with her favorite pen on top. The next stack to the left were visitation orders, mandated counseling, and parenting classes. The largest stack was on the floor next to her desk, secured in a lock box where private lives were exposed and bared through hatred, all to prove who was the better parent.

There was no science to it. The decision-making process that Delma went through rested on one very important factor: the best interest of the child. Who would provide a stable, loving, and caring environment? Which of the parents had the best interest of the child and not just the best interest for themselves. Delma's bullshit meter easily picked up on the one who used the child as nothing more than a way to seek revenge on the other parent.

Most of her peers based their decisions strictly on the law. Fairness played little if any role in their decisions. Unlike her, most of her peers could care less about right and wrong, good versus bad. That's what the laws were for. Precedents were set to make life easier. Thinking beyond the written law could make one lose sleep, get an ulcer, or take up drinking. Or in Delma's case, take up with a pint of double fudge Breyers in one sitting, all to make the voices go away.

"Time to go," Hudson spoke gently, so as not to startle her. "Ten o 'clock, lady. Let's move it out." He came behind Delma's chair and placed his hands on her stiff shoulders, giving them a powerful squeeze.

Delma moaned. "Yes. One more time, right there." She pointed to a higher spot where the tension in her neck and shoulders rose into one thick clump of muscle.

"These late hours are wearing me out," Hudson had the nerve to say. "I'm getting too old for this. What do you say we run off to a deserted island and make babies?"

Delma twisted her mouth with a smirk. "That would require one or both of us to get naked and I'm trying to keep what's left of my eyesight as long as possible." She breathed out the tension as he worked her shoulders. "Did you notice the McKinley case got restraining orders filed on each other? So how are they supposed to be able to agree on any kind of visitation for that child? Lord, I wish these people would get some sense."

"Right now I wish you'd go home and get some rest." Hudson rolled Delma's chair back with her in it. "All this can wait. Up," he demanded, snapping off her desk light.

Delma was on her feet and packing her leather attaché. It was their ritual every evening. She pretended she didn't want to go and Hudson did his part to make her. She peered over her reading glasses to see him making sure the windows were locked before closing the wood blinds.

Their cars were parked side by side in the spaces with reserved signs posted. They were supposed to be for judges only, but Delma made sure Hudson had the green sticker so they could be in the same area. Nine times out of ten they were side by side.

They walked in the night air that was as thick as the day. There was awkward silence between them while they listened to crickets and the sound of the fluorescent parking lot lighting going on and off overhead. "Straight to bed, you hear. You have a big day tomorrow," Hudson said as he held the car door open for her.

"You're talking about the Trevelle Doval case." Delma shook

her head. "That woman . . ." She tried to not let on that even the sound of her name made her bristle with fear.

"Don't let her bully you. Just because she's famous doesn't mean she gets special treatment." He gently closed her door.

Delma was quick to stick in the ignition key and roll down her window. "Since when have you ever seen me bullied, by anyone?"

Hudson took in a long deep breath even though the humid heat made it difficult. "Right, what was I thinking?" He tapped the hood of her car. "Buckle up. I'll see you in the morning."

"Bully me," Delma Hawkins whispered while she pulled out of the parking lot. *Please.* She wasn't afraid. She had no reason to be afraid. Trevelle Doval would never recognize her. Delma only knew who *she* was by chance. One night as she lay in bed flipping channels knowing nothing was on but late-night preachers and *Girls Gone Wild* commercials, it struck her like a brass band blowing in her ear. The voice she'd remember for the rest of her life belonged to Velle Wilks. The deep throaty lilt of her words. The way she sang the last bits of her sentence, even back then when she was nothing more than a teen prostitute, drug fiend, and petty thief standing before the juvenile judge pleading her innocence.

Twenty-seven years was a long time. She sincerely would never have recognized Trevelle Doval if not for hearing her voice say the closing words, *Peace be unto you for God grace has no bounds.* God's grace definitely has bounds. Delma was sure of that. Thou shall not kill, and if Delma had seen it, then surely God had witnessed the whole thing, too. The woman preached nightly about coming clean to Jesus yet there was no confession of having killed a man.

Delma pulled into her garage and pressed the remote to let the door slowly fall. She sat in her car for a few moments, wondering how far she should take it. The smartest thing to do would be a recusal, take herself off the case. Impartiality was a requisite. Lord knows she was only human. All of her peers had some sort of prejudice lurking in their psyches, though they'd practiced denying it so avidly they even believed their own lies.

This was far more than prejudicial. Delma would need every compassionate bone in her body to make a fair and just decision. She'd need something close to a hypnotic state to not see the young prostitute Trevelle was thirty years ago sitting in that courtroom instead of the holy evangelist Trevelle Doval had become today. She'd also need a guarantee that she hadn't come back to Atlanta for the one thing she'd left behind. Because if she had, she'd be sorry. Not even that woman's faith and holy high horse would be able to save her. When it came to what was best for her child, Delma didn't mess around. There was only one answer, get rid of her and her husband, in and out, as quick as possible.

She'd read the case. The biological mother, Venus Johnston, had been accused of child neglect and endangerment. She was married to Jake Parson, arrested, but never tried, for manslaughter. The biological father had not seen his daughter in three and a half years, claiming the mother had moved without him knowing. Normally, it would've been a clear and easy decision. She would've given the father exactly what he'd wanted. But Delma couldn't see past the ugliness she knew of Trevelle, Velle, whatever she was calling herself these days. She couldn't stop being reminded of that night all those years ago. Seeing the way she'd violently beat a man over the head, and watched while he bled to death.

Normally, there wouldn't be a question of who got custody. She didn't tolerate unstable mothers, and attempted suicide shouted instability. There was no other form of selfishness greater than a mother trying to end her own life. What if the child had found her? What if the child herself was hurt from being left alone while the mother toiled into her oblivion? Delma didn't understand it and had no sympathy for a mother who didn't put her child first.

In any other case, there'd be no question of what to do. But now she was faced with the dilemma of choosing the lesser ills. She'd need two pints of Breyers chocolate on this night. Lord knows she had her work cut out for her.

8

Venus

A court of law brings out the fear and vulnerability in a person. The bland walls and dark heavy pews are like being in church, only there was no forgiveness. Words could not be taken back. Lies could not be recanted. Sins could not be prayed away. I wasn't in a forgiving mood anyway. I would never forgive Airic. It was the first day of the officially declared war. He was seated in between his lawyer, a narrow-shouldered man with weeping eyes, and his wife, dressed in a cream knit suit in a quest to look angelic. Jake and I arrived without representation with express orders from Georgina to keep our mouths closed tight, hand the judge the request for an extension, and offer nothing in the way of confidence. Not having a lawyer there would make us look like the underdogs and underdogs usually won in these types of situations.

I hoped she was right. The same way she was right in Los Angeles when she told me not to worry. "Jake will be home before Jay Leno finishes his monologue. Relax," she'd told me. I should have listened. Worrying had unleashed a cataclysmic war inside my head and body. Jake came home as Georgina had promised, tucked safely in bed by midnight. At four-forty that morning I was being wheeled on a stretcher into an emergency room. One shot and the premature labor was stopped in its tracks. We were out of the woods. I went back home prepared to spend the next three months off my feet as the doctor had ordered. Two days later I was back in the hospital. Our baby son came into the world and never took a single breath. *Who was to blame?*

"Please rise."

Jake was helping me stand since I obviously hadn't heard the request. The judge, a black woman with robust color on her lips and cheeks faced the courtroom. Her obvious wig tilted slightly to the right. The bailiff and clerk gave her a double take as if this was the first they'd seen of her new look.

"Good morning." She swept her eyes across her audience. "Matter of *Johnston vs. Fisher* on this date July 25, 2005."

"Yes, your honor. I'm Anthony Young representing Mr. Fisher." The lawyer slid a paper toward the bailiff.

Jake took notice and did the same. "Yes, your honor." He slid a request for continuance to the edge of the desk then took his seat, putting his head down.

"You're the representation for Venus Johnston-Parson? I don't have your name here."

"No, ma'am, I'm her husband, Jake Parson."

The sound of a throat clearing in the hollow room made everyone look in the direction where Trevelle Doval sat innocently.

The judge asked, "Do you need some water?"

"No, thank you, I'm fine." Trevelle gave a dismissive wave.

"So you're Mr. Jake Parson. Very nice to meet you, sir. My daughter was a big fan of yours not so long ago. And I won't lie, I bounced a few times to the beat."

Jake visibly flinched, surprised by her earnest approach. "Thank you . . ."

"Judge Hawkins," she finished for him. "Let's see what we have there." She read the papers the bailiff put before her. "What to do, what to do," she whispered too close to the microphone sitting on her podium. "Mr. Fisher, you are the birth father of Mya Parson and are requesting joint physical custody. I understand you hadn't made contact with your daughter for two years, is that correct?"

"Three," I said, before feeling Jake's hand grab mine under the desk, giving it a polite squeeze.

His lawyer stood while adjusting his long thin tie. "Mr. Fisher wasn't sure the child was his, your honor."

"Really?"

"Ms. Johnston had a relationship with another man while she and Mr. Fisher were engaged to be married."

Mouth closed, mouth closed. What happened to the continuance request?

"What gives Mr. Fisher the impression that she is his child now?"

A conscience. A new wife who prefers a husband with a spine.

"First thing's first. I'm requesting a DNA test," the judge continued.

"Mr. Fisher is sure of his paternity. There's no need for a test."

"If he is so confident he is the father, there shouldn't be a problem."

"Subjecting my client to needles and unreliable tests isn't necessary."

"Mr. Young, welcome to the twenty-first century. All we need is a small swab of the cheek, a strand of hair, perhaps that won't be too painful . . . for your client. And the tests are extremely reliable." She shook her head, miffed by the fact that the lawyer didn't know this. "Ms. Johnston, do you have a problem with a DNA test?"

"No. No problem."

"My clerk will give you the information on where to take your daughter for the lab test. Okay, let's all go enjoy the rest of our day, shall we?"

"Judge Hawkins," Mr. Young spoke weakly into the microphone. The judge shot him a look.

He only backed down slightly. "Mr. Fisher would like visitation with his child. He is legally the child's father as stated on the birth certificate and he has a right to visitation."

"Really?" Judge Hawkins said, her voice dripping with sarcasm. "He has a right?"

"Mr. Fisher never gave up his parental rights, your honor, regardless of how long he's stayed away."

"In some states that may well be the case, Mr. Young. But as you know, in this peach of a land, we have something called—"

"Legitimization, your honor. We filed the necessary paperwork."

"Interrupt me again and see where it gets you," the judge threatened before turning her questions to me. "Did you make contact with Mr. Fisher?"

"No, he made it clear he didn't want anything to do with me or my daughter."

"So you never requested child support?"

"No," I said, unable to stop my lip from trembling. "He said he didn't want to be a paycheck dad. If he couldn't be my husband, and a full-time father, he'd rather not be involved at all."

"And of course Mr. Fisher never volunteered child support?" The judge scribbled something else down.

"The mother immediately married the man she was having an affair with, moved two thousand miles away to Los Angeles, and never once contacted Mr. Fisher. He wouldn't have known where to send the money even if he wanted."

I object.

"What did I tell you?" Judge Hawkins slammed her gavel down.

"My client has a right to full representation."

"I asked you not to interrupt me and you did it anyway. Now if you can't keep a lid on it, you're out of here. So back to you, Mr. Fisher, and I do mean *Mr. Fisher.* Why didn't you try to contact your child?"

"Financial circumstances made it difficult for me to establish a relationship while she lived in California. I'm ready to take full responsibility for my child, your honor, before any more time passes."

"How sweet," Judge Hawkins said without so much as a glance in Airic's direction. "I'm in possession of a continuance filed on behalf of the mother. I will grant the continuance and we'll meet back here after we have the results of the paternity test." There was silence in the courtroom.

Another throat clearing from Trevelle along with uncomfortable chair squirming. Airic and his lawyer huddled quietly for a moment. "We have no problem with a continuance as long as my client can have weekend visitation during the waiting period."

"You just don't let up, do you?" For the first time, Judge Hawkins found my face and zeroed in on my eyes. "Do you have a problem with visitation?"

Mouth closed, cooperate. I shook my head no.

"Visitation set for two Sundays a month for no more than three hours per visit."

"That's a problem, your honor. My client lives in another state. He would need at least a full weekend visit."

"At this point, Mr. Young, this child doesn't know this man from Adam. Let's take it one step at a time. Let's get a paternity test on record before we start with overnight visits, shall we? Court adjourned. I'll see you all back here on the twenty-first at eight A.M." Judge Hawkins rushed off.

Shallow as the victory was, I somehow felt redeemed. I could hear Trevelle in a high-octane whisper switching between Airic and his lawyer, pissed and not caring who knew. Glints of perspiration rose past her well-matted foundation. The crisp polished cuffs on her white blouse waved around like flags as she made her point of sour disappointment. "This is ridiculous," Trevelle exclaimed. "The woman was locked up for mental instability. Her husband is a known felon. What was so difficult?"

"Lower your voice," Airic said, doing his best to *shh* his wife, while escorting her toward the doorway.

I watched and waited for Jake's reaction. The muscles clenched under the smooth skin of his jaw. "Let's go."

"Wait until they're gone, okay." I pulled him back down, nervous, listening intently for the voice of Trevelle to sail away. Funny thing was, even when she was gone I could still hear her: Jake, a known felon, and me mentally unstable. She was right. What made it so difficult? If I were a judge, I may have made the decision right on the spot. From the outside looking in, Jake and I shouldn't have stood a chance. Just the possibility made me fall apart.

"Don't, babe. Please. We're going to get through this. This is us," Jake said, looking me straight in the eye. "This is you and me. Have faith."

I leaned into the warmth of his neck and let him rock me back and forth.

Sins of the Mother

She pulled the wig off as soon as she closed the door to her chamber. "Fool," she muttered to herself. *How you gon let that woman make you act a fool?*

The knock at the door wasn't a surprise. She shoved the wig in the drawer and pulled her fingers through the rough patch. She needed a touch-up in the worst way. Penny, her hair stylist of well over two decades would shake her head and groan the entire time she sat in the salon chair, wondering why a high-paid public official couldn't make time for something as crucial as a hair appointment.

"Come in."

Hudson had his arms folded over his narrow chest. "What in the world is going on?"

Delma grabbed a couple of sheets of Kleenex out the box and dabbed the gloss off her lips. "Can't a girl add some shine?"

"Not jazzy pink, no." Hudson sat down, something he rarely ever did. "Are you going to tell me or do I have to hold you down and tickle you till you say uncle?"

"I wish you'd try." Delma rolled her eyes up and down his lanky frame.

"Was it JP, Mr. Juicy Hips and Fat Lips himself? Wanted to give him something to remember you by?" Hudson chuckled, but his face was strained. "I didn't know you liked rap music."

Delma didn't respond with a nod or a *C'mon, I was just kidding* smirk. In fact she was downright ashamed of the way she'd carried on in there. She knew nothing about JP what's-his-name. She'd never heard of him except after she'd looked him up on her computer the night before.

Delma averted her eyes. The bulb went off over Hudson's head and the wiry Afro that needed a trim. "Trevelle Doval? You're trying to impress her?"

Delma knew Trevelle Doval wouldn't have recognized her, wig or no wig. She wouldn't have recognized the young woman from twenty-seven years and thirty pounds ago. Oh, who was she kidding, more like fifty pounds ago. Delma sat still, wondering how much she could tell Hudson without breaching a right to privacy. Hudson waited with baited breath.

"She's always preaching about the duty of a woman to be all that she can be, her constant message of modest beauty. I just wanted to look decent."

"Do me a favor, leave the costume props to the drag queens over on Locust Street. You don't need wigs or lip goo. You're beautiful au naturel."

"Hudson." Delma felt her cheeks get warm. Was she blushing? "Thank you."

He stood and stretched his lean frame. "Guess I better get back to work."

"Do you ever eat, man?" She didn't wait for his answer. "Come on. We're heading to M&M's. They got a po'boy sandwich make you want to scream and holla."

⊙⊙

Sitting across from Hudson, Delma wondered why they hadn't done something like this sooner. It wasn't like a judge and her clerk couldn't get out and have lunch together once in a while. She also wondered why she didn't know more about him when he knew practically everything about her.

"We'll have two number elevens," Delma said to Mavis, the patient waitress who double-shifted as the cook and owner.

"Extra fries?" Mavis began scratching on her notepad before Delma could answer.

"No. Not this time."

Mavis gave a perplexed look to Delma and her date. "What about the coleslaw?"

"Of course."

"But do you want two? You usually get the one that comes with it and an extra on the side."

Delma felt like saying, *If you know what I usually get, why are you asking?* Instead she meekly responded, "Yes, but today, the regular order will do. Two number eleven's." She held up two fingers.

"Something to drink for the gentleman?" Mavis understood and decided to play along.

"I'll try your famous sweet tea."

"Not as sweet as Delma here, but we'll see." Mavis winked before walking away.

Awkward silence followed. Delma watched the other guests chatting away. The restaurant sat smack-dab in the middle of a gentrifying neighborhood. Mavis and Marnie, sisters and excellent businesswomen, refused to move out of the way. Luckily they owned the building and couldn't be pushed or bribed. They'd refused the offers that kept coming in, occasionally showing Delma a threatening letter or two asking if the city could do this or that. Sometimes she felt like a mole. "No, they can't do that. Ignore them," she'd say. Or sometimes she'd just laugh at the pure silliness of the ultimatums. Eventually, she pointed them in the direction of a good lawyer that she knew so she'd never be accused of taking bribes of coleslaw and po'boy sandwiches.

Mavis set down two icy cold glasses dripping with condensation. "Your food will be up shortly."

Delma knew what Mavis was thinking. This wasn't a date. Midafternoon in broad daylight? She'd at least have the good sense not to bring a man around a public place. Judge Delma Hawkins did not date or besmirch her spotless reputation.

"I've never seen you so quiet." Hudson sipped his iced tea to the last drop, leaving lonely ice cubes to keep each other company.

Delma hadn't realized how long the food had been sitting in front of her. She'd been thinking about Trevelle Doval nonstop, wondering if she should remove herself from the custody case. Wondering what her life would've been like if she'd taken a different road, literally and figuratively, that night so long ago.

Enough, she told herself. Daydreaming was for sissies, people who didn't have the guts to move with the ebb and flow of real life. The daily drudge was too offensive to deal with so they checked out in their fantasies to change the past or future.

The po'boy sat untouched on her plate. She stabbed at it with her fork then dipped inside for a fried shrimp, leaving the bun behind.

It didn't feel right keeping this secret from Hudson, who knew both nothing about her and everything that mattered most. He knew she drank her coffee cold without sugar or cream, her way of facing the day's contempt with one morning shot of bitter brew. He knew she was left-handed so he always put her pen where she could reach it. He knew she and her daughter Keisha were close, better than best friends. Her daughter, who was the air she breathed and the sun that shone across her face each morning, was truly her only reason for living.

"I have something to tell you, Hudson. I know I can trust you. This thing on my mind is wearing me down."

He reached across the table slowly. Delma felt the eyes and ears of the M&M sisters and the rest of the people in the place pay full attention as their hands connected. She didn't care.

"You know you can tell me anything and I'll never repeat it," Hudson said, and she knew he meant it.

10

Trevelle

Trevelle led the way into the hotel suite after Airic opened the door for her. She tossed her Gucci bag on the shiny marble-topped table at the entrance. She went straight to the ten-dollar bottle of Voss and poured a glass of the overpriced water.

"We're going to have to get a new lawyer. That man is an imbecile."

"He's a good Christian lawyer," Airic said, taking off his suit jacket.

"In this instance, those two traits may be a contradiction. We need someone who's going to rip Venus and her husband apart. Someone without a moral bone in his body."

Airic plopped on the sofa. "His hands were tied. A continuance was filed, it wasn't like he could go into detail right then and there. And that judge, whoa. I thought he handled himself pretty well considering she was one tough bit—" He caught himself. "One tough woman."

"He could've at least mentioned she was a danger to her child."

"I don't think that's going to be necessary. Venus knows what she's up against. She'll come around to making the right decision."

"You mean like a couple of pity visits a month. No. There's only one outcome I want and that's full custody. That woman is unfit. Who comes to a courtroom with hair spiraling all out of control? An Afro? Did you see her? Look like one of those mother earth women. Girl never heard of a hot comb, or any comb for that matter?"

"I don't know," Airic said. "I don't know if this is the right thing. Yes, I want visitation, but the whole full custody thing seems a bit much."

She stood over him with her arms crossed then leaned close. "'For I know him, that he will command his children and his household after him and they shall keep the way of the Lord, to do justice and judgment, that the Lord may bring upon Abraham that which he hath spoken of him,' Genesis eighteen. What I'm talking about here is a *thing* called responsibility as a man of God.

"Do you know how many fathers are running around this world not taking care of the children from their loins? All of them are going to burn in hell, you can believe that. The husband is the head of the household and his first and only responsibility is to teach his children the way of our Lord and Savior Jesus Christ." She strutted toward the table and picked up her white leather-bound Bible.

"First Timothy, five:eight. Listen to this, 'But if any provide not for his own, and specially for those of his own house, he hath denied the faith, and is worse than an infidel.'" Her voice rose, "That child, will not see the inside of a church living with those people. Unholy, that woman. No respect for herself or that child. She's unstable. How is she going to take care of a daughter and teach her to respect herself in the ways of Christ?"

Trevelle sat, exhausted. Court had been a drain on her spirit. Airic scooted close to her. One could see Airic was a good man. While she had prayed over his lack of spiritual backbone, she'd also been grateful for his sensitivity and complete openness to change. Being raised by a single mother who barely had time to put a potpie in the oven while holding down two jobs, let alone get her son to church for a Bible study lesson, was not his fault. But the makings of a God-fearing heart were there and ready to be molded. He'd graciously waited until they were married before being allowed to enter her celibate garden. Six months was a lifetime for any man to wait and he did so without complaint. Difficult for Trevelle as well, spending so much time around his charismatic scent, his words of comfort and sincerity. He'd still be a lowly professor if she hadn't entered his life, and been proud of it. His days of worshiping the all-mighty dollar were long behind him. He merely wanted to live and let live. His honesty and humbleness had been refreshing, but now it was simply getting on her nerves.

"How many times do we have to go over this?" She leaned on his shoulder, careful not to smudge his suit with her makeup. Her hand grazed his tie before loosening the knot and pulling the fabric away.

Trevelle knew a thing or two about men. One thing she knew for sure, a satisfied and happy man was far more pliable than a callous one full of contempt and spite. Her fingers trailed the buttons of his shirt, undoing them as she went along. She leaned into the smooth blank canvas of his chest and used her tongue to begin a work of art. The full thickness of his arousal called out to her. She worked his belt and zipper with one steady hand, the same as she'd been taught so many years ago. Old habits died hard. She couldn't wait to feel his hardness against her tongue.

"A woman's duty," she whispered before taking him in her mouth. Just a taste, she chastised herself and yet couldn't force herself to stop. Old habits never really died at all, only hid in the dark waiting for a chance to be free.

Airic certainly didn't mind. She held the way to his heart and mind in her throbbing mouth. A few moments later he was a withering mess.

In the bathroom, where Trevelle washed the foulness out of her mouth, she prayed for forgiveness. Such a filthy depraved need . . . *hers*. After all these years no matter how much she prayed the desire away, the want never left her mind. Cain had taught her how to suck and control every movement with her tongue. She learned there was nothing a man wouldn't do for a quick and efficient blow job. The thrill of victory, maybe, the triumph of reducing a man to pure jelly after completion, she wasn't sure why she received as much pleasure as she gave from such a one-sided act. "The flesh is weak. The soul is strong. Thank you, thank you," she whispered. Grateful to God for sending her a husband, one man who understood her need and did not cast her out or judge her for the depravity.

She went back out and tossed a towel to Airic, startling him. "Clean yourself up. We have more to talk about."

11

Venus

Before the garage door was all the way up I could see my mother's pants legs in the open doorway. She bounced lightly with impatience. Pauletta had flown out the day before, determined to do some butt-kicking. My father had wanted to come, too, but she made him stay put. Henry Johnston was a levelheaded softy, always the voice of reason. If things got ugly and needed to be taken to another level with, say, eye-gouging, character-slaying, or knife threats Pauletta didn't want lucid Henry to get in the way with rationality and calm.

No one messed with her babies and got away with it. In school I swiftly got a reputation for having the mother who used her visitor's pass regularly. Nine times out of ten she was there to observe the teacher, not me. Any treatment she deemed unfair was quickly resolved with her ability to question you to death.

She moved to my side of the car. Her stylish brown jogging suit was a safe bet for our pleasantly cool house. "So, how'd it go?" she asked.

"Went fine," Jake answered for me. He was next to my mother giving me a hand to help me out of the car.

I needed them both to move back if I was ever going to get out.

"What'd the judge say?" my mother asked impatiently.

"Pauletta, let's go inside." Jake gently eased her out of the way for clearance.

Inside the house I'd noticed things were a bit more organized. Boxes that were once in the middle of the floor were shoved against the wall. The couch was clear of stacked dishes and pots from me looking for a single spatula. The first thing my mother said when she arrived was "You haven't even unpacked. How are you living?"

My answer, "One minute, one hour, one day at a time." Tomorrow wasn't promised, so I stopped planning for it.

"Mya's taking a nap, so don't mince words. Tell me everything." She sat with her hands in her lap, back straight, bracing herself for the worst.

The last thing I felt like doing was rehashing the details. I made a long story short and told her, "Airic gets Sunday visitations with Mya every other weekend." I may as well have said he won full custody the way Pauletta slumped.

"He doesn't deserve a minute of her sweet preciousness. I know he has rights as her biological father, but it's still not fair."

Jake stood over me with a tall glass of water and the little white pill I thought I'd never want to see again. For two months after the loss of my baby I took the antidepressant to help me function and, on occasion, sleep. "She needs to go lay down." He spoke to my mother but kept his eyes on me. "She's exhausted." He brushed a hand across my shoulder with a soft rub around my neck.

"What are you doing?" Pauletta stood up and grabbed the pill out of my hand. "I thought you said you'd never swallow another pill, not even if your head was pounding, not even a Tylenol? You said a pill would not pass your lips, that's what you said."

"Pauletta," Jake intervened. "Nothing like that's ever going to happen again. I have the pills in my possession so there's no possibility of an accident."

"Oh, is that what we're calling it now?"

I threw my head back and covered my eyes. "Mom, please, it's one pill. I'm not a drug addict. I'm not suicidal. I just want to get a minute of peace so I can sleep."

"Um-hum. Can't nobody drive you crazy unless you give 'em the keys. I tell you, Jesus is the only pill you need. Both of you need to get on your knees." She moved past me with disgust and mumbled her way out of the living room, something about knowing better. The last part I heard for sure, ". . . like somebody else raised you."

"Go lay down," Jake said to me. "I'll talk to her."

I held out my hand for a replacement. He slapped it lightly. "You're mom's right. I'll be up with some hot tea and give you one of my relaxing foot massages." He kissed me on the forehead and sent me on my way.

I knew a setup when I saw one. I'd asked Jake for the pill when we were in the car. We agreed anything prescribed would be kept in his possession. He could have given it to me discreetly, but he wanted to do it in front of my mother so he wouldn't have to be the bad guy by saying no. I took his advice and made my way upstairs. I stepped into the bedroom expecting the obstacle course of boxes and instead found a true miracle. My mother had managed to turn the oversize space into a real bedroom suite filled with comfort and coziness. The beautiful framed black-and-white pictures of Mya when she was only months old sat on the center of the dresser. Pictures of Jake and I when we were happy, mainly the Christmas picture we'd taken snuggled against one another with Mya sitting on Jake's lap near the fireplace lit in an effort to look seasonally correct. Lord knows it was eighty degrees that Christmas day in California. We were sweating like pigs and pleaded for the photographer to speed it up.

I stared at the picture until the realization hit me, I was pregnant with our son in that picture. I turned it facedown and sat at the edge of the bed. *Please, please, please.* Please what . . . ? Let Airic be hit by a bus? Please let the earth crack open and he and Trevelle fall straight to the hot core and disappear forever? *No, stop it.* I tried to control the anger but it wouldn't go away.

I dropped to my knees and kneeled at the rear of the bed.

Please give me strength.

Please let Airic see the error of his ways.

Please stop the hurt and hatred flowing through my veins. What Airic was doing was downright deplorable. Hearing Trevelle Doval call me mentally unstable hurt me to my bone. She would be unstable, too, if she'd lost a child after carrying him in her womb, feeling his every movement. Loving and caring each day, waiting to see the sweet miracle of life, only to have him ripped from your body, lifeless.

I lay with my eyes closed, knowing sleep was an obstacle course I'd never get through. The bedroom door opened. I heard my mother. "Venus, you sleep?"

"No, Mom. I never sleep."

"You're going to be fine." She climbed in the bed beside me. She pressed her cheek against mine while I hugged her for life support. My mother brought out the child in me as I assumed all mothers did for their children, regardless of age. The moment when you can put down your weapons of defense, admit to vulnerability and sometimes defeat, and just be the small scared child who depends on Mommy to make it all better.

"Don't let this drag you down. Don't let it get between you. If anything, it's time to bond together and squash whatever's causing the strain."

"We're fine," I protested. Then I rose up on my elbows and asked, "Is it that obvious?"

"Not to everyone, only to the people who care." She brushed back my pile of hair, running a hand along the edge. She'd grown to like my hair natural. When I first cut off my long straightened coif she'd hoped it was a phase. It just wasn't done. Why run around with an unruly head of hair when Dark and Lovely promised adventure and romance with one dose of creamy chemical assistance? Why live with what nature gave you when you could have man-made silky ease? Because I'd had enough of the promises that had been broken. Straight hair didn't get me the job, career, the house, or the man. And it certainly never took me horseback riding, convertible cruising, or any of the other magical journeys shown in the commercials. I didn't get anything remotely close to love and adventure until I cut off every shred of my hair and started over from scratch on my own terms.

"You know what I think? After this custody thing is over, you two need to leave Mya with me, take a nice long vacation. Go somewhere and just relax." She kissed me while I inhaled her scent. Thirty years and I still didn't know the name of the perfume she wore. All I knew was that it was the only perfume that didn't send me into a fit of runny nose, watery eyes, and raised welts if I got too close.

"We're doing better if it's any consolation."

"He loves you like nobody's business. I can see it in his eyes, in everything he does, all for you. I'm mostly worried about what's in your eyes."

"Mom . . ."

"Listen, women have been giving birth since Adam screwed Eve. Losing a child is devastating, but it's a natural reality. Women lose their babies. You are lucky to have Mya. You're lucky to have a husband that loves you."

"You've got it all wrong. I'm the one keeping Jake together," I said, ready to defend my position.

"I see who's keeping who together. He's not the one in need of little white pills."

"I'm tired. I'm exhausted from *trying* to keep it together for him and me. I figured since you were here I could at least zone out for a minute. I haven't slept in like a year," I said. "Do you know what that feels like, Mom?"

She shook her head no. "Worrying won't bring your baby back. It won't stop Airic from wanting to see Mya, and it won't bring you and Jake any closer together. Close your eyes, sweetie." She scooted next to me and pulled the cover up around my shoulders. "You have to trust everything is going to be all right." She kissed me lightly on the forehead and put her arm snuggly around me. For the first time in so long I rested. I gave up the fight and let my body relax and waited for sleep to come.

12

Good for the Soul

Delma stood at her daughter's front door. She put her finger near the doorbell but waited, unable to press the button. She wasn't home. She knew this, of course. But she always pressed the button so as not to barge in. Keisha was an adult now, one that made her mother extremely proud. At twenty-seven she already owned her own home and had a nice car and all the high-tech accessories her upwardly mobile salary could reasonably afford. Knowing there were strong theories about nature versus nurture, evidence proved an apple didn't fall far from the tree. Delma had steered Keisha with a steady hand. She'd given her a good home, sought out the right teachers from ballet to Bible study, and made sure the bar was set high for achievement. Still with all she did right, she couldn't help but fear the day Keisha's true DNA would rear its ugly head and ruin everything.

After all, Keisha's biological mother had been a prostitute and dope fiend, her father some demented john who hadn't the sense or morals to know having sex with underage streetwalkers was foul, despicable behavior. Delma watched for signs of self-degradation. The teen years were the worst, wondering if one day she'd come home to boys lined up outside Keisha's back window, waiting their turn. In her work she'd seen just about everything. Girls as young as eleven and twelve having sex, getting pregnant, and not knowing which boy or man was the father. So Delma watched with a cautious eye. Other parents warned her it was normal for teens to start wrestling for independence, acting out. Raging hormones and awkwardness. Needing acceptance from anyone and everyone except the mother who loved her.

Keisha had the requisite temper tantrums, a few bouts of depression because a boy she liked made it a point to choose her best friend over her. She was suspended once for fighting, tired of the other girls' teasing that she talked white and thought she was better than everyone else. Delma wasted no time moving her out of that school and into a private academy where "talking white" equaled straight As and not an ass-whupping.

They survived the teen years without serious incident. As she watched her daughter mature into a woman she thought about telling her the truth. *Adoption* seemed like such an ugly word. *Fate* was far better. In Keisha and Delma's case, *divine fate.*

Delma finally rang the doorbell. She heard Pearl scamper on the other side of the door, barking in her tight little terrier voice. "Just use your key," her bark insisted. Pearl couldn't understand why they must go through this every time.

"All right, I'm coming." Delma didn't like letting herself into her daughter's house. Respect. Courtesy. Fear. The same nagging fear she'd endured the child's entire life. Walking into some scene, witnessing with her own eyes the inevitable. *Stop it,* she told herself. *Just stop it.*

"Hey, Pearly. How's the precious baby, huh?" Delma cautiously pushed the door open, not wanting to hit the excited doggy. Pearl stood on her hind legs while Delma patted and smoothed her shiny white coat.

Delma washed the water bowl and poured a fresh bottle of Evian into it, as Keisha instructed. The dog even ate gourmet doggy food bought online, shipped in dry ice. What else could be expected? This was Keisha's child. She was treating Pearl the way she understood a child was to be treated, given the best, honored, loved, sacrificed for. Delma thought it ridiculous the way Keisha researched the dog's pedigree, met with the breeder several times to get a feel for the temperament of the doggy parents, as if she were interviewing them. It all sounded familiar. Keisha wanted to make sure she was getting a good dog, from good stock, mentally healthy, who wouldn't piss and poop all over her thousand-dollar rugs, or chew up her expensive Jimmy Choo collection.

How fortunate for Keisha to be able to choose, to insist on the best pedigree. Lucky her. She was never given the opportunity to make a choice, to interview or investigate the biological parents. There was no time to think, only to act. No waiting period. No background check.

She simply had accepted the responsibility of what may come from the minute she held Keisha in her arms when she was only a day old, malnourished, dehydrated, and more than likely damaged from the mother's drug use. Didn't matter.

"Mom, you're already here." Keisha said as she walked in the door. She was wearing her hair long these days. Gone was the short corporate raider look. Since taking the job with the Peabody law firm she looked more like a member of a girl singing group, always in spiked heels and fitted dresses that showed her compact booty and thin waist. Delma was familiar with the Peabody Group; they specialized in sports and entertainment law.

Keisha knelt down and rubbed cheeks with Pearl. "Hey, sweet pea, you miss Mama?" The shaggy dog ended up in Keisha's arms. Delma couldn't help notice their resemblance. The big glossy coal-black eyes peeking underneath a sheath of straight bangs. At least Keisha hadn't gone platinum blond like a lot of the young black women these days, crying out for attention.

"I . . . we need to talk." Delma grabbed the pocket-size package of tissues from her purse. Tears were sure to fall.

"You're scaring me," Keisha said, sitting on the couch next to Delma. "When you called and said you wanted to meet me here, I was a nervous wreck. I had to talk myself straight; now you're scaring me again." Pearl squeezed between the two of them on the couch. "Just tell me, what's going on?" Keisha nervously ran her fingers through her doggy's silky strands.

Delma licked her lips and tried to remember Hudson's words of encouragement. *Secrets only hurt when they're secrets. Once it becomes the truth, it can't hurt anymore. She'll understand because she's your daughter and you raised her with love, strength, and compassion.*

"Keish, sweetie, I should have told you this a long time ago. I was afraid because you were all I had and I never wanted to see hate in your eyes or in your heart. My mother died when I was eight years old, and I hated her for leaving me. I know that's silly, hating someone for dying, but it's true. I wasted a lot of time and years feeling that way until I was pretty much empty, until you came along."

"Mom, I know where you're going. I could never hate you."

"Me?" Delma caught herself. "Of course, no. I mean, our relationship is solid. But I know you've always wondered about the missing pieces."

Keisha leaned across and kissed Delma on the cheek. "I've never needed a father, I had you. You think because I'm still single I don't know how to have a balanced relationship with a man, right? How many times are we going to have this same conversation? I'm right where I want to be. I could be in love, married with children, if that's what I wanted, but I don't. I like my life. And yes, I owe it all to you because you taught me I could do it on my own . . . I don't need a man to validate me."

Delma squeezed the tissue package. "That's not it. I mean, not today. This is about your biological parents."

Keisha swept the hair away from her face, pushing the long straight ends behind her ear. So young, so pretty and full of life. She was the spitting image of that woman, her seed mother. The only difference was, Keisha was also beautiful on the inside where it counted.

"You've always told me you didn't know who . . . what are you saying?"

Delma suddenly got cold feet. Not just cold, solid ice blocks hinged to her ankles.

"I don't want to know. I don't care." Keisha stood up and Pearl was quickly clipping at her heels. "I have to go. I have to change. The firm is sponsoring the Coalition for Black Women in Business, a fund-raiser. Of course they're sending me to represent."

Delma followed her daughter to the large master suite, the size of Delma's entire living room. "I guess we can talk later, some time when it's more appropriate." She turned to leave.

"Why are you scaring me like this, Mom?"

Because secrets only hurt when they're secrets. "I'm tired. I'm just feeling a bit lonely these days. Needy. I simply wanted to talk, spend a little time with you." Delma couldn't believe how contrived she sounded. Surely her daughter could see through her façade. She braced herself, ready to make the confession, hoping Keisha dragged it out of her.

"I know I haven't been spending enough time with you, but things will calm down at the law firm around the holidays and we'll do something. Go on a vacation. Hang out at the beach and drink mai tais."

I don't want to hold this inside anymore. Something's happening and I know it's happening for a reason. Sins revisited, I don't know why . . . I don't. All I know is you're all that matters to me, all that's ever mattered in my life.

"You're right. I've been so stressed and I shouldn't take it out on you." Delma leaned in and hugged her precious daughter. "Go represent." This time it was she who pushed the hair out of her daughter's face. "I'll talk to you tomorrow."

"Bright and early," Keisha called out behind her.

13

Venus

I held Mya steady in my lap while the lab technician ran a swab across the inside of her cheek. Mya sputtered like she was about to choke from the dry cotton too near her throat. Her lip poked out ready for a wail.

"That didn't hurt at all, did it?" The large red freckles on the woman bloomed to a kid-friendly smile.

Mya was led into subliminal agreement. *Right, it didn't hurt at all.*

I kissed Mya on her head. "Such a brave girl."

"Now I get my pop?" Mya softly whispered against my ear.

"I heard that. You deserve two lollipops," the lab tech said, reaching into her pocket and pulling out the shiny hard candy she'd used earlier as a bribe. "You also have your husband's sample?" she said to me, taking advantage of the distraction.

"Um . . . yes." I reached in my purse and pulled out a baggy with barely enough hair shavings to be visible to the naked eye. Jake hadn't volunteered for the test. "What's the point," he growled. "We know who her daddy is."

The technician held the baggy up and inspected it in the light. "Good enough. And the second party's sample is already on file. So you're all done."

"When do I get the results?"

She flipped through a couple of top sheets in the file. "Since this is a court-ordered test the results will be sent directly to the case clerk."

Mya began unwrapping one of her lollipops, her large eyes on the prize.

The technician smiled. "You did good. Most kids are not happy customers."

I thought about the onslaught of "customers" in the waiting area. Dozens of children from every age and race sitting patiently, most with no idea why they were there, some with a definite knowledge, obvious by the scowl of injustice on their faces. Why was it their fault that their parents had screwed up, slept with the wrong man, or seduced the wrong woman?

As we walked past, Mya held up her glistening red lollipop as proof for the other children, the experience wasn't bad at all. *And look, you get a reward.*

I drove home glad to have the test over and behind us. It was the last thing I wanted to put Mya through, the last thing I'd ever want her to know. A test was needed to prove who her father was. What does that make her mommy? I wasn't sleeping with two men at the same time. There was definitely a solid month or two between them. I'd already made up my mind to end the relationship with Airic long before Jake and I sealed our deal. Not to mention Airic had been experiencing technical difficulties. Erectile dysfunction wasn't the biggest issue but damn if it didn't throw a monkey wrench into the possibility of reconciliation.

Bottom line, it was plain old wishful thinking on my part. Deep down I wanted there to be a shred of hope that Mya was Jake's. Up to the last second before Mya's head came peeking out of my womb I'd wished by some miracle she was the love child of the hottest, sexiest, best thing that had ever happened to me. Everything would've been so much simpler.

Though anyone could see the similar features of Airic, the lightness of her skin, the sun-bleached frizzy edges of her hair that separated from the pack regardless of what kind of miracle-claiming product I used. Her sharp chin and piercing eyes could have come from either one of us, but there was no denying the overall presence of Airic became more pronounced as the years went by. Anyone could see it was his child. I lived with this fact every day. Though I disliked Airic immensely there was no denying my love for Mya.

As a treat for being such a brave girl, I promised a trip to the big park, the one with the waterfalls randomly spurting out from the ground, making a game. The children could never guess which hole would shoot the water so they ran to each one like it was a game of musical chairs.

There were a few children already surrounding the shooting water streams when we walked up. She sprinted past the water and straight to the sandbox. Maybe she'd play in the water later after she got hot. The child became a butterfly in springtime when other children were around. I watched her jump right in like she'd known the two other children all her short life. I headed to a seat on a bench a few gigantic steps away, which is all it would take for me to get to her if she fell off a slide or met some other daily threat of being a child.

"Is this seat taken?" I asked about the only shaded spot in the park.

"No, go ahead." The woman hadn't bothered looking up from her knitting. She pulled a long strand from the bag of yarn next to her. Someone's grandmother I presumed, just like the ones in storybooks, with her sharp bifocals hanging on the bridge of her nose and her hair neatly pinned in a bun like she'd probably worn it all her life. I sat down to get a good view of Mya and all the children and wondered which one was under her watchful eye. Although in this case she was only watching her needles wave back and forth at record speed.

"Which one's yours?" I asked, staring out at the sandbox where Mya had pushed her way through the thick of things. A little boy was suddenly without his shovel and Mya was digging away.

"Right here," she said, reaching past her bag of yarn. She adjusted a light knit blanket with holes big enough to see through to where a baby slept peacefully.

"Oh my goodness, I didn't even see him over there."

"Yeah, he's a sleeper. But of course nighttime's an entirely different subject. I've tried everything to keep him awake during the day but no sirree, he's got a serious aversion to daylight hours."

"That must drive his mother crazy." I smiled.

"Well for now, that would be me, and I'm all right with it. I don't sleep much at night myself with this old bladder acting up. We got ourselves a rhythm. I wake up right about the same time each night and he knows I'm coming, no need to even put out a cry." She pulled the light blanket back over the rocker.

"Your grandbaby?" I said for confirmation of what I'd already assumed.

"Foster mom. I'm on my twentieth child. Been taking care of little guys like this since my husband passed away eleven years ago. Why be on earth if you're not going to do something worthwhile with your time?" She winked. "And you have just the one there." She nodded toward Mya.

"Yes, just one."

"Thinking about having any more? I say one is the loneliest number," she chided me before I can get in a word. "Kids need siblings. Need somebody to tattletale on them to keep each other in line."

"I only had a brother. Well, I shouldn't say 'only' . . . he was my best friend."

"There you go, my point is proven. So you plan to have any more children?" she asked.

I turned my head and did my best to hide the well of tears attempting to break free. The odds were slim for Mya to have a brother or sister. Getting slimmer with each passing day. The tiny nagging voice in my head warned me there would be no more children. Mya sustained me. Such a heavy load to put on a small innocent child. My entire state of being depended on seeing her sweet face each morning and holding her for tender good night kisses.

The woman cleared my stifling thoughts with her voice. "When

I was growing up we had a house full of my seven brothers and sisters and me. We had two bedrooms and one tiny bathroom. Guess that's why I can't imagine my big house empty. When this little guy leaves, there'll be another one right behind him. No shortage of unwanted babies." She twirled her yarn and started a new row. "Such a shame, too. I see all those big movie stars and celebrities flying all over the world looking for a child to love when there's plenty right here in our own backyard."

As if on cue there was a tiny cough from underneath the blanket. Then a second dry cough.

"Poor thing have a cold?" I asked.

"I wish it was just a cold. He's got asthma. Found out early so that's a good thing." She put her knitting down and checked on the little guy. She reached inside and lifted the thick bundle against her chest. The baby opened his eyes and looked directly at me, but only briefly.

"He's an angel," I said quietly, reaching out and stroking his wispy head of hair, bald in the back where he'd spent too much time laying down. "Can I hold him?"

"Of course," she said. "By the way, my name is Alverene Henderson."

"Venus," I said, anticipating the weight of the child in my arms. She handed him over without asking any more questions, like last name or any time served in a mental ward. Maybe if she'd known I'd suffered from the loss of my baby boy a mere six months ago and ached and yearned with every passing minute, hour, and day for his return, she would've thought twice before handing him over. Lucky for me she was a trusting soul.

"What's his name?"

"Ralph."

"Ralph?" I tested the name out loud and thought for sure it was all wrong for such a sweet little boy. I could feel the familiar tremor of his body with each raspy breath; it was the same way Jake felt when he was fighting an asthma attack.

Mya must've sensed her territory being breached. Before I knew it she was at my side making inquiries. She touched his foot and gave it a shake. Ralph smiled. If I wasn't mistaken, he even let out a sly laugh. "Does he like peanut butter sanmiches?" Mya asked, stroking his chubby arm.

"Probably, but not yet. He likes milk. Lots of it," Alverene said.

"Oh, milk." I shook my head. "It's not good for babies with asthma. My husband's asthmatic," I added, as if it made me an expert.

Alverene ignored my milk warning and faced Mya. "And what's your name?"

"Mya." She held up three fingers knowing the next question. Alverene couldn't help it, she asked anyway.

"How old are you?"

Mya skipped her usual hand to the forehead like she did when she was at her wit's end. She leaned on Alverene and whispered, "Three."

"You sure are a smart girl for three."

"She is," I agreed, "very smart." She could count to ten, only skipping the number nine along the way. She'd mastered all her colors and wasn't afraid to tell Jake or I when she was in a pink or blue mood. I pulled her up on the bench to sit next to Ralph and me. For a brief second or even longer the missing piece to a puzzle had been found and snapped gently into place. I snuggled against Ralph's warmth and watched Mya make baby conversation.

"If I didn't know better I'd say you all came this way," Alverene said. "I believe families are made, not born. Such a big job. So much work to do, giving birth is only a small part, wouldn't you say?"

I wondered if there was a sign on my back with my tragedy written in permanent marker. She pulled out a package of tissues and handed it to me, and went back to her knitting as if having a stranger balling her eyes out right next to you was the most natural act in the world.

14

Do Tell

Bright and early came with a vengeance. Mr. Sun slithered through the mini-blinds, sneaking under Delma's closed lids, making her wish it was a Saturday instead of hump day. She wasn't an early riser by nature. She could easily sleep till noon without so much as fluttering her lashes. But duty called. Duty always called. She never had anyone else to depend on but herself. No man around to pick up the slack. Mortgage, light bill, gas, and water, all had one name on the account: Delma J. Hawkins.

She rolled over, wishing for ten minutes' more rest. All night she'd fallen in and out of sleep, fighting off visions of Trevelle Doval from nearly thirty years ago, bloodied and battered. Remembering the constant fear of being found out was like a thousand pins and needles pushed through her eyes. Always waiting for the day when the sheriff would walk into her courtroom and take her by the arm. *Delma Hawkins, you're under arrest.*

How is it after all those years Trevelle Doval lands in her courtroom, of all the courtrooms in the land? She wasn't a big believer in coincidence or accidents, collision courses. Cause and effect was what Delma subscribed to. The last few days felt like a cruel joke someone decided to play, bringing Trevelle front and center in her life. All those years of watching and waiting only to have her past land right on her doorstep.

Delma turned on the shower and waited while the water turned to hot and the steam rose on the mirror. Her phone started ringing the moment she was about to step into the glass enclosure. *Let the machine get it,* she thought. No, it was probably Keisha. She'd better answer. She'd already worried her baby to death with her talk of secrets and confessions. She didn't want to be any more of a bother, making Keisha drive all the way over just because she hadn't answered the phone.

Delma stood shivering, with the towel draped around her body.

"Hello," she sang out, expecting to hear Keisha's voice on the other end of the line. The line clicked and quickly went dead. She stared at the receiver and tried to pull up the caller ID. PRIVATE CALL showed on the small window. Delma placed the phone back and it instantly rang again.

"Hello," she snapped, expecting the same caller.

Keisha's voice was a relief. "Hey, Mommy."

"Hey . . . did you just call a few seconds ago?"

"No. This is the first time I dialed. But that must be why you answered on the first ring. I wanted to check on you. Did you sleep okay?"

"Yes, yes. I told you I didn't want you to worry about me, Keish. I'm fine."

"Good. I'm going to look into a trip for us to Jamaica or Barbados, somewhere we can just relax, the two of us."

She thought about being difficult, saying something silly like *That's not necessary,* or *Go with a friend who'll be a whole lot more fun.* Instead Delma was thankful for her good fortune for having a daughter who cared enough to want to spend time with her, let alone vacation together on an exotic island. "I'll get my bathing suit whenever you tell me." Delma chuckled, picturing herself hiking up a calm sandy shore in a one-piece. "Just let me know the dates and I'll clear my calendar."

Her daughter was all that mattered, all that had ever mattered. Only a mother could understand complete and utter self-sacrifice.

Not even a husband or wife knew the kind of love between a mother and her child.

"Go on now. I've got to catch a shower and get to the courthouse."

They hung up. Delma headed back to the bathroom. The minute she reached for the shower handle the phone rang again.

Keisha, always with one more thought.

"Yelllo . . . ," Delma sang out.

"Somebody's got a secret," a man's voice whispered, too low to identify.

"What . . . ?"

The phone clicked and the line went dead. Delma couldn't move. Her heart raced fast and hard against her chest. *Somebody's got a secret.*

She dropped the phone. She spun around, suddenly feeling exposed. She stood shaking with nothing more than a towel wrapped around her body. She eyed the windows, then the bedroom door. She swung it open, peeking out quickly as if she'd catch someone standing right in her living room.

It took a minute to get a hold of herself, to calm her nerves. Must've been a crank caller. Her own paranoia was leading her down a crazy imaginary path. No one could know . . . Trevelle Doval hadn't even known and it was her child. A real mother would've sensed her child was still alive somewhere, walking the earth. That was the very reason Delma had lived in a state of constant dread during those first couple of months. The day never came. Because no one knew. Except . . . she'd told Hudson everything only days ago. And now she was getting phone calls.

She hurried with her shower, got dressed, and rushed to work.

◎◎

Delma waited in her car instead of going right into the courthouse. Hudson should've already arrived ten minutes ago. She had to appear unaffected. Pretend she wasn't mad to get him to tell her the truth. All she wanted to know was *why*. She'd been good to him over the years. There was no reason he should want to harm her, cause her stress. No reason whatsoever.

"Hey, there," Hudson said through the open window. Delma nearly jumped out of her skin.

"You scared me half to death."

"What're you doing waiting out here?" His orange polo shirt collar was folded inward.

Delma reached out instinctually and straightened it out. "I wanted to talk with you, but not inside." She knew without a shadow of a doubt the courthouse cameras picked up more than pictures. In her early days in the district attorney's office she'd listened to plenty of taped conversations in the courtroom between a defendant and his lawyer. Why would a judge's chambers be any different?

"I needed to ask you something. I need you to be honest with me."

"Wait . . ." He did his best to rush around to the passenger side of her car and got inside. "What's going on?"

"Are you calling my house . . . trying to scare me into doing the right thing? I can't think of any other reason, no other motivation for these phone calls. You're my friend. I've been nothing but good to you. I gave you a job when no one else would touch you with a ten-foot pole." She went on, never having realized Hudson's mouth was hanging open in shock.

"What in the world are you talking about, woman?" His eyes bugged out like she'd seen on very rare occasions, usually sending her into a fit of giggles. Not this time. She was serious and too tired for games.

"Someone's called my house, whispering about a secret. Now you're the only person I told about Keisha . . . I trusted you—"

Hudson Hinkler reached over with both hands, pulling Delma in for a full-frontal kiss, taking her completely off balance. It happened so fast, yet lasted forever. His mouth still tasted of the toothpaste he'd used before coming to work. His tongue roamed over her bottom lip ever so gently, getting one last taste before letting her go. "I'd do anything for you, Delma Hawkins. You need to know you can always count on me . . . don't you know that by now? Now what in the world are you talking about?"

Delma nodded up and down, still dazed with shock. She brought her fingertips to her lip where the tingling moistness still lasted. He took ahold of her hand. "We'll figure it out. Whoever, whatever's going on, we'll figure it out together."

15

Trevelle

"My life is an open book, just like the Bible," Trevelle said to the television camera. "I'm here by the grace of God just like you." She pointed out to the supposedly millions watching. "We all have trials and tribulations that bring us to the door of salvation. Yet, all we have to do is knock and we are granted entry. But you know what, it's easy to get in; the work comes when you earn the right to stay in. You ever had a guest come to your house doing everything you asked them not to do, drinking, smoking, putting their shoes on the couch? Maybe they spill some food on your white carpet after you specifically asked them to not eat in your living room?" She paused. The television audience filled in with laughter. Trevelle smiled and shook her head. "God don't want you in his house if you're not going to follow the rules."

Trevelle pressed the power button. The television turned off and she sat in silence. She enjoyed watching herself, unlike most television personalities she knew. They complained incessantly about their inability to watch themselves, lamenting over their hair, makeup, the angle of their mouth or the nervous tic no one else would notice if their life depended on it. Trevelle spent a great many hours studying her tapes, figuring out what she could do better, how to reach her audience and close the show with every eye in the house wet with emotion.

Her mission in life was to teach, so all that she'd been through was not in vain. She wanted to save others from the hurt and suffering she'd experienced. If she couldn't save them, she could at least help them in healing. Her desire to help others was genuine. One day Venus Johnston-Parson would thank her for saving her child, giving her the foundation of God and Christianity.

It was the least Trevelle could do. She wasn't able to save her own daughter but she would save Airic's baby girl from a life of ill repute. She looked at the clock and set the alarm before pulling the silk mask over her eyes and facing her demons head-on. She fell asleep, accepting the fact that Cain visited her in her dreams every night and would probably do so for the rest of her life. She closed her eyes and welcomed his visit.

She craved Cain and couldn't wait to see him every day. Soon, her education was an afterthought. He picked her up right outside of the middle school before the first bell rang. It was clear how much he cared, how much he wanted to take care of her. If only she were older, if only she weren't a virgin, they could be together, he'd told her. What else was she to do but take things into her own hands, to prove to Cain she wanted to be with him just as much?

He wanted a real woman, he'd told her. She took it as punishment that she was relegated to her knees as her only duty, although she enjoyed it just as much as he did. She thought she understood why he was called "Cain," like the wild sugar plants growing in the Mississippi fields in the back of her grandmama's house. She'd only been there once when she and Kevin were little. The field was anybody's paradise. All you had to do was break off one of the wild-growing canes and chew and suck away.

At thirteen years old, there was only one way she knew how to be a real woman. The reasonable choice was Boomer, one of Kevin's friends who'd been steady on her case the minute she entered Banner Junior High. Kevin no longer went to school. Instead, he spent all his time downtown selling drugs to the lunch crowd, so the coast was clear. Boomer was short and small for his age and tried to compensate with an eight-inch round Afro and oversize shirts that made him look even shorter. The conclusion: He was small so he wouldn't hurt her.

By the end of lunch, in the back of the rotten wood bleachers, Boomer had helped himself to all that was offered. He poured his soul into her believing their consummation would become a ritual. "Now you're mine," he'd panted in her ear before she tossed him off her. No, she belonged to someone else and she couldn't wait to spread the good news, the chains of virginity had been unlocked.

As the words spilled from her lips, she watched Cain's hand rise up before coming down hard across her face. He grabbed the back of her neck and slammed her head into the dashboard. Two, three, four, she lost count how many times her head was shoved into the thick leather, shocking her face numb, beyond pain. "You want a be a whore? I'm a show you what whores do."

Four hours later Cain dropped her off at her mama's house and told her he'd be back for her the next day. She'd better not try to hide from him or he'd find her and hurt her. That evening she wept while she sat in the tub of hot bathwater, too ashamed to tell anyone. Cain had showed her exactly what whores do. He'd taken her to a sad apartment on top of a Chinese restaurant. He led her into the stuffy room filled with smoke and the suffocating potency of Chinese food. A woman lay sleeping on the couch. Cain swept across the room and slapped her so hard she fell onto the floor.

"What tha—?" She tried to get up and Cain slapped her again.

"Get yo' lazy ass up and get to work." He turned his gaze back on Trevelle. "Come here. I got somebody I want you to meet."

"Who this, Cain? She what, twelve, thirteen?"

"She old enough. Ain't that right?"

Trevelle nodded out of sheer and outright fear. Her eyes scanned the woman's hard chapped lips and yellow teeth. The woman took in the welt growing underneath her eye. "My name is

Nadia," she said, getting back up on the couch. "What's yours?" Her
tone was almost motherly.

"Velle."

"Get her some ice and stop all this lip jabbing. I don't want her
looking bruised up on her first day on the job."

"Cain, no," Nadia said, her eyes big hollow circles. "You ain't
gon do that. She a child."

He raised his hand and she cowered, hiding from the strike that
never came. "I said get her some ice." He turned and faced Trevelle
and put a soft hand against her cheek. He kissed her throbbing forehead where he'd slammed her into the dashboard. "It won't hurt for
long." How right he was. She'd forgotten about the pain in her face
where he'd hit her. The new pain was so much louder and stronger.
It hurt like a million daggers pushing through her body. Three different men, grown men who'd had no problem taking a little girl and
shoving her in the backseat of a car for five minutes' worth of pleasure. All the while she screamed until her throat burned raw with exhaustion leaving behind the sound of a teenaged girl mourning her
childhood once and for all. It was only the beginning of her nightmare, the never-ending vision that seeped into her sleep at night.

16

Jake

He pressed the power button on the flat screen television's remote when he couldn't take it anymore. He stretched his legs and leaned his back against the couch. He'd been up all night unable to get Airic Fisher out of his head, so he turned on the television and just his luck, landed on Trevelle Doval. He watched her every move, listened to her every word, and realized he was only getting more outraged at the situation. Surely he had more to be worried about than Airic and his holy wife. There was the small matter of his financial situation. Not that he was broke by any stretch of the imagination but money was relative. He had a life and a family to take care of. Lots of money going out and not a dime coming in would eventually present a problem.

Then there was the matter of his past creeping around his mind like a noisy ghost. The ghost was named Byron Steeple. The house was quiet. *All the better to hear your cries with, my dear.* Between Byron and now Airic Fisher in his head, Jake could've easily been the one to turn to the little white pills he held in his possession. He could use some mind-numbing assistance but thank goodness he'd never resorted to drugs of any kind. A taste of rich cognac on a late stormy night listening to Coltrane, now that was his fix. He leaned forward and picked up the glass and swirled the dark liquid around until it coated the sides. He took a sip and felt the sweet burn slide down his throat.

When he'd first come on the scene as a hip-hop artist, he'd been offered every kind of mind-altering drug known to man. He could admit now, fifteen years later, that he had been too scared to take anybody up on their offer. Too scared of losing control of his faculties. Afraid of what he might do once outside of his own mind.

How many times had he witnessed it? The aftereffects of too much crystal, an OxyContin mixed with a cocktail creating the ultimate aphrodisiac, turning anything with two legs into hunted prey. The penalty came in the form of rape charges, incurable diseases, and paternity papers. Jake ran with a small crew. He couldn't afford entourages of six or twelve deep. He had a mother and brother who needed all the goodwill payments he could reasonably come up with at the time. So he kept his friends list to a minimum. *Associates* may have been a better term.

When his hotness played out, so did they. He'd have to say his failure on the second CD was the best thing to happen to him. Otherwise he'd probably still be out there trying to profile. Pretense was all it was, all it would ever be. Anybody who got the opportunity to escape through an open door would run like hell. An opportunity to produce, act, host, was like a get out of jail free card. The music industry was filled with nothing but leeches and frogs hopping onto the next best thing. When your lily pad sank, no one was there to offer a hand.

Jake had bought his freedom with his clothing business, JP Wear. It was still going strong with his name on the label, only he wasn't there to make the decisions. All because of Byron Steeple. He'd lost his business because of one man; he wasn't about to lose his family, too.

He checked the time on his cell phone. 5:00 A.M. It would only be two on the West coast. If Georgina wasn't up, she should be. He was paying her enough money to be on the clock twenty-four seven.

Her voice came on the line groggy but completely aware who'd interrupted her sleep. "Mr. JP."

"'The one and only," he said with a smooth, tired voice. "When's your flight?"

She stuttered slightly as she said, "I plan to be there for the court date, Jake. On time and accounted for."

"Nah . . . Sunday. He's coming to pick up my little girl for visitation and you need to be here."

"Listen, don't even think about doing anything stupid. Do you hear me?"

"Exactly why you need to be here . . . keep me from doing something stupid." He slapped the cell phone closed before letting out the harsh groan of frustration. Any moment he expected his wife or mother-in-law to come rushing downstairs to see what the noise was. Then he remembered no one could hear anything in the big pretty house. When the hoarse groan seeped out of his throat, he didn't try to hold back. He let the moment take him. If there was one thing he knew, anger should never be bottled up. Whoever created it, deserved to have it back tenfold.

17

Trevelle

Sundays were important to Trevelle, but not because she had work to do. Her shows were taped Monday through Friday and played nightly. By the time Sunday came around she was spent with exhaustion and simply needed time to rejuvenate. On occasion she accepted a Sunday invitation to visit a church and bless them with her words of gospel, though invites were getting fewer and fewer. Churches simply couldn't afford her anymore. The honorarium wasn't something voiced or put on paper. Trevelle Doval knew what she was worth and so did her fellow captains of ministry. They simply respected her enough not to insult her. Good thing, because this Sunday would have been cause for cancellation.

This particular Sunday was all about the child. Trevelle's heart palpitated with nervousness, wondering how Mya would take to her, their first outing together as a family. The plan was to pick her up at nine, have breakfast, then go to a local church, something she was sure the child knew nothing about. Prayer. Devotion. Praise. The silly mother did her best to keep the child sheltered from God's blessings under a veil of ignorance and damnation.

Trevelle snapped her makeup bag closed and checked her glowing smile in the mirror.

"Sweetheart are you ready?" She knocked on the door of Airic's room. Inside, his clothes were strewn about, slacks, shirts, ties hanging on the edge of his bed. "What's going on?"

He came out of the bathroom wearing boxers and socks. "I don't know what to wear."

"Sweetheart." Trevelle opened her arms and let his head weigh on her shoulder. "You're nervous. It's okay. Everything's going to be fine. This is your child. She will have an inherent love for you that not even her mother will be able to deny. A child knows instinctively who has their best interest at heart. She'll know, she will know."

He lifted his head. His eyes glistened with fear and regret. "I don't know. Maybe—"

Trevelle put her finger to his lips. "Relax. Get dressed. Trust me, everything is going to be fine," she said. She had no proof of that. Her nerves were on edge, too. She closed the door to his room. She sat on the couch and put her hands together; her long nails clicked, finding their place against each other. "Dear God, give him strength, give him peace of mind."

Moments later Airic stepped out of the room wearing a white linen shirt with beige linen pants. He looked breezy and casual like they were preparing to take a walk on the beach instead of going to the Lord's house.

"I want her to be comfortable around me. I think a suit'll put her off a bit."

"You can at least wear a tie, Airic. We're visiting Mount Ebenezer, a Baptist church. Respectfully speaking, you look like some tropical gigolo, and where in the world did you get white shoes?"

Airic turned all confident, picked up his keys and said with a bright outlook, "My shoes are light tan. You coming?"

Trevelle took in a breath and held it. She didn't want to ruin the small steps of progress, but this was not what she meant when she prayed for her husband to have his own mind and strength.

☙

Pulling up to the house and seeing the extravagant, stylish mansion threw Trevelle for a loop. Not what she'd expected at all. Unemployed rappers weren't supposed to live in palatial spreads fit for kings. All completely unexpected. The car idled. Airic's jaw flexed against bone, then his Adam's apple went up and down two or three times.

Trevelle handed him the bottle of water she'd been nursing to ease his obvious parched throat. "We're already late as it is." Her way of telling him to get a move on. *We've come too far now.*

She watched as he strode the straight pathway and rang the doorbell. Venus answered, and then darted a look past him to eye Trevelle sitting in the car. The front door closed but Airic remained standing in the same spot.

The little snarly haired woman was so predictable. Trevelle checked her watch to start timing before she'd make the call to the sheriff's office. She held the judge's order in one hand and her cell phone in the other with the number already typed in, fully prepared to do all that was necessary.

18

Venus

"Is she ready?" Airic stood on the porch with his hands in his pants pockets, giving off cool confidence.

I folded my arms across my chest. "Why are you doing this, Airic? Why now?"

I felt Jake arrive by my side, radiating heat from his five-mile run on the treadmill. He wiped his face with the towel draped over his shoulders. His arms glistened with a sheen of perspiration. He stood firmly but didn't say a word. Soon Georgina Michaels was next to Jake, followed by my mother. We were a solid unit but still powerless to stop what was about to happen.

"I'm not going to have this conversation with either of you," Airic said, shoving his hands deeper into his pockets. "Just get Mya."

I slammed the door closed. Jake gave me a reprimanding look but remained silent.

Mya had been standing behind my mother the whole time, peeking past her thigh to see if this was really all about her. I bent down and looked her in the eye. "Sweetie, you remember what I told you. It's just for the afternoon, and you're going to have a great time. Daddy and I will be waiting when you get back." I kissed her lightly on the nose, then the lips, then the forehead before getting the gentle squeeze on my shoulder.

"It's okay, babe." Jake's way of telling me to calm down, telling me I was scaring Mya. I gave one last hug then took a second to get myself together. I opened the door to Airic, who hadn't budged or moved a muscle. He simply waited patiently. After a certain period of time he was within his right to call the sheriff to come and escort the child out of the house. Georgina had warned us of the exact same thing. "You don't want to have any unsportsmanlike behavior on record. No authorities involved. You're going to follow orders, do exactly as you've been told to do by the court. Explain to Mya about her visit with a relative and how much fun she will have. Tell her you'll be waiting when she gets home and that you love her very much."

Even as Mya bucked, kicked, and screamed, calling out for Mommy while Airic led her down the cobbled pathway, all we could do was watch. Powerless. Jake gripped my hand so hard I thought he would crush it. Pauletta simply locked herself in the bathroom, unable to watch another minute of her grandbaby screaming in tears.

Few moments were as intense as this one. Nothing came close to having your child wrenched from your hands and dragged off. Didn't matter that it was Airic. He knew nothing about Mya, her likes or dislikes. How she would drift away while no one was paying attention. *Come find me, Mommy.* But what if I wasn't there to find her? What if she was lost and Airic didn't know the game?

"Mommmmy," Mya wailed. "Daddeee."

"She'll be fine," Airic called back toward us. "We'll be fine."

Georgina blocked the door when Jake attempted to take the first step out. "Okay, so the hardest part is over." She clapped her hands together as if we'd all won a prize. Her crisp white blouse was unbuttoned low enough to see she was tanned to perfection on every inch of her body. "You cooperated fully with the judge's orders." She gave us a sympathetic nod. "We're doing the right thing here. There's nothing a judge hates more than to hear a parent didn't comply with a court order."

19

Trevelle

Trevelle pulled the sunshade down and flipped open the mirror. Heat built up in the car, making her perfect foundation break out in oily sprinkles all over her nose. There was a time when she needed no makeup at all, a time when she awoke beautiful with no assistance whatsoever. Those times she tried not to remember, when her youth and beauty had taken her down an unexpected and very wrong road. So long ago and far away her past floated overhead every now and again, coming down to remind her that she'd been a foul piece of work. Thank God for divine intervention. Even more proof of God's good grace was the little girl coming toward her. Not of her own free will of course, but these things took time.

Mya wore jeans and a sky-blue T-shirt and a bow in her hair to match. She pitched a fit, screaming and yelling for her mommy and daddy as Airic carried her to the car. Understandable. Poor thing didn't know any better. Trevelle sat still, though she really wanted to jump out of the car and meet them halfway and give the little one a stern talking to.

But of course Venus and her husband were still watching. She wouldn't be surprised if they followed them to every destination out of spite.

The car door opened and Airic helped Mya into the booster seat they'd ordered with the car rental. Mya's wailing turned into soft sobs in between still calling for Mommy.

"Hi there, Mya. You look so pretty today. Remember me? I'm Trevelle and we're going to have lots of fun." Trevelle batted her long lashes and did her best to ignore the large erratic bush of hair on the child's head. The bow tilted to the side and did nothing to tame the wild mane. What a sight. Uncombed hair sent a shiver through Trevelle's spine. Obviously no one cared for the child or she wouldn't be running around unkempt.

So now she had both of them to deal with, Airic with his open collar and loose linen pants like he'd just left the set of *Miami Vice*, and the child, in jeans with uncombed hair looking like an orphan. Trevelle's first thought was to skip church altogether. She couldn't walk into Mt. Ebenezer with this motley crew. Her second thought, however, was to make a stop at the local Wal-Mart, pick up a tie and some hair products and fix all that was wrong in her small part of the world. Resourcefulness had always been one of Trevelle's strong suits. There was no time like the present to sharpen her skills.

20

Jake

Jake squeezed his arms tight one over the other to keep from slamming a fist into the wall. He realized if he loosened his grip even slightly, he could single-handedly destroy everything in his reach.

Yes, he'd agreed to play nice. Yes, he'd accepted the fact that Airic had a right to see Mya. It didn't stop the pain. There were no words, no way to make anyone understand. There were no visible signs of injury, no blood and guts. Then why did he feel like his insides had been ripped out?

Georgina failed to notice he was hanging on by a thread and continued with the plan of action. "This is going to play out perfectly," she said. "We'll ask for a psychological evaluation of Mya, explaining the rampant nightmares followed by this little visit."

How right she was. Nightmares vivid and haunting, of being led out the door with a perfect stranger. Mya didn't know who Airic was, and wouldn't understand if they'd tried to explain. Saying he was a close relative of the family. *Stupid!* Going through this was ridiculous.

"Do you have any idea . . ." Pauletta was back in time, speaking the words no one else could. "Does anyone realize we're dealing with a real live child, a baby, three years old? She doesn't know about your grand strategy. She only knows her mother and her father let a strange man take her out of this house. Uh-huh, you can bet there'll be some bad dreams, we won't have to make 'em up."

"Mya is going to be fine. Children are resilient," Georgina said, inching toward her briefcase to make her escape. She threw her suit jacket over her arm. "Let's keep it simple. We don't want to do anything stupid." She eyed Jake harder than the rest as she said her warning.

"You don't care," Venus said quickly. "I already lost one child, I can't lose another." She turned her face up to Jake, looking for support. But he shook his head instead. "Stop," he reprimanded. "Keep it together."

"She doesn't care," she repeated.

"Of course she cares, it's going to be okay. Mya's going to be back before you know it."

"Did you see Mya kicking and screaming like she was being kidnapped right in front of us? We did nothing, Jake."

Georgina tilted her head slightly like a dog who didn't understand such human antics and wasted emotions. She seemed unfazed until she spoke. "I wouldn't be here if I didn't care. You're forgetting I was there. I know what you went through. I'm not going to let it happen again." She reached out and shook Jake's hand.

"I'll walk you out."

When they reached the edge of the walkway, Jake faced Georgina. "Look, something's gotta be done to end this. I can't see her go through this nightmare. I can't watch her fall apart again."

Georgina unlocked her rental car. "Have I ever let you down? Leave it up to me. Just be patient and don't do anything stupid," she warned again.

"*How* stupid?" he said. "What exactly is it you don't want me to do? Kill him? Shit Georgina, all this time and I thought you actually believed me." He slammed her car door closed and backed up. She started her car but didn't leave.

"That's not what I'm implying," she said, letting the electronic window flow effortlessly down. "I just don't want you to jeopardize your chances by hitting him because if it were me, I probably would've decked the guy. Call me when Mya gets home." She pulled her long red hair over her shoulder. "Damn, it's hot."

"Hot as hell," Jake agreed.

"How long you plan on hiding out here?"

"I'm not hiding. If anything I'm trying to get some exposure. I'm invisible in Cali."

"You'll never be invisible to me." Georgina hunched her shoulders. "Guess I'm the one that shouldn't do anything stupid."

He raised both his arms. "Later." He didn't give Georgina's obvious flirtation a second thought. He was flattered, but impervious. He'd had enough women to last him ten lifetimes. He'd lived his life full and complete as a bachelor and the only benefit he'd noticed was that the roll of toilet tissue lasted longer. Women were pushing up on him at every turn, married or not. Rich or not. Famous or not. He didn't need the stress of running game.

He had exactly what he needed, his family, and he had no plans of losing them.

21

Dead Man Tales

Delma knew better than crossing the personal boundaries. Over the years it wasn't hard, she had but one thing on her mind: be success-ful. Take care of herself and Keisha first and foremost. She hadn't time for personal liaisons unless they were going to get her a bigger raise or a lower interest rate on her mortgage.

The waitress set the steaming cups of coffee down in front of her and Hudson. He grabbed four packets of sugar and tore them open all at once, pouring them in the same fashion.

Delma sighed. "You're right, I could be blowing this out of pro-portion. The secret . . . could mean a lot of things. Doesn't have to be referring to Keisha."

Hudson blew on his coffee before taking a sip. He leaned back in the booth. His long legs pushed out, bumping against Delma's thick knees. "Exactly. You shouldn't play into it."

"But here, in my heart, I know it's time to tell her everything. The secret has been too much of a burden."

Hudson nodded but didn't want to push. She knew what he was thinking. If she told Keisha the truth, then there'd be no more need for fear. There'd be no secret to threaten her with ever again. Any-one else knowing would be inconsequential.

Why couldn't the past stay the past? Delma didn't understand people always in need of bringing up old stuff from eons ago. There was surely always one aunt, uncle, or cousin around the dinner table who deemed themselves the chronicler of all things distant. As if it mattered. As if anything that happened in the past could affect what was happening now. She did what anyone would have done in the moment. She shouldn't be held accountable for that. She looked down at her perfect black coffee, which she knew would taste like snake piss because she refused to add cream or sugar, and took a huge swallow of the bitter brew. She began to rehearse her side of the story.

◯◯

June sixteenth, 1978, she'd been working late on a trial as usual. Why not give the heavy loads to Delma, she had nothing better to do than work her butt off to make everyone else look good? She'd loaded two boxes of files into her car, to continue the work over the weekend that she couldn't do while sitting ramrod straight in the hardwood chairs of the DA's office.

She was driving home when she saw the girl walking, stumbling, barely able to stay upright. Delma's headlights landed on her face. She put up a bloodied hand to protect her vision. She'd been beaten, that much was obvious. Delma put the car in park and jumped out, startled to see even worse up close. Her face was covered with bruises, a swollen eye, and gashes on her lips and cheeks. "What happened to you? Who did this?"

"I killed him," the girl sputtered, then nearly collapsed if not for Delma's grip on her arm and around her waist.

"You killed who?" Delma asked, worried that she was hearing more than she should in her capacity as an assistant district attorney, but unable to resist. "You say somebody's dead?" She helped her get into the car. The hospital was only a mile or two away but Delma knew it would take forever for an ambulance to come.

"Cain. He's dead," she said.

Delma's mind was racing. Cain. The man's name was actually Devon Little, very well known for preying on girls, turning them out before they could figure out how to wear lipstick and high heels, let alone have sex with a grown man. When Cain was only thirteen he and his little brother got into a fight while they were home alone. He claimed his brother fell and hit his head on a glass coffee table. He bled to death and Devon went to juvenile detention for five years. That was where he picked up his little nickname for the Bible story of Cain killing Abel. The man was pure evil as far as Delma was concerned, so he probably deserved whatever he got.

"Are you sure he's dead?" Delma asked, putting the car in gear. She pulled out, thinking to check first but thought the bloodied girl was more important. She was covered in it from head to toe.

"I killed him," she cried out, ". . . and my baby."

"Don't you tell another soul what you just said to me, you hear? Don't repeat another word of it." Delma drove fast, barely slowing through yellow lights, speeding through the red lights, running them altogether. She pulled into the emergency bay at the downtown community hospital. She helped the girl out of the car. "Emergency," she yelled for anyone able to hear her. The girl was heavier than she looked. Delma practically dragged her as she slipped in and out of consciousness.

"Over here." The receptionist appeared and called out from behind her bulletproof window.

"What you mean, 'over here'? Does it look like I can carry this girl another step? Get somebody out here, now."

The buzzer opened the double doors. A male nurse was waiting on the other side with a wheelchair. She guided the limp body as best she could and plopped her down. "Get her help. She's been beaten up pretty bad. I'm from the district attorney's office." Delma flashed her badge to the receptionist. "She's not to leave this hospital." Delma tore off in a bigger hurry than she'd come.

She drove and sped through the very same lights, this time going in the opposite direction. When she got close to the point where she'd originally picked up the girl, she slowed, looking for *the car*, what car? Think, think, Delma told herself. *Cain.* He'd pimped the streets long enough that she would know . . . should know, and she did, the minute she saw the gold Cadillac parked haphazardly with the back passenger door left wide open, the headlights on.

The shadow of the streetlamp made it even harder to see the man's face. But there was no denying it was him slumped over the steering wheel with shattered pieces of glass stuck to his stiff dry perm.

Delma's hand shook with fear as she reached out to touch his shoulder. "Wake up. You okay?" She gave him a shove in the off chance the girl was mistaken. Maybe he wasn't dead, case closed and everybody could go about their merry way. "Hey," this time shoving him harder. His body fell completely off to the right into the passenger seat. Delma jumped back, never having seen a dead body unless it was prepped nice and pretty in a casket. Her district attorney assignments mostly included white collar crimes, the worst being rape and assault. Not once had she been front and center with a dead body.

She took a cautious step closer, peered inside, this time looking for the baby. A blue slither of light landed on the backseat, showing the blood-soaked rag and tiny hand sticking out but not moving. Her own shadow made it difficult to see. But she knew blood for sure when she saw it covering the leather interior like spilled paint.

It was a tragic scene, one she'd never forget. First things first, she needed to call the police. The girl was probably going to jail. If there's one thing Delma had learned working in the DA's office, one crime didn't cancel out another. Just because he'd hit the girl, beat her senseless, didn't mean she would get off scot-free for winning the fight. And a dead baby to boot. She leaned forward one more time, almost sure she'd seen movement. Maybe her exhaustion was making her eyes play tricks on her. Then she heard it, a small desperate breath and a weak cry.

"Oh, dear sweet heaven." Climbing inside the backseat of that car took every ounce of strength in Delma's arms and legs. She was weak and shaking with fear. "Oh my God." She gently scooped up the child and gave plenty of thought to taking her directly to the hospital. Then something stopped her.

Delma surmised two things about that night. She was meant to find that child alive. She was meant to find the mother and be the first to tell her to keep her mouth quiet about Cain, because if it had been anyone else the poor girl would've been in handcuffs, regardless of Cain's debauchery. One man's sins didn't null and void another's. That much she knew about the law she helped enforce on a daily basis. The final thing, having worked in the district attorney's office, she'd seen enough travesties to know they would simply put the child in foster care, a system riddled with indifference and neglect. So she did what she had to, she took the baby to Dr. Yancy, even though he'd only seen a year or two of medical school before being kicked out for stealing pharmaceuticals. He'd earned the name "Doctor" for helping out the girls on the street. He performed abortions for half the going rate, ignoring nosey laws about age and consent. He delivered babies for the girls on the street who were too busy getting high to realize they were pregnant in the first place. He conveniently ignored the law of reporting a mother for drug abuse while carrying a fetus, a prosecutable crime.

Delma wasted no time getting to Dr. Yancy's door carrying the baby, who was still attached to the umbilical cord and placenta. His only question: "Where's the mother?"

Her only answer: "Somewhere getting help."

22

Trevelle

The entire church gave her a standing ovation. The pastor pushed his hands together like a ten-bout champion in a ring, happy and blessed Trevelle Doval had chosen to visit his congregation. She stood and waved with Mya and Airic by her side. Trevelle knew it was going to happen. That was precisely why she'd insisted on making a respectable presentation.

"Won't you come up and say a few words, Ms. Doval?" Pastor Clarence showed a sincere hope that all he had to do was ask in front of hundreds and she'd be obligated. The answer was still no.

Trevelle blew a kiss to the pulpit and shook her head no, gracefully. If the word got out she took the podium by mere request, she'd be inundated with invites by Monday morning. The congregation spoke in various measures of pleading. "Oh, please. Thank you, Lord. Praise his name."

She felt a hand touch hers. It was Airic. He gave a loving nod of approval. He should've known better. In front of all these people he'd given her the nod. She couldn't possibly turn a deaf ear to her husband's direct order, not in front of all those who knew her mantra, *put him first,* God, husband, family. She'd even written a book about it since her marriage to Airic and sold half a million copies. She couldn't, she wouldn't dare disrespect him by disobeying his will in front of these people. When they got home would be another story.

Her smile turned to one of compliance. From where she stood in the front row it only took a few steps before she was up the stairs. A booming applause moved her toward the microphone. Once Trevelle was up at the podium she was a moth to a flame, a person born for the limelight. "Praise the Lord." A huge chorus from the congregation returned her greeting, "Praise the Lord."

"Yes, God is good, amen. I am so blessed today to be with you all. But to tell you the truth, I'm blessed every day." The crowd was hanging on her every word. She released the microphone from the stationary stand and tested the line to see how far she could travel. Trevelle was famous for her stroll.

"I said, I'm blessed every day. You want to know why? 'Cause I'ma super Christian. Yeah, that's right I said it," she sang out. "Someone asked me, what's that mean . . . does it mean you can fly? Do you have super powers? Can you turn water into wine? Can you . . . can you make someone walk who's not taken a step in years?" She beamed quietly, letting the congregation get out their "Yes Lord" and "Amen."

"Waiting for the answer?" she asked. "Well here it is. I'm a super Christian and yes, I can fly. My wings are being sized as we speak. Yes, I have super powers. Because there is no greater power than faith. And yes, I can pour a glass of water and take a sip and feel higher than any alcohol poured from the devil's bottle. You know why . . . say it with me." Her signature high heels strutted from one side to the other. She refused to say another word until the entire congregation was on their feet. She stared in silence, one hand on her hip tapping her foot.

"Are we there yet?" she said in a low whisper, then raised her hands like a bandleader. "Say it with me," she shouted and then in succession everyone shouted with her. "I'm a super Christian." Her eyes swept across the church, she felt glorious. Triumphant. Trevelle's gaze fell on Airic clapping, sending up love and support. He was her biggest fan. What more could she ask? she thought before her eyes fell on Mya. A second chance. The truth of it overwhelmed her with joy. She was going to have her second chance to be a mother, to make up for that night so long ago.

"Today," her voice broke through. The crowd hushed. "My husband and myself took a very important step in our lives, praise God. We have just taken in a beautiful young baby girl, her name is Mya. We are in the process of adoption."

The shouts of "Hallelujah" and "Praise him" came in waves. Trevelle had to calm them once again. "We of course intend to give her a good Christian home and teach her that God is a loving God and one that will protect her and nurture her into a good Christian woman." The crowd started to murmur as if talking among themselves. Trevelle was a pro at getting the congregation riled up and making them hang on every word that came out of her mouth.

"I am reminded of a significant passage, 'And ye shall teach them your children, speaking of them when thou sittest in thine house, and when thou walkest by the way, when thou liest down, and when thou risest up.' We can't be true Christians unless we not only follow the word for ourselves, but administer to the children, as well. It's so important to get to them early. You see them, don't you, the sagging pants, the foul mouths, the lack of respect for themselves or anyone around them? It's never too late to find a child who needs God's word. I dedicated my life to the Lord to share his ways with all of God's children, including you and you." She opened her palm to spread her message. As if on cue the piano began playing and Trevelle's magical voice sailed over the congregation.

"Yes, Lord," shouted from the crowd; one by one, people were standing up to give her a standing ovation. Like a conductor that just finished a masterpiece, Trevelle bowed her head, leaving the crowd screaming and shouting in praise.

 ◉◉

Airic leaned into Trevelle's ear as he opened the car door for her. "What was that?" he hissed. "Why did you make that kind of announcement? We barely have visitation and you're bragging about

the care and nurture of this child. Adoption papers can't be filed until the biological parent's rights are terminated. Do you see that happening in the near future, honestly, do you?"

Trevelle slid into the car, ignoring Airic and the heat radiating
off the smooth leather seat. She twisted around to face Mya, who
was already buckled in and ready to go. "I bet you'd like some ice
cream. What's your favorite flavor?"

"Chocolate," Mya said. Her long legs extended far past the
booster seat but she was under forty pounds and Trevelle was determined to follow caution to the letter.

"Then chocolate it is."

"We're taking her home." Airic started the engine to show he
meant business.

"We're going for ice cream," Trevelle said through gritted teeth.
The little show of submissiveness had already gone to his head,
making him forget who was really in charge. They rode in silence
until he conveniently pulled into the shopping center parking lot.
Trevelle scanned the buildings and pointed with her acrylic nail.
"Perfect. Baskin-Robbins." She craned her neck around to face Mya.
"My favorite flavor is chocolate, too."

Airic said nothing, putting the car in park. He refused to get out
of the car or lift a finger to help Mya out of her car seat. Normally
Trevelle would have read him his purpose. Instead she got out of the
car, unlocked Mya's seat belt. She helped the child out of the car and
didn't glance back as they entered the ice-cream shop.

23

Truth or Consequences

Delma hadn't thought about the details in such a long time. Surprisingly, she remembered every moment, every word spoken. Every choice made that night.

Dr. Yancy had worked diligently, cleaning up the tiny infant, checking her heart and lungs and clearing her air passages, all the while talking in soft whispers to the barely breathing child. Whatever he said must've worked. She sputtered then coughed out a loud, healthy wail. He put a clamp on the stump where he'd finally cut the lifeless cord. "Thank goodness the umbilical cord was still attached or she would've bled to death. More importantly, thank God you were there." He dropped the gorged placenta into a yellow bucket with a warning sign of skull and crossbones on it, hazardous materials.

He wrapped the baby in a clean towel before handing her to Delma. "She's good, no shakes, no signs of addiction. Close to dehydration is all."

Delma held the tiny baby close and stared down at the eyes that wouldn't open before. "She's beautiful." She pushed the white towel tighter around her body so she'd feel snug.

"She's lucky. Start her out on this formula, start her real slow." He threw a couple of cans, a plastic bottle, and a few diapers so tiny Delma thought she could've mistook them for sanitary napkins.

"From this point on every day she should do better than the day before. Get her to the hospital if you see any signs of trouble."

"Of course."

Dr. Yancy gave her a knowing nod. "If you can't take her to a hospital, bring her back here."

"Oh no, I'll take her to the hospital." Delma kept the pretense to protect the innocent. "Thank you," she mouthed before slipping out into the night where what's done in the dark usually belonged there.

She took the tiny infant home and did nothing but hold her and stare at her for hours while she slept. "Keisha Marie," she whispered. "Your name is Keisha and I'm going to love you forever."

Delma called in to work three straight days before asking for administrative leave. Stress, she claimed, reached her breaking point. All the while she held the baby close and stared down into her pretty brown eyes as long as they were open and awake to stare back. And even then while she was sleeping Delma couldn't put her down, not for a minute.

Dr. Yancy had said to keep her hydrated. Bring her back if she wasn't doing well. The miracle baby was perfect, more so with each and every day counted on the calendar. She thought about the mother, even called to check on her and found she'd been released the very same morning. No one had any idea where she'd gone. They didn't have an address or phone number, which Delma knew wasn't unusual. Most of the young prostitutes had been taught to never reveal anything about themselves using made-up names like Poison, Lickety Split, or Hard Candy. Most of the time unless a parent came to lockup to claim them, they were forever lost with the fake names their pimp had labeled them and eventually disappeared or were buried as Jane Doe.

But one life was saved. She knew what would've happened if she gave the baby up to the system. Foster care. Possibly even given back to the mother if she got away with probation and could prove she could clean up her act. Two, three years later, if at all, the mother would be back on the streets, back on drugs, and a precious child would soon be living in harm's way waiting to be sold into the same hollow hell her mother was living in. She watched the clichéd scenario unfold day after day. Those poor children had no one to fight for them.

The reality of the situation was the girl had committed a murder. If the true story came out, she would be in prison far too long to ever get her baby back. The ideal would be for someone to adopt her. Why not Delma? She was a good person. She was a smart, ambitious woman who'd give a child a real home, with a strong foundation in education and self-reliance. Her grandmother had raised her alone with no one to help. Delma could do it, too. She didn't need a man to have her own family.

Her next move was securing the child in her possession without questions. Delma had to have legitimate paperwork. She couldn't suddenly show up with a child, a bright beautiful baby girl, without proof of where she'd come from. Delma remembered being choosey about the print, not wanting it to look too archaic, or too contemporary. Somewhere in the middle. She'd spent an entire night in the office she shared with two deputy assistants on the computer, printing and reprinting. She'd named her baby girl that night, Keisha Marie Smith. She typed with one hand, pecking the keys, while the other held the small bundle against her chest.

Mother. She used a cousin's name, Eugena, a bothersome child the last time she'd seen her. The last name . . . sitting at the desk she looked up and saw the law encyclopedias all with the same name stamped in gold across the spine, Thompson. Perfect. Delma typed the name with swift confidence. Eugena Thompson. Surely Eugena should have known better than to get herself knocked up by . . . Kevin Smith, who had no future, no desire to love her unconditionally. Kevin Smith, a good solid name, and so many in the world no one would ever be able to pinpoint the real one, whether he existed or not, and he certainly did not.

She took the perfect copy and made another copy on fine linen paper she'd bought at the new high-tech print store where doing everything yourself was supposed to be a privilege. All the while she

f of air-conditioning coming out of the Baskin-Robbins.
t some ice cream," he said, making the moment feel like a
and that we weren't just killing time with distractions.
line was short. A few patrons already had their large glob-
rozen cream and sugar. I stared at the smorgasbord of fla-
re dropping my eyes to the ice-cream counter. I thought I
ng things. Mya? No, couldn't be. I'd know my own child any-
Wouldn't I? Yet I stood paralyzed, confused. This little girl
same bow in her hair, only it was slicked back in a greasy
d curl. I thought about those desperate mothers who'd lost
ld in the store or at the amusement park, racing to the famil-
t, or hat, only to find out it was the wrong child. *Tsk, tsk* and
hame on a mother who didn't know their own baby, front,
d, or sideways. I could never be one of those women grab-
eone else's child only for them to face me in fear, calling out
my because some crazy lady was accosting them.
asn't Mya, couldn't have been. I studied the long gangly legs
out from underneath a pretty pink dress. I examined closely
y patent leather Mary Janes and thought *How cute.* I eyeballed
streaks of hair popping up around the edges that refused to
and secure. Then she turned around and I nearly fell over
d. She faced me, taking the first lick of her ice cream.
mmy." She rushed forward. "Ice cream," she sang with
izz Trevelle got me chocolate."
ened my arms, "Sweetie." I kneeled down and kissed every
her face. My hands traced the edges of her hairline that was
ack so tight I could see tiny white pores threatening to give
hat . . . what happened?"
zz Trell make me purrty." She proudly modeled her new
fore taking another lick of her scoop.
watched the whole scene as if it were in slow motion, with
hose *aw shit* faces. He knew what I was about to do. I cut my
ay, landing on Trevelle, who was still at the register paying
ice cream. Before I could stop myself I was reaching over

held the newborn close against her body, feeling her heartbeat, her strong stretch, and occasional yawn.

Once she had the fake birth certificate, the rest was easy. She forged the paperwork, relinquishing the parental rights. She typed up adoption forms, signed them, and used her very own file stamp to make them legal.

⤬

She was thinking about that day and the many more that came, presenting challenges so big Delma thought she would be swallowed up whole, never to see the light of day again. Hudson leaned over and patted her hand before taking hold of it. "What about this doctor? You think he may have something do with the calls, maybe planning a retirement fund with a few extortion dollars?"

Delma let out a short sigh. If only it were that easy. "Dr. Yancy died years ago. He was a good man but eventually got beat to death when some junkies thought he was a real doctor with real meds. The best he had was some penicillin that he used to treat the women on the street." She shook her head. Then her eyes went bright as she remembered. "There was someone else."

24

Venus

"It's your turn to go lay down, Mom." I kissed Pauletta on the cheek and hugged her as hard as I was able. Her soft body caved under my grip. Watching Mya get taken out of the house seemed to affect her more than the rest of us. She was physically weak and tired. Maybe the jetlag had caught up with her, too. Not to mention the physical labor of making our unhappy house a home. The hard work had paid off but also taken its toll. I hoped that's what it was. Her bout with breast cancer years earlier had weakened her immune system. She never played into it, letting it control her life. If anything she lived each day to the fullest, letting nothing slow her down.

"Thank you for being here for us, Mom. But I think things are going to be okay from here out. You should go home. We'll be okay."

"You're my baby. The same way you would fight for Mya, the same way I'd fight for you . . . till death us do part." She kissed me on the cheek. "I think I'll take you up on your idea and go lay down. I'm tired. You know that's not easy for me to admit."

Jake came back inside after what seemed like forever, having walked Georgina out to her car. He found me in the living room. The compassion in his eyes met the defeated shift in mine. If we weren't in the midst of battle I'd want to reach out and run my hand across his smooth cheek, kiss him fully on the mouth, and tell him how much I loved him. But we were in battle, the biggest fight of our lives.

He sat next to me on the couch. "I k . . . know you want someone to lash out a . . . true ally. We're going to get through this . . .

He pulled me close with a warm . . . should get out of the house instead of si . . . We could see a movie, or go out to lunch . . . took mine and pressed them to his lips. H . . . against my skin as he closed his eyes. "Ev . . . I can honestly make that promise here ar . . .

I closed my eyes as well, and for a l . . . lieve him.

Jake and I settled on a movie at the nearb . . . what we were watching, only relieved t . . . having to sit across from each other and . . . had a bucket of popcorn filled to the t . . . We'd at least drank our sodas, giving me . . . the bathroom. There I closed myself in . . . fifty layers of tissue around the toilet s . . . comfortably cry my eyes out in the priva . . .

By the time I returned to the theater . . . and the credits were rolling. Jake leaned i . . . entire time and couldn't tell you what I saw . . .

All we wanted was for Airic to retur . . . again.

Afterward we walked around the p . . . took ahold of my hand. We hadn't walk . . . long time. In the beginning we'd walk outs . . . barefoot in the sand. We'd go for miles u . . . ther, stopped by boulders as big as buildi . . . side of the beach. Too tired to even conte . . . turn around and start back the other way, . . .

Here in the land of stifling humidity . . .

Mya and doing my best to grab a piece of Trevelle Doval's hair. Trevelle shook and flailed like a rag doll.

She leaned back with the force of my grip, screaming, "Call the police. Someone call the police, I'm being attacked."

Jake grabbed me by the waist and spun me around to the other side, facing out. I saw Airic through the window getting out of his car, rushing inside. Customers scooted their chairs back, not sure if they should clear out or get a better angle.

Airic rushed over to Trevelle. "She attacked me, did you see her? Lord father," she huffed, straightening herself out. "She attacked me in front of all these people." She pointed her bony finger at me. "You're going to jail. I have all these people as my witnesses."

"No. Everything's fine. You don't have to call the police." Airic lifted a hand to the shocked girl with the pastel sun visor and pink shirt, her mouth gaping open in shock. She held an ice-cream scooper in one hand, and the other held the telephone ready to dial.

"Yeah, call the police. A crime has been committed." I lunged again unable to control myself. Jake kept a tight grip around my waist. "How dare you put a hand on my child."

"I did not. I would never hurt Mya." Trevelle Doval was stunned at the accusation. She batted her long silky lashes. "What would make you say something like that?"

My eyes fell on Mya's hair. I managed to loop my finger through the tight band and loosened it in spite of Mya's cries of protest. "No, Mommy." She gripped my hand. "I like my hair," she whined.

Trevelle looked on with smug victory. "You should be thanking me. No child wants to run around unkempt. At least let her start life with a little dignity."

I'd give her dignity, a right hook would do fine. Jake kept me at bay while I struggled breathlessly to get at her. By the time the police arrived, there was a crowd of looky-loos outside the ice-cream shop window. Mya stood in the middle holding her dripping cone, the front of her dress covered in milky chocolate stains, and tears streaming down her face. The two large policemen entering with their hands resting on their guns must've been the cherry on top. As soon they stepped inside the ice-cream shop Mya started wailing and doing a jig dance like she was on fire.

I rushed to Mya and immediately felt shame and embarrassment for acting like such a fool in front of my baby. Not that she hadn't seen her mommy make a fool out of herself before. Just not recently, and not while she was old enough to remember.

"Her." The young girl with the pink hat pointed toward me. The officers beelined in my direction.

"Ma'am, you want to step outside." The officer opened the door and cleared the way for me.

"I want charges filed. She attacked me." Trevelle could still be heard after we were outside.

"Calm down." Airic did his best to console her. "Everything's going to be fine."

"Come out here and I'll give you something to file charges for," I yelled back. *Okay, stop it,* I told myself but my mouth wasn't listening. Defiance seeped out of me like water from a leaking faucet. Who was she to put her hands on my child's hair?

"Ma'am, if you won't calm down, we're going to have to put you in the backseat of the squad car. Let me tell you, it's not a nice place to be." He scrunched his nose to give me a clue of the stench real felons left behind. "Now let's start from the beginning."

Jake came outside holding Mya, who was heaving with tears. She reached out for me and I took ahold of her. "I'm sorry, sweetie. I'm sorry Mommy acted like that." I put her down and unleashed the rubber clasp holding her hair. All I wanted to do was get home and scrub the whole jar of grease out of my baby's head.

"This is what I'm talking about." I held up my hands, glistening in the hot sun. "She did this." I pointed to Trevelle, who was holding court with the other officer.

"What is it I'm looking at? I don't see any bruises."

I sighed heavily. "That woman is married to her fa . . ." Somehow the word *father* couldn't leave my lips. "They had visitation.

The first thing she does is slather all this greasy goo on my baby's hair, without my permission. She pulled it back so tight she's got bumps all along the edges. See?"

The officer's face tightened in confusion. "Okaaay? Sounds like there's another issue at work here because I'm not seeing the problem. Let me ask a simple question: Did she provoke you in the form of bodily attack, did she try to harm you or your child?"

Jake intervened. "Let me explain," he said, knowing the officer would never understand. It was a hair thing, more specifically a woman-against-woman-hair thing, a timeless war that no one would ever understand. "They had a court-ordered visitation for the first time," Jake said plainly. "We just happened to bump into them here. Already everybody's nerves are on edge, then my wife sees they've completely given her some kiddie makeover, new clothes, changed her hair, like she wasn't good enough the way they found her."

The officer nodded. "Got it."

I was busy pulling the dress over Mya's head. I gathered the ice-cream covered fabric in a ball. Jake saw what was next but couldn't catch me fast enough. I hurled it in Trevelle's direction, catching her in the face.

"That's it," she sputtered. "If you don't put her in handcuffs right now, I will have your badges."

The officer took me by the arm. "Okay. I can see this isn't going to end nicely."

"Sir," Jake said calmly, though I could see desperation in his eyes, "please, this is a domestic situation. Nobody's life is being threatened here."

Trevelle yelled out, "He'd know a thing or two about that, check his record why don't you? This man was arrested for murder not too long ago. *Murder*," she enunciated. "He's a known criminal."

The earth dropped from underneath my feet. We were no longer kicking sand in a playground. She'd crossed the line and entered into the real battlefield. This time it was Jake moving in Airic and Trevelle's direction. I caught Jake's arm as he started toward them.

"Jake, no. Let's go." I took his hand and pulled in the opposite direction. Mya reached out and took his other hand, pulling, too.

"C'mon, Daddeee," Mya pleaded, sounding more mature than the whole lot of us put together.

"So will I be on your hit list next?" Trevelle snarled. "Maybe Airic? This is just one more example of your degradation. Both of you, unfit. Attacking me like an animal," she continued even though Airic was doing his best to quiet her. She was on a roll. "God is watching. He is the last and final judge."

The crowd seemed to have grown. The officer was quick behind us. "Sir, there are some more questions I have for you two."

Jake turned around as if he'd had enough. "Look, no harm no foul, you have charges you want to bring against us? If not, me, my wife, and daughter will be on our way."

"You're going to have to sit still while I sort this thing out." The officer's big hands rested on his belt. Obviously the other officer was on the horn checking to see if Jake was a wanted man in any of the fifty states.

If I could push rewind and take it all back I would. I was responsible for what was about to happen. *Me.* I put myself between the officer and Jake. "Really, it's just a misunderstanding. I shouldn't have let her upset me like that. I'm willing to go with you, I'll go to the police station, whatever you want."

The other officer came from behind and tapped his partner on the shoulder. "Joe, we don't really have anything here," he said to my relief. "Everybody just go on your way. Found out they have a court day coming up. We'll let Fulton County deal with this nonsense." He nodded toward Jake. "Have a nice day."

Jake stared him down. "You, too, officer."

Later that evening Jake and I drove my mother to the airport. I could feel her wondering if she was doing the right thing by leaving. If not for the fact her ticket was nonrefundable and my father,

Henry, hadn't eaten a decent meal in the two weeks she'd been gone, she would've told us to turn the car around. I reached over the seat and grabbed her hand. "Don't worry."

We pulled up to the curb at the Delta terminal. The Atlanta airport was a city in itself. The sheer size and mass was like a sci-fi thriller where there was no getting out once you were in. I knew when my mother hit those doors, we were on our own.

"You two going to be all right?" she asked Jake, while kissing him gently on the cheek.

"We'll be fine, Miss Pauletta. I'm not going to let anything go wrong." His voice dragged a bit, fighting off exhaustion. He offered a bear hug, the kind that promised indeed he would protect the mama bear and baby bear.

"And you . . . come here." My mother bent over and waited for Mya to come into her arms. "You be a good girl," she said, hugging and kissing her. "Grandma will see you soon, very soon."

Mya nodded up and down with her spastic new hairstyle of barrettes and ribbons on as many strands of hair as she could reach. She'd brandished her doll baby with a matching set of pink, yellow, and white clips. I could thank Trevelle Doval for Mya demanding to look like a Kizzy doll.

"We'll come visit as soon as this is all over," I confirmed. I kissed my mom and held on for a minute too long.

"You're going to be fine," my mother whispered near my ear. "Be strong for your family."

The ride home in silence seemed to last longer than a cross-country road trip. Brake lights trailed in front and on the sides of us, all the way up the freeway. If someone had told me traffic like this existed beyond California borders, I would've scoffed at the possibility. No one, no city, had traffic like California. You could leave your house at 2:00 A.M. and still be stuck in a bumper-to-bumper surge.

"This is ridiculous," I said. "It's confirmed. Now I can add claustrophobia to my many new anxieties." My elbow rested on the window that I thought about rolling down until remembering where there's traffic, there's exhaust. "It's only a matter of time before this place is layered with smog. Why is it so crowded? And everyone has the nerve to talk about Los Angeles's smog. I was at the grocery store and the cashier looked at my ID and then went into this whole thing about California smog. I asked her, Have you been there? She said no. I said, Well this place is next, I can guarantee you that. Yeah, we'll see who has smog—"

Jake interrupted, holding up an *I surrender* hand. "I get your point, okay?"

"I didn't realize I was annoying you. I was just making conversation that doesn't revolve around our usual."

"Well, I'm tired. I'd rather just get home without making small talk."

"Nice," I said. But I wasn't about to let him piss me off with rudeness. I stayed quiet . . . for a minute. More like thirty seconds. "Since when is having a conversation with your wife small talk?"

"I don't give a damn about the smog in L.A. or this fucking city!" his voice boomed.

My first reaction, as always, was to turn around to see if Mya was here or in dreamland, where mommies and daddies didn't curse each other out or throw random punches.

Sleep. Good.

"What the hell is wrong with you?"

"What the hell do you think is wrong? You know what we're already up against and then you're in a public place swinging on Trevelle Doval like you don't have no damn sense." He drove with both hands in a death grip on the steering wheel.

"I was defending—"

"Defending what? We're in the biggest fight of our lives and you're giving them exactly what they want. Exactly what they need to finish the job."

I folded my arms over my chest to prevent the involuntary

movement of my hand reaching out with a slap. "She had no right to touch my child. She's not her mother, not her stepmother, she's nothing. I don't care if she owns the Taj Mahal and preaches from the mountaintop. She had no right."

"All I'm saying is we got enough against us already."

"And whose fault is that?" I said. *Damn it.*

"What took you so long? I knew it was coming." He leaned up to the steering wheel and rested his chin there for a brief second before getting back in the fight. "So all this is my fault?"

"You started the blame game."

He pressed the brakes too hard, sending me jerking forward. "My fault for having a homicide charge? My fault you swallowed half a bottle of pills and ended up in a psychiatric ward?" He was now officially mad, where before he was only pissed. "Was it my fault you were still sexing old school after we were already together?" he said calmly. "My fault, huh, that you gotta carry another muthafucka's baby for nine months when I was the one there for you from day one. Day one," he repeated.

Here is where the book gets closed. Here is where the chapter ends and the world cannot witness what real ugliness looks like. Those moments when you're sure if someone else heard this conversation they would sit with their mouth hanging open wondering, *How do you come back from this one, girl?*

Exactly . . . no coming back.

"What're you doing?" he asked in disbelief when he followed me upstairs. I moved with unorthodox speed, throwing clothes into a bag, grabbing some toiletries. Then even faster to Mya's room, grabbing a few of her favorite clothes, the kind that couldn't be replaced easily. Her favorite yellow SpongeBob nightgown. Her Dora the Explorer slippers.

"Move," I said when he tried to block the doorway to her bedroom.

"Calm down . . . stop it. You run every time somebody yells fire. Stop and think for a minute. How's it going to look if we're splitting and breaking up at the drop of a hat?"

"Move." I shoved past him, hurting myself, butting against his solid arm and shoulder. I bolted down the stairs. Mya was still asleep where I'd left her on the couch. Jake had carried her in, but I would have to walk her out. "Mya, sweetie, wake up."

"Don't do this," Jake said.

"It was already done when I carried some other man's baby in my stomach for nine months . . . right?"

I walked Mya to the car. I threw my bags inside and backed the hell out. He followed, trailing in front of us to the end of the driveway. He rested his hands on his hips and shook his head. Mama bear was fleeing the scene with baby bear. Papa bear had the bed all to himself.

25

Sins Revisited

"There was another call last night," Delma whispered to Hudson. "They said the same thing, *Someone's got a secret.*"

They'd already gone down the long list, the obvious choices of ex-coworkers. Plaintiffs and defendants done wrong with an ax to grind. But there was one person Delma remembered better than the others. One who truly had the artillery to do damage, because he knew about Keisha and where she'd come from.

Shep was a sweet, laid-back, and fine as hell courier who showed up every day at the downtown district attorney's office. He delivered documents or picked them up at the same time, with the same sexy brown shorts tight against his brown muscular thighs, same buttoned-up shirt, with the top two open to reveal a slight patch of dark hair in the center of his wide chest.

Delma played the hard-to-get role, offering up her delicacies with a smile and bat of the eyes, turning him down the four times in a row he'd asked her out. She was a lawyer after all and he a lowly courier. Finally she said yes with no other reason on her mind but getting some of his sweetness to satisfy a whole decade of celibacy. Anybody with good sense knows you can't go that long without getting some and not expect to be struck with a stupid stick once you do. She was instantly dick-notized. The state of hypnotic glory of one man's big long richness making her do things she was ashamed to say out loud. She couldn't see straight once Shep got ahold of her.

They'd become expert at tasty quickies in her office, where she'd exclaim loudly enough for everyone to hear that the box was too heavy to carry, so she needed his assistance. Inside with the door closed those big arms would swoop her up. He gave her all the assistance she needed. Their crazed heated bodies attracted each other like magnets.

Shep was all man, 100 percent pure grade. None of that dipping in both sauces, that male and female mess that was going on these days. Delma knew it was she he wanted by the urgency and combustion of their lovemaking. Everything ran smoothly until he started having needs. First it was the car. He only needed to borrow it until he got his fixed. A week turned into three. Then he needed an $800 loan. It was back child support or jail. Couldn't have that, dick-notizing sessions would be cut short. If only he hadn't needed a place to stay *temporarily*, of course. He'd made up some lame story about the landlord exterminating his building for mice. She knew better. Didn't stop her from giving it some grave thought and consideration. But the answer was still no. Keisha was always first in her life no matter how good the dick-notizing sessions were. No way could she have some man living in the same quarters as her young beautiful daughter. She'd seen it enough times in the courtroom, the mother's boyfriend helping himself to the females in the house like a Sunday buffet after church. Why invite trouble?

"I think we ought to cool out for a while," she'd told him. "It's not you, it's me. I'm just not ready to keep going." The spell was broken. She kissed him good-bye after paying for their dinner and refused to take his calls after that.

He was bitter and downright aggressive, leaving notes on her car, messages on her phone, and waiting for her after work since she refused to come to the lobby for deliveries. "Delma, how you gon treat me like this? Did I do something to you? What'd I do?" He stood next to her, breathing erratically while she unlocked her car door.

She gave it a great deal of thought to go back on her word. The sensation between her legs was ready to blow like a volcanic eruption every time she got within smelling distance of the man.

"I need a break," she told him. "I'm not concentrating at work. I have a big case these people heaped on me at the last minute and you know how it is. I can't show any signs of being less than perfect, not in a law office full of white men."

Shep looked less broken, like maybe he believed her excuse. Some of it was true. She did have a huge case; a black female employee had filed sexual assault charges against her plant manager, who was also black. It drove Delma nuts how cases involving people of color always got thrown her way. She was under immense pressure, always being evaluated and constantly judged. It didn't help when she started missing meetings from oversleeping, taking long lunch breaks, and falling asleep in depositions. Though being with Shep had actually alleviated some of the stress. Companionship had its benefits: laughter, good times, sex. Oh, the sex. She'd lost almost twenty pounds just keeping company with Shep. If only he hadn't asked about staying with her.

"The truth is, Shep, I wanted to break it off because I have Keisha at home. I know you've never met her, but she's my life. I can't have you asking to move in with me, I can't take that kind of pressure."

"When did I ask to move in with you?"

"Don't play dumb. You asked if you could temporarily stay with me . . . anybody that can add two plus two knows where it'll lead, one week, then three months, then a year. I'm nobody's fool."

He licked his thick moist lips. "So it's like that, huh?"

"Like what?"

"You think you're better than me. Right, right. I got your number Miss Lawyer," he spat.

"That's hardly the issue, Shep. I'm just trying to keep myself above water, I can't keep taking care of your mess when I got my own."

"It's always the issue. You sistas get a little education, nice pay-ing gig in the big house, got your house, your car, then you don't need a man. Man can't do nothing for you."

"Since we're on the subject, maybe you have a point. Maybe just once I'd like it if you paid for a meal, or brought me some flow-ers, candy, something. Maybe I find it offensive to be offering you loans and wondering if you didn't call when you said you would 'cause your phone is turned off or some other sorry excuse. I'm taking care of my business. I can't be taking care of yours, too, which includes you laying up in my house. That's not going to hap-pen. We're through, okay? Enough said." Delma attempted to get into her car and Shep slammed the door closed, nearly catching her elbow.

"You ain't gon never have nobody," he hissed.

Delma wiped the spray of moisture from her face. "I will have your black ass thrown in jail. Now you need to step back, right now."

"You think somebody want to be with you for free. Nah, baby, no such thing as free. You ain't gon have this fancy job forever. You ain't gon have your daughter forever. You think I don't know. I saw your diary. I read every page. You gon need somebody, but you rather be a lonely bitter bitch." He turned and began to saunter away with his hands in his pockets, as if he hadn't just ripped Delma's heart out and stomped all over it.

"I rather be alone than have some no-good Negro sleeping in my bed," she yelled after him. The streetlight bounced off his clean-shaven head. She got in the car and gave thought to hitting him. The rubber bumper wouldn't kill him, just maim him a little. Bastard. The tears streamed down her cheeks while she sat for close to an hour trying to get herself together.

◉◉

Hudson leaned forward. "This guy might know you took Keisha, but why would he surface all of a sudden . . . now?"

"Maybe he heard I was getting nominated for the superior court."

"You don't even *know* you're being nominated for the superior court." The whites of his eyes rolled into a huge circle. "Are there any more scorned lovers I have to hear about? If so I'd like to get through them before dinner. My stomach can't take much more."

26

Trevelle

Chills ran up and down Trevelle's arms. She'd hoped the hot shower would help calm her nerves but her humiliation and anger could not be tamed, thinking about that Venus woman attacking her in broad daylight and getting away with it. She wrapped her robe tighter, unable to stop her teeth from clattering. "Get it together," she whispered to herself. She leaned across the marble hotel sink and wiped the fog, clearing the mirror. She stood cleansed of makeup with her hair pulled back. The dull lines around her eyes revealed a hard life. Sadness. Regret. Anger. Right now she was more furious than she was sad. Still there was no ignoring the heaviness of her heart.

She closed her eyes and whispered a prayer, asking for lightness of heart. When she opened her eyes all she saw was bitterness. Years of hurt and anger that reared its ugly head during her most weak and vulnerable times.

The knock on her suite door shook the entire room. Trevelle knew it was Airic, tired of waiting. He'd demanded they talk about what transpired. She told him later, after they'd both calmed down. What she meant was, after *she'd* calmed down. She could care less about his insipid anger. He had no idea of the fury burning, itching and clawing to get out. She would have said things she couldn't take back if they'd carried on their conversation from the car.

The knock again. Trevelle took a deep breath, splashed water on her face and realized the cold had gone away, eerily replaced by heat radiating around her body. She tossed the robe aside and stood naked, shaking her arms as if to peel the suffocating cloak away.

"I'm coming," she finally said, lifting the robe back over her shoulders.

Airic stepped inside, still dressed in his Sunday worst, still wearing those awful white shoes. "Where do you want to start?" he asked, pacing the floor.

"We can start with you disrespecting me. An apology would be nice," Trevelle said.

"I didn't call you a 'bitch,' I said you were acting like a bitch. There's a distinct difference."

Trevelle leaned close to his face. "There is no difference. You let that word fall from your lips again there better be a pack of wild female dogs at your feet."

"All right, I'm sorry," he said. "Can we focus on the real issue? I told you it wasn't a good idea to touch Mya's hair, her clothes. Didn't I tell you that? No, you wouldn't listen. We had them. Right here." He slapped his palm. "Now—"

"Now *what?*" Trevelle asked. "So I tried to comb the child's hair, it's not a crime. But I'll tell you what is." She walked over to the desk and picked up a manila folder. "Let's see, 'Venus Johnston-Parson arrested October 20, 2004, Los Angeles, California. Disorderly conduct. Assault on a police officer. Resisting arrest. Unlawful protesting.' Then not more than six months later, Jake Parson arrested March 2005, indicted for murder." She enunciated the word. "*Murder.* It doesn't get worse than that. Then let's top off this delightful meal with the crème de la crème. Venus Johnston-Parson held in a psychiatric hospital for a suicide attempt. These facts speak for themselves. The judge has to make a choice: put Mya in a home with two good Christians or leave her with two parents with arrest records." She dropped the folder on the coffee table in front of Airic. "There is no fight. This is what's called a KO."

He shook his head. "Maybe they'll pull up the fact that you used to be a prostitute."

"Oh please," Trevelle weakly scoffed. "My life is an open book, literally. The difference is that was thirty long years ago. These people are acting like fools in present day with a child in their care. There's nothing they can do." Trevelle became resigned, sitting on the edge of the bed, suddenly overtaken by exhaustion. "Are we done?" She lay down on the soft pillow and closed her eyes. Airic remained in the room.

She could hear Airic open the folder and flip through the police records. Nothing money couldn't buy these days. She'd paid for the initial Internet search the very day Airic informed her that he had a daughter he hadn't seen since birth. She asked Airic all the pertinent questions, who this terrible woman was who wouldn't let him see his God-given child. She listened with a sympathetic ear. Within days she knew everything about both Jake and Venus Parson, credit scores, driver's records, income, and the prized criminal reports. Eventually she took it to the next level and hired an old friend, Eddie Ray, a private investigator, to find anything she might have missed. That's when Eddie announced the last and final straw, Venus had been hospitalized for a suicide attempt by overdosing on antidepressants. Trevelle had counseled enough lost souls to know one had to be deeply unbalanced to attempt to take their own life. That poor child, that poor sweet child. *Don't worry, Mya, we will save you.* She opened her eyes, wondering if she was hearing correctly, the distinct sound of a zipper and belt buckle knocking together.

"Airic. I have a busy day tomorrow. We both do." Her way of telling him it was time for him to leave.

"Yeah, right." Airic walked straight to Trevelle's bed.

"What do you think you're doing?"

"I'm going to bed, just like you said, we have a long day tomorrow."

"Go to your room."

"I'm in *my* room."

"Airic, not now. I don't feel like playing any games."

"I'd have to agree with you. I'm tired of playing games, too." He

pulled the covers back and slid between her cool sheets. "I sit and listen to you preach about being there for your husband, your family, I
just want to hold you tonight. Is that all right?"

"No. Not tonight. Trust me, now is not the time." Most likely
she was hurting herself more than him. She'd probably feel so much
better with him inside of her, losing herself to his control. Instead
she kept her steely glare on Airic until he finally relented, rising
from the bed in defeat.

She wanted to be a good wife, the kind that closed her eyes in
the comfort of her husband's safe arms. She would if it were possible. Her greatest fear was falling into a deep sleep, Airic beside her
and waking to the sound of her own screams. Always the same
nightmare. Once her eyes closed, the hands squeezing her could
have belonged to any of the hundreds of men who'd used her flesh
for their pleasure.

"Let's not have this discussion again. Not now," she said, near
tears. "I'm tired. We've had a long day to say the least and I don't
have the strength to fight with you."

Airic rose and slipped his pants on. He stroked a comforting
thumb across the tear as it rolled down her cheek. "I'm sorry. I
didn't mean to make you cry." He kissed her gently before leaving.
"I'll give you some peace."

If only it were that easy. She slipped into the covers and placed the
silk lavender-scented mask over her eyes. She said a gentle prayer,
then relented. Not even she could pray away the maddening visions.
"Come and get me," she said to the darkness of her closed lids. "I'm
not afraid of you."

Cain was the host of her dreams but he wasn't the culprit. He'd
never once had sex with her in the traditional form. Never once slid
into anything besides her mouth. He'd never wanted her that way,
only delivering her for someone else's taking. "Just like a virgin,"
he'd say, grinning. "Feel that tight pussy." He'd grip her between the

legs in the middle of the street, like she was a slave on the auction block. If there weren't enough takers, he'd lower the price. "Five dollars extra and you can take her from behind."

Trevelle squeezed her eyes tight. The tears ran down the sides of her face. Even in her dreams she felt the pain.

27

Right May Be Wrong

Normally Delma would take the next case, keep them coming fast and in a hurry to clear her calendar. Not this time. Delma saw the names that were next on her docket and decided a break was necessary. "Hudson, taking ten." Delma fanned her hands to show all ten fingers. Hudson gave a knowing nod.

He probably thought she was going to go find her wig, spread on a little blush and lipstick. He was wrong. Delma was going to pray, something she wasn't too familiar with. She depended on man's laws. Real laws that kept people civil. If not for laws, the entire world would run amok. But this was bigger than what was right or wrong, or written in black or white. She had no control over the outcome. She needed strength to face Trevelle Doval, wondering when the glass house she'd built so carefully was going to shatter in a million pieces. Someone had already made it clear this was no coincidence. *Someone's got a secret.* Then the second part the caller spoke raised the bar on the teasing. *You should've given her back,* the caller said before hanging up last night.

She heard Hudson's knock before he entered her chambers. He silently walked behind her chair and let his hands rest on her shoulders. He rubbed lightly as if testing the waters. "You're going to do fine." He massaged and squeezed, taking her silence as license to dig in.

"I should take myself off this case." Delma's shoulders had fallen, not with the weight of Hudson's hands, but with her own

impending doom. The worse thing a judge could do was have a recusal on file without a legitimate cause. She couldn't very well tell
that she knew Trevelle Doval from the past without incrimination.
Speculation would haunt her spotless record, barring her from her
lofty dreams of a seat on the Supreme Court, or a posted position
on one of the administrative boards. "I keep thinking she's behind
this whole setup. She could've easily found out I was the one that
helped her that night. Now she's back to right the wrongs of the
past. Maybe she expects me to just hand over that little girl to her
and her new husband because of my guilty conscience."

"Sounds to me, she was in no condition to remember names. I
think her being in your courtroom is simply a coincidence."

"I flashed my district attorney's ID to the receptionist at the hospital," Delma said. "I don't think anyone wrote anything down
though. Everything happened so fast."

"But she wouldn't have known you went back for the baby, anyway . . . a presumably dead baby. I think it's time you put this out of
your mind. Pray about it, do a forty-day fast, but let this thing go. It's
eating you up." He reached in front of her, brushing his rib cage against
her back. The warmth of his body against hers caused a brief shudder.
He picked up the wooden gavel with her name engraved on the curved
handle. "Judge Delma Hawkins, you are an excellent judge. I admire
your dedication and your honesty. Bottom line, you're going to do
right by this child, like you always do. Children first. Parents, steppar-
ents, and regrets be damned." He handed the slim gavel to her. "This
case has nothing to do with the Trevelle Doval of thirty years ago."

Delma shook her head. *She has everything to do with it.*

He gave a final pat and squeeze on her shoulders that felt like
love. "Put the past out of your mind. You have a job to do."

"You're too good for me," she said with new confidence.

☙☙

"Good afternoon," Delma said, sidling up to her judge post. She
plopped in her chair. The leather chair felt too low and sunken. Her

first thought was to get a new one. Her second thought was of the
sweat dripping underneath her hot robe. She took a sip of water and
scanned the room. The mother of the child was almost as uncomfortable as Delma.

"Well, let's get started. The matter of Johnston and Fisher regarding minor child Mya Fisher." She spoke clearly for the recorder's
sake but her mind was miles away. She searched all the faces in the
courtroom to see if anyone present could've made the cryptic
phone call. Someone with a knowing glare or an ominous smile.
Somebody's got a secret. She took another sip of water. "Mr. Young,
Ms. Michaels, have you two introduced yourselves?"

Georgina Michaels gave a short polite smile. "Yes, we have met,
your honor."

"Could I be so lucky that you all have come to an agreement?"

"Not so lucky, your honor."

Another sip of water. "Who wants to go first?"

"I'd like to go first." Mr. Young took the bait. He rubbed his narrow chin before standing up.

"Standing isn't necessary," Delma said. "I can hear you from
here."

He sat back down, an instant blow to his potential success. Trevelle rolled her eyes and let her hand fall to the desk with a slapping
sound.

Delma would have taken offense to the obvious show of disrespect. Seeing as how she'd made Trevelle invisible she couldn't very
well notice such a thing, now could she? The only way she'd get
through the proceedings was to pretend Trevelle Doval didn't exist.

"Please continue," Delma said politely.

"This past weekend my client, Mr. Fisher, visited with his
daughter. During the course of the day, they went for an innocent
stop for ice cream, encountering the mother who became enraged
and physically attacked Ms. Doval in front of the child for absolutely
no reason."

Georgina raised a well-manicured hand. "I object. She had specific reason, your honor. Ms. Doval took the child to a hair salon and altered her appearance."

"I did not." Trevelle almost smiled. "I simply put a comb to the child's head. Is that a crime?"

Mr. Young continued. "This kind of behavior sends a clear message of the instability of the mother. She's clearly unfit and we have record that she's been hospitalized in the past for mental incapacity. Furthermore, with her arrest record, and that of her husband it's clear these two people are without boundaries and should not be trusted a minute longer with the responsibility of taking care of this child when there are two respectable loving adults waiting with open arms."

"Praise him," Trevelle Doval sang out, her eyes closed. She swayed gently to a tune no one else could hear.

"Speaking of two loving adults," Delma spoke into the microphone, "where is Mr. Parson this afternoon?"

Georgina leaned forward and cleared her throat. "Mr. Parson is on his way from clear across town. He's run into a bit of traffic. He'll be here as soon as he can," she offered. "Make no mistake, he's dedicated to the well-being of Mya and is working very hard to get here."

Mr. Young continued. "I'd like to file an immediate motion for removal of the child from the home until a psychiatric evaluation can be presented."

"*My child* isn't going anywhere."

"Please, have a seat, Ms. Johnston," Delma instructed. *I got this,* her eyes said. "Mr. Young, motion is denied. Secondly, do you have a police report on the alleged attack?"

"Yes . . . I have an incident report right here, your honor."

"So that would be a no. An incident report is a far cry from a police report for an arrest." Delma slammed her gavel down for effect. "Let's move on."

"My clients filed a formal complaint the very same afternoon."

"I'm sure the district attorney is going to get right on it," Delma said smugly. "In the meantime, let's deal with the facts. Mr. Fisher had a visitation with his daughter. Did you enjoy your visitation, Mr. Fisher?"

"Yes," he answered meekly. "I did up until the time Venus attacked my wife."

"Tell me how that started." Delma leaned back with her arms folded under her ample chest.

His lawyer touched his sleeve and spoke for him, "It's all explained in the incident report, your honor."

"I can read, thank you, Mr. Fisher. Please, I'd like to hear your interpretation of the events."

Airic Fisher cleared his throat. "I didn't hear the exact words exchanged. I was sitting in the car and saw Venus lunge toward my wife. I ran inside and stepped between them, since her husband seemed to condone her irrational behavior."

The doors creaked open and Jake Parson entered. He took a seat next to his wife. Delma noticed she didn't turn to greet him, instead stared straight ahead as if he didn't exist at all. There was real tension between them. Common at this point. Delma knew it was never easy on a relationship. Tempers. Emotions. Finger-pointing.

"So you're saying you have no idea what prompted your ex to attack your wife?" Delma did her best not to suck in one side of her jaw. Hudson pointed out the small tic when she felt obvious disbelief. Instead she covered her hand against her face and tapped her cheekbone. "Okay, Ms. Johnston, why don't you tell me what happened?"

"May I stand?"

"Yes you may."

"First, I'd like to apologize to Airic and Trevelle for the outburst. I was upset and shocked. When Airic picked my daughter up she was wearing a cute little top, jeans, and sandals. My daughter actually picked out her clothes. I mean, I want her to feel empowered with her choices, you know. Same goes for her hair. I don't straighten her hair with hot combs or try to slick it down with a whole jar of grease because I think it hurts a black child's self-esteem."

"Excuse me, your honor, I don't see how this is getting to the facts," Mr. Young interrupted.

"Go on, Ms. Johnston," Delma said.

"I spent my life feeling pressured to wear my hair the way society expected me to wear it. I made a promise to myself I would never do that to my daughter. I wanted her to learn to accept her natural beauty and not have her self-esteem determined by her hair."

"Oh that's ridiculous," the voice called out.

She doesn't exist. She's not here. "Go on," Delma said, ignoring Trevelle's interruption.

"The point is, when I saw my daughter I didn't recognize her. My heart nearly leaped out of my chest. The realization that I didn't even recognize my own child sent me in a tailspin. She had on different clothes and her hair was in this painful-looking press and curl pulled back so tight she still has the tiny red pus bumps at the edge of her scalp." Her hand pressed against her chest. "My first reaction was of a mother defending her child. It wasn't personal. I respect Trevelle Doval very much and do believe she had the best intentions in mind."

Delma couldn't help but smile. This girl was good.

"It was a misunderstanding, and I'm sure it won't happen again now that we know where each other stands."

"Oh, please." Trevelle Doval stood up. "Both of these people are documented criminals. This woman attacked me in public. There are witnesses and I want something done about it."

Delma almost fell out in laughter. She had to control herself. She slammed her gavel down. "Mr. Young, control your client or I will have her removed."

They whispered back and forth among each other before Trevelle finally sat down. She was fuming and had no choice but to button up and fly right. Delma was in control. Satisfaction came in the form of silence.

"Now, fighting is never a good thing when it comes to the best interest of a child. This process should be about getting over yourselves, your needs, your hurt and bruised egos. Because such selflessness is such a rarity, I usually do three things. I speak directly with the child in question. I speak directly with the parents in question. I speak with the custody adviser and I come to a decision."

On the other side, Trevelle went into a damage control mode. She clawed her long fingers over the microphone so no one would hear what she was saying. Moments later, Mr. Young stood up. "Your honor, it's crucial that the criminal records of Mrs. Johnston-Parson as well as her husband are taken into consideration."

"Mr. Young, are you trying to tell me how to do my job?"

"No . . . no ma'am."

"I didn't think so," Delma said. "I have the parents' file. I will take it into consideration. Okay, please see my clerk to schedule your meetings, hopefully very soon. By the way, I still don't have a paternity test." She turned to Hudson. "Why do I still not have a paternity test on record?"

"I'll get right on it," Hudson said.

"Let's hope there are no more delays. I encourage you all to put on your happy faces. Custody advisers aren't nearly as nice as I am." Delma slammed her gavel down.

28

Trevelle

She and Airic rode to the airport in silence. She was more than happy to leave, to get on the plane and be miles away from the circus clowns and ridiculousness of baby mamas, ineffective lawyers, and crazy judges. Trevelle knew there was something amiss. Court day had been a train wreck. Nothing had gone in their favor. Continued visitation. What a joke, as if Trevelle would set foot near those wretched people without armed police protection.

The judge, that jungle woman with the wrinkled collar peeking underneath her robe, that woman, Trevelle decided, was against her. She had a knack for knowing these things. She was used to the Trevelle Doval–haters, the ones jealous of her success. Jealous of her beauty. Judge Hawkins appeared neither self-righteous nor petty, which was made obvious by her lack of personal esteem, running around half-dressed and hair uncombed. Then what? Simple disdain for Trevelle having once been a prostitute and drug addict? It wasn't a secret that she'd lived a wild and ignorant childhood. She'd read a few articles on herself where even the journalists thought they were disclosing something rare and secret, outing her, when they truly weren't. The part that was private and sealed was her criminal record, at least from the public, but someone like Delma Hawkins could easily get access. It all made sense. The judge knew more than anyone else could possibly know. More than Trevelle herself ever wanted to remember.

"Ma'am, you're going to have to step to the side." The airport security guard stood with a solid body and bland expression. "Female pat down." He waved at another guard.

Trevelle was so busy thinking about the judge that she mindlessly walked through the metal detector wearing her Dolce & Gabbanas with the gold-plated clasps. Setting off the alarm was like volunteering for a strip search. She spun around looking for Airic, wondering how he could let her make such a mistake. She spotted him ahead of her, already gathering his wallet and watch from the plastic tray.

"This way, miss." Clear blue eyes and blond lashes blinked at her without seeing. "How's your day so far?"

"Blessed. And yours?" Trevelle tapped her now bare stocking feet impatiently on the filthy floor. She'd have to soak her feet in hot boiling water with half a cup of hydrogen peroxide. Extra strength.

The woman waved the magic wand across Trevelle's chest, where the beeping amplified. The wire in her bra, her earrings, even her diamond cross hanging on her neck set off the alarm. There was no easy way to travel anymore. The country was under siege, not by terrorists but their own lack of spiritual trust and faith in God. The young woman patted and ran her hands along Trevelle's body, barely paying attention to what she was doing, incapable of saving lives, securing a plane.

"Okay, you're free to go. Thank you for your patience." The woman's glazed eyes focused on nothing. "Your things are over there."

Trevelle knew the sad hopeless expression all too well. She reached out and touched the woman lightly on her arm. "We are all God's children and he will not forsake you. You are loved." She opened her palms and waited with closed eyes.

Without pause, the thin cold hands of the woman slid into Trevelle's. "Lord, I ask you today to guide the heart of this young woman, give her strength and peace of mind. I ask that you give her direction, oh Lord, so that she may find her voice, her strength, her passion. Give her heart the warmth and calm of knowing she can do and be anything in this world with you as the light. Show her your blessings, dear Lord, so that she may follow and know your greatness."

"Thank you," the security woman whispered as she clung tightly to Trevelle's hands.

"You're going to be fine. God knows what all his children need." Trevelle squeezed the bony hands of the woman one last time before walking away. She could still hear the soft whispers of "thank you" over and over, as if the lady was walking by her side. It happened more often than not, someone's energy and spirit clinging to her out of sheer desperation. She understood. She would not abandon the woman and would keep her in her prayers until she was strong enough to take the journey on her own. Trevelle understood how someone could be afraid of God's abundance and power. She'd been in those very shoes before she'd been saved and made to see her true calling.

Airic led her by the arm at a hurried pace. "You've already had a rough week. I wish you wouldn't exert that kind of energy unannounced—not to mention, we could miss our flight."

"That poor woman was lifeless, soulless. I couldn't let her go on that way. Besides, I wouldn't have run into her at all if you'd been mindful. How could you let me go through security with my shoes on?"

Airic paused, then changed what he was about to say. "I love you," he said unexpectedly.

"Okay," Trevelle said with fear and questioning. "Is there something you want to tell me?"

"Sometimes, you give and you give of yourself and I wonder if there's anything left for me."

"Of course there is, Airic. I don't understand where this is coming from."

He shook his head. "I didn't think you would."

"I do love you, sweetheart." The softness of her voice promised she would try harder to make him believe. They held hands the rest of the distance to the gate. All the passengers had already boarded. The crew members patiently looked on as the final two passengers took their first-class seats.

Trevelle plopped down into the leather comfort, exhausted. Her eyes closed and she was in a deep sleep before the plane left the ground.

She'd been on the streets a whole year with only one goal: survival. Unless she learned to adapt and take advantage of her situation she would've ended up nothing but used meat. She figured out how to be the sweet desirable pussycat. That way she'd get more money, be treated nicer, and get on Cain's good side.

It was the very same vulnerability that attracted Lieutenant Kellogg, or Lieutenant K, as he was known. Most of the girls giggled at the sound of his name, teasing him for being named after a cereal. She didn't take him serious at first, either, treating him like a Boy Scout. He worked the downtown area on a special task force called "S.A.F.E." Small Accomplishments for Empowerment. On Sundays he had his own church in an abandoned storefront on Baker Street. He never berated any of the girls for doing what they did. He carried bottled water and boxes of trail mix, offering nutrition and a word of encouragement here and there. He only arrested the girls when it looked like they could use a good night's rest.

In lockup they could get some sleep with a hot meal the next morning. Needless to say, riding in the back of his patrol unit became the most welcome part of her night. She made sure her misdemeanor crimes were conducted between the hours of ten and midnight; walking off with an armful of hygiene products from the brightly lit convenience mart, leaving the diner without paying, or pretending to hitchhike and being ashamed when it turned out to be Kellogg's headlights instead of a paying trick.

"You know it's past your bedtime, young lady," Kellogg would always say to Velle, rolling down the window. The large dark gap in the center of his teeth was a welcome sight. "Get in."

"Yes, sir." She'd curl up in the backseat, take off her high heels, and rub the burning start of a blister. She trusted him, which was unusual for two reasons: he was white and a police officer. She could honestly say he was the only one walking the earth she could be herself with. She told him her real name, something she knew was against the rules. Still when he booked her, he always left the initials "N/A," pretending he didn't know.

The rearview mirror tilted to eye her directly. "It's time you made a decision," he said with more persistence in his voice than usual.

"I don't have a decision to make. You act like I got a choice." The dirty yellow streetlamps offered barely enough light to capture the silhouette of him. She could make out his jawline, the distinct pockmarks left by splatters of hot grease intended for his father when he was only six years old. He had told her the story of standing too close to the stove when his mother decided she'd had enough of the man's lying and philandering. She picked up the skillet she'd heated to fry chicken and flung the sizzling grease, burning both himself and his father. Third-degree burns, a matching set. "If you think mine are bad, you should see my daddy's," he'd said, when she had the nerve to cry from his sad story. As if her own wasn't the saddest of them all.

"Tonight, I'm either going to drop you back off on that corner or you're going to the Grant Reed Shelter. They got one bed open. I made them promise to keep it for me." He turned around and faced her but his face was unreadable. His tone said it all. "This is the last time I pick you up, Velle, unless it's at the Grant Reed Shelter."

That's why she loved him, because he cared. But she shook her head. "Cain found me last time. He pulled me out the front door by my hair and nobody even stopped him. He stuck a knife to my throat and said if I went back he'd kill me."

"I'm not going to let that happen. Not this time, I swear." He turned the police radio down to mute. "I worry about you," he added, dropping his eyes.

Her hands tingled with fear, but more from the thought of not being able to get her hands on a little PCP, or red dragons, than the threat of Cain beating her upside the head.

"Your choice," he said, using his Lieutenant K voice. But something told her he was tired, and wasn't going to make the offer again.

"Okay, but you promise to come get me first thing in the morning?"

"I promise."

She spent the night in the four-story brick building that used to be a bank before the area fell to ruin. The cot smelled like piss and vomit, but so did she.

The next morning, Kellogg showed up bright and early. It was the first time she'd seen him in the daylight and almost didn't recognize him. She didn't know he had light brown hair or dark gray eyes. Even with the thick scarring on his face, he was handsome. He had a solid, trustworthy face. "You ready?" He handed her a miniature carton of orange juice and a bag of donuts with colorful sprinkles.

"Thank goodness. I thought it was gonna be something healthy like those nuts and berries you always pass around."

"It's a special day." His voice deepened. "I wanted you to have something sweet and special, just like yourself. I'm proud of you for taking this step."

Nothing tasted so good. The warm buttery sweetness of the fresh donut melted on her tongue. She rode in the front seat next to Kellogg, taking moments in between bites to watch his profile. "Why are you so nice?" she asked. "So many bad things happened to you and you're still a good person."

"Bad things happen to people all the time. It doesn't have to make you angry. Eventually you'll see that. You can take a tragedy and grow from it, become a better person."

"No, I don't see how being raped and being used up will ever make me a better person."

"I do. One day you're going to help other people, other women, who've gone through the same thing you have. You're going to be able to say, look at me, *If I can change, anyone can."*

The trees got bigger, greener, and taller with every passing second as they drove. The quiet peacefulness of the thick wooded countryside with only glints of sunshine passing through was something she'd only seen on TV shows, or in pictures. They arrived to a large country mansion. The outside was lined with white rose bushes. The garden plaque on the gate said, GROW WHERE YOU'RE PLANTED.

In six months she did just that. She blossomed into a young woman who stood in front of her rehabilitated group with Kellogg looking on and read the poem she'd written as a semi-commencement speech. It was time for her group to go their separate ways. She took a deep breath and read aloud with more confidence than she knew she had.

> *One dream at a time.*
> *One hope at a time.*
> *One step at a time.*
> *My heart and mind lift with angels who guide me*
> *One day at a time.*
> *One hug at a time.*
> *One man, woman, and child at a time, will see the power in me.*
> *The glory in we.*
> *The hope and the dreams in all of us.*

Kellogg was the only one who'd shown up, even though she'd invited her mother and her brother, Kevin. Six months and she hadn't so much as sipped cough medicine. She was clearheaded and sober. She'd gained ten pounds of healthy weight eating food she'd helped grow. Daily Bible study gave her a foundation to stand on her own two feet and not be afraid of what someone else thought of her. There was only one problem; it was time for her to leave and she had nowhere to go.

Being only fourteen meant foster care or back to the streets where Cain would be happy to welcome her home with a beating worse than all the others. "I don't know what I'm gonna do. I've never been so happy and now I don't have anywhere to go."

Kellogg hugged her and gave her a fatherly kiss on the top of her head. "Have I let you down, ever? I'm not about to start. We'll find someplace."

"What about your place? I can sleep on the couch. I'll cook. You won't even notice I'm there."

"Velle, I wish I could take you home with me. You know I can't."

"Why?"

"I'm a police officer. I have a family, a wife, two little boys."

Brimming with tears she said, "I can help . . . babysit, or clean." Her folded arms couldn't stop the overwhelming chill of insecurity. Only minutes before she was brave and full of hope. In front of him, she began to wither. "I'll do everything I'm supposed to do. I'll go to school. You won't have any trouble out of me, I swear."

"We'll have to find somewhere else for you to go," he said with regret.

"Right," she said, turning to walk the distance to the well-kept mansion. His footsteps quickly caught up with hers.

"Listen, okay, you can stay with me until we find a good home, a family who's willing to take you in. It's temporary. You understand?"

You understand?

"Mr. Doval, is your wife all right?"

The entire first-class cabin beamed concern in her direction. She'd fallen asleep. Her cries could be heard loud and clear over the roar of the plane engine.

"She's fine," Airic said. "Some water would be helpful." The fear in his eyes said otherwise. She wasn't fine. "You scared me half to death." He squeezed her hand and brought it to his lips. "We're almost home."

She leaned against his shoulder and held on tight. Just *once* she wished she could close her eyes without living her worst nightmare over and over.

29

Venus

Fighting, along with everything else on our plate, seemed like a waste of good energy, which neither Jake nor I had to spare. When I left with Mya, I ended up at the Embassy Suites about ten miles away. I spent the entire night on the phone with Jake. I was back home the next morning. I knew it was only a matter of time before the lure of his voice or the promise of doing better would no longer work. I'd lost count of the number of times I'd scooped Mya up in the middle of the night or day, claiming I was through. I was tired of restarting the race from the same spot. Ready, set, go . . . only to be tripped up by his insecurities. The clock was ticking on our relationship, I knew it. He knew it as well.

I'd been looking forward to my appointment with the custody adviser, a chance to tell my side of the story. As soon as I entered her office, I was struck with the fact she held my entire life, Mya's life, in her hands.

"Have a seat." She offered a choice of either chair with a smooth sweep of her hand. She was casually dressed in a scoop-neck top and tailored denim. Her amber locks were pulled up and twisted over her head, landing in spirals. "I'm impressed with your little girl. She's smart and full of energy. You're a lucky mom."

"Yes." I gulped air along with my fear. "She's the best thing that's ever happened to me."

"First of all, don't feel like this is an inquisition. I can see how much you love your daughter. I just wanted to go over a couple of issues that I have to deal with." She opened the file in front of her.

I braced myself for what I knew would be the first question. *Why did you try to kill yourself?*

She offered a warm smile. "You spent a week in psychiatric counseling. Can you tell me a little bit about that . . . what you remember?"

"Of course. I accidentally took a few too many pills."

She gently leaned to the side and rested her face in her hands. "Why don't you tell me how that happened?"

"My son was born prematurely. He never took his first breath. He was this beautiful tiny baby, the most beautiful I'd ever seen and he never took a breath." I slapped my hands in my lap to say *end of story*. "That's it."

"How far along were you?"

"I . . . seven months."

She was quick in handing me a box of Kleenex. "Take your time."

"I had a difficult pregnancy. My blood pressure shot up. There were complications." I wiped and blew and counted slowly. "I had a hard time dealing with the loss. I didn't mean to take so many pills but they didn't seem to be working. I wanted the sadness to stop. I had a family to take care of, a daughter, a husband. I just wanted to be myself again. Honestly, I wasn't trying to die."

"I understand." She made a couple of notes. "Are you still in therapy?"

"No. I'm fine. I mean, really." I wiped at my nose before taking a few more tissues just in case. "Don't I look fine?" I'd hoped she got my joke.

She did not. "Don't take offense. It would be in your favor. Therapy is a good thing. It would show that you're being monitored and focused on being whole and healthy. Mental health . . . especially in this situation, is a huge factor in a child custody case."

I cleared my throat. "I understand."

She flipped past a couple of pages. "Quite a colorful life. Busy lady."

"You're referring to the arrest in Los Angeles. I was protesting the closing of a community hospital. Harmless protesting."

"And your husband, also harmless?"

"He is . . . the kindest man I know. The most gentle, loving man I know. He had nothing to do with that man's death. Nothing. He was investigated and the case against him was dropped."

She stood up, signaling the conclusion of our time together. "I'm going to refer you to a few therapists I know in the area. Some-one you can trust, all right?"

"Thank you."

Outside, Jake sat with Mya in his lap. We switched places. He saw the obvious signs of my tears and kissed me between the eyes. "It's going to be all right," he said reassuringly.

"I know," I whispered to Jake before he went inside.

When we got home, we headed off in separate directions. I'd meant what I told the custody adviser. Jake was kind. He was loving. He was gentle. He was all those wonderful adjectives and more. He was also a man who had a nagging voice in his head that reminded him daily he was raising another man's child.

I could hear his determined footsteps through the long hallway. He stopped, checked our bedroom first, expecting to see me wallow-ing in bed or taking a deep hot soak in the tub. Wrong, I was wallow-ing in the room down the hall, next to Mya's. I could hear him peek in on her with a slower, more careful opening of her door. Hopefully she was still fast asleep.

Three door openings and closings later Jake found me. "There you are."

"Here I am."

When Jake noticed the box in my hands, there was a small detectable change in his breathing before he looked away. "The custody adviser asked me if there was some tension going on between us."

"Hmmm, maybe it was something you said." I found what I'd been looking for. The small white box was at the bottom underneath all the other baby clothing. None was as special as what was inside this one. A christening gown, the precious white bonnet, and baby mittens all lightly wrapped in tissue paper.

"I made sure she understood I was Mya's father, I was in for the long haul. No walking away."

"Good. Thank you," I said curtly. "Glad you're doing your civic duty."

"It's not going to work, so give it up. We're going to get through this. I'm not going anywhere." Though strangely enough he left me sitting there alone in the middle of the floor.

☺☺

Falling out of love was a torturous process, never as easy as falling into love. The warning signs were everywhere. The basic and most obvious: Jake and I hadn't made love in nearly a year before we moved to Atlanta. No sex, not even Bill Clinton–style. Some might find that completely odd and unbelievable, even insane. Why live with someone you couldn't share the basics with a, such as the mating game? Easy. Far too easy as it turned out, one week turned into two, one month into three, six, nine, and on to twelve. Starting with the second trimester I was pregnant with our son.

I wasn't buying the *sex won't hurt the baby* story. They obviously had no idea of what I was working with. Jake was blessed with a large endowment and I wasn't talking about a trust fund. We played kissy face and touchy-feely but I didn't trust penetration.

Into my sixth month, the Byron Steeple case opened wide and swallowed us whole. I spent day and night worrying about Jake. I worried and prayed till my stomach charged in fits of acidic shock. I

couldn't keep any food down. What went in came right back up. I
lost ten precious pounds in seven days when it should have been the
other way around. Dehydration and a blinding headache sent me
straight to the emergency room where I was finally diagnosed with
preeclampsia, a condition that causes high blood pressure and could
possibly damage vital organs in the mother as well as the baby.

After getting the condition under control I was sent home,
where everything seemed fine for the next few days. Then I was
back in the hospital again. Midway into the seventh month I knew
there was something wrong but I kept praying it was my imagination. Praying that I felt a kick where I knew it was only a faint
nudge. Talking myself into believing he was one of those gentle
souls who decided not to give his mother any grief by staying in one
position. The final time I arrived at the hospital the doctor said I had
to have a cesarean.

Jake was by my side the entire time. He held my hand and
kissed each fingertip, promising everything was going to be fine. I
had my first hint to the contrary when the doctor made it clear he
wanted me under full anesthesia. Putting me under was the best
way to make sure I didn't send myself into cardiac arrest. My blood
pressure was sky high and my head felt like it would explode. I fell
asleep hearing Jake's soft whisper at my side. "Baby, I'm so sorry." I
heard the sadness in his voice and knew before my eyes closed that
my baby had died.

The christening gown was never worn. I peeled back the tissue
and ran my hand across the white satin. He was so perfect in every
way. Perfect fingers and toes, a mass of black hair slick against his
tiny scalp. His eyes, I never got to see, but I already knew they were
Jake's eyes. From all those nights having watched Jake sleeping, face
to face, our heads against the pillow, I'd ask myself how I got so
lucky to have a man like him.

We no longer faced each other on the pillow. Always one of us
turned in the opposite direction. One of us wide awake at night listening to the other's breathing, trying to guess if the other was really

asleep. Then the question would push itself into the darkness to join us. *Are you ever going to stop blaming me?* Sometimes it was me who asked, sometimes it was Jake. We proudly took turns in our guilt, sharing it like housework and cooking duties.

The sadness never proved to be a deal-breaker. I always believed true love surpassed the physical. The very thing my mother asked me each and every time I came home with claims of newfound head-over-heels love: *Can you picture yourself spoon-feeding him, or changing his Depends? 'Cause that's real love. Running around looking for passion and excitement will get you nothing but emptiness in the long run.*

I'd go into my sunny room and ponder the question. I'd try to picture Johnny, Frank, or fill in the blank, sitting in a wheelchair, broken with old age and I'd be immediately shocked into a bleak reality. No. I absolutely did not love Johnny, Frank, or fill in the blank.

And it went on that way. I loved, but not really. I'd convince myself my mother's grand standard was far too high. Until of course when I asked myself the question about Jake. And the answer was an unequivocal yes. Yes, I could spoon-feed him, change his Depends, curl up next to his limp warm body and still be completely, happily in love. Real love.

But what happened when both of you were broken? No one to spoon-feed the other. No one to wipe up drool and misspoken words. What then? Who would save us if we couldn't save each other?

I folded the tissue back over the christening gown. I put it away, closed the box, and shoved it toward the others. Then I kicked it hard, using my heel to chase it down. Before long I'd stomped all over the box until the sides were torn and the contents spilled out of every corner. Cute little onesies and two-piece sets I'd spent endless hours shopping for, all still with tags attached. Stuffed animals and the mobile for over the crib made of plush cars. There was more of the same in the other boxes. Tons of never-used baby goods.

I carried the boxes down the stairs one at a time. I came back with a trash bag and shoved any strays inside and carried that down, too. For a moment I felt invincible strength, like I could lift the entire house, so a few boxes were no problem. Weightless. By the time I was finished, sweat poured off my brows and stung my eyes. Where I thought I was invincible now felt like I'd been carrying concrete blocks. My back pounded and throbbed. My arms and shoulders felt stretched beyond repair, and the bruises against my thigh had already started to darken.

I picked up the yellow pages and found a shelter for battered women. I made it short and sweet. "I have thousands of dollars' worth of never-worn baby clothes, car seats, strollers, all brand new," I said. "Please come pick them up."

I gave the tongue-tied woman my address. She must've heard it in my voice, recognized it from voices like mine before. "I'm so sorry for your loss," she responded, assuming what was true. "I'll send someone over right away." She paused, the sound of papers shuffling in the background. "I have a number you can call if you need to speak with someone."

"No, I'm perfectly fine," I managed to say. "Just fine."

◎

The only sign that sleep had visited me was seeing Jake's side of the bed empty and not knowing what time he'd slipped out. I'd woken up thinking about the status of my life, and the changes that had to be made. I had to call the recommended therapists. The last thing on my list was to call Wendy and update her on the goings-on of the south. Over the years I'd learned the last thing on your list is usually the one thing you should do first.

So I dialed and put the rest of my burning duties on hold.

"Girlfriend, that you?" she answered on the first ring.

I smiled. "Yes, it's me."

"I've been worried about you." Wendy sighed. "But what else is new? I'm always worried about you, right?"

"I'm in a state of denial," I said quickly before she could lead me down the path of more palatable discussions like health, weather, or the status of the latest "new man" she'd met on her way to the grocery store. "I don't see how Jake and I are going to make it work. This thing will always be between us, always."

"This *thing* have a name?"

"No . . . no names to protect the innocent."

Wendy paused. "You two have been through so much. It's going to take time to put everything back in place. Don't you remember how happy you were? You used to always tell me how perfect Jake was, and after a while I actually believed you."

"I believed *me,* too." I took a long deep breath. "I don't think I'm ever going to stop blaming Jake. And if I lose Mya, I'll blame him again."

Wendy stayed silent, a clear indication she thought I was off center.

"I know it's a stretch but try to understand."

"No . . . no, I get it," Wendy said, reserving judgment. "It makes sense in a strange Venus kind of way. You blame him for losing the baby, therefore you blame him for the depression that followed, therefore you blame him for giving Airic the ammunition against you he needed to take Mya . . . it's sad but I get it." Once again she had a way about repeating everything I said to make me hear it from a fresh perspective.

"Thank you, Dr. Wendy. And to think I still have to pay good money for a real doctor," I said with a much brighter outlook. I clicked on the television and saw the news channel with the caption at the bottom of the screen, SHOOTING AT SUGAR HILL STUDIOS. That's where Jake was working.

"Wendy, I have to go . . . I'll call you back." I hung up and dialed Jake's number. The call immediately rolled over to voicemail. "Jake, I saw something about a shooting. Call me."

After rushing around gathering Mya and my purse I jumped into the car only to realize I had no idea where I was going. I called information. Got the address. Punched it into my navigation system and sped away.

Blue shiny police cars parked along the street as far as the eye could see. The giant SWAT vehicle angled to keep everyone out shook me to a whole other level of panic. If there was a SWAT team someone was being held inside. Hostages. Bodies. Jake.

A police officer with a thick mustache and bald brown head put up his hands to stop me from going farther.

I rolled down my window. "My husband is in there."

"Is that a fact?" He pulled out a small notepad. "What's his name?" By this time a helicopter was flying overhead casting a shadow on the street. NEWS TEAM was printed on the side of it, while it rained noise and a solid gust of wind. The officer was talking but I couldn't hear a word of it before he walked off.

"Mommy, a helicopter."

"A-huh, sweetheart."

I picked up the cell phone and tried again. "Please, answer."

" 'You've reached JP. Be honest, be sincere, live life without fear. I'll hit you back.' " The *beep* sounded. "Jake, I'm in front of the building. Please tell me something." I hung up and was just about to dial again when my phone rang.

"There's a man in here with a gun," he whispered. "I love you." His voice trembled. Shouting from the other end and a loud popping sound. The phone must've dropped from Jake's hands.

"Oh God." I whispered under my breath. I signaled for an officer, waving like a madwoman. He stared straight through me, ignoring my desperate pleas. "Hello, please, my husband is in there." I held up the phone. "I just talked to him," I yelled.

"Mommy?" Mya worked her way out of the car seat. "What's wrong, Mommy?"

I've done a lot of stupid things in my life. A lot of things I would always regret but none could top what I was about to do. I stepped on the gas, gently at first. The car lurched forward and I was making my way past the cornered-off street. I stepped harder on the gas moving faster than the two officers who gave chase.

My car window was still down. "Stop her," one of the officers yelled. Three or four blue uniforms moved in front of my Land

Rover, obviously willing to sacrifice their own lives because I had no plans on slowing down. Footsteps trampled in my direction. Thick arms reached inside and unlocked my door. Those same arms pulled me out of the car and to the ground. The female officer charged me off in the opposite direction.

"My daughter's in the car." I fought with all my might.

"Move!" the female officer ordered. Her grip tightened, twisting my arm behind my back. She shoved me to the ground and crouched down, too. "You could've been hurt," the woman officer said. "Not to mention your daughter."

Another police officer carried Mya toward us. To my surprise, Mya was calm and cool. She reached out and grabbed ahold of my neck. I kissed her face and held on for dear life. "Oh baby, I'm so sorry, you all right?"

"Okay, let's go." The female police officer grabbed my arm.

"I'm not going anywhere. My husband's in there at gunpoint with a crazy man. You've got to get him out of there."

"You talked to him?" The female officer's interest piqued.

"Exactly. That's why I was trying to get through there. No one would listen to me."

"Hold on. Don't move from this spot," the woman ordered before trotting off. She returned with a large-faced man wearing a SWAT vest and a hat. He kneeled down to where Mya and I were still crouched on the ground against the back of a squad car.

"You say your husband called you?" The large man stood over us blocking the sun.

"Yes."

"What's his name?"

"Jake Parson. He's working in the studio. He said the man had a gun pointed at him and he only had one chance to call," I said, trying my best to keep it together. Mya stared between me and the dark figure hovering over us.

"I want you to call him back."

"I've tried, he's not answering."

"One more time. Please." He handed me a black cell phone. I dialed. The phone went to voicemail.

"Again," he said.

Again. Again. No matter how many times I dialed, I was sure Jake wasn't going to answer. As hopeful as I was, I knew something had gone terribly wrong. My lip quivered and my hand shook as I pushed redial one more time . . . the last time.

"Yeah. Who this?" The voice didn't belong to Jake.

"Where's my husband? Where's Jake . . ." The phone was snatched out of my hand.

"This is Sergeant Floyd with the Atlanta Police Department. Everybody doing all right in there?" He spoke with nonchalant confidence while waving a huge hand to signal to another officer. Heavy military boots lined up around us. He made another hand sign and they all dispersed as quickly as they came.

"I can get some medics in the building to help anybody who needs medical attention. Right now, nobody's lost their life, am I right?" He paused for the answer. "Don't do anything more you'll regret. Nobody's going to hurt you. Just walk right out the front door. We'll have a car waiting for you."

I could hear the gunman yelling through the phone. The sergeant clicked the phone off and turned his attention toward the building.

"What's happening?" The knot in my throat was dry and filled with regret. Only minutes ago I'd told Wendy of my doubts and fear of the relationship with Jake being doomed to failure. Yet all I could do was pray to have him back in my arms. *Please let him be okay. Please.*

A huge cloud of black smoke pooled through the broken windows.

"Got 'em," the sergeant said to himself before starting a slow trot toward the brick building.

The female officer had a tight grip on my arm as I watched the sergeant disappear. "As soon as they know something, I'll tell you," she said answering my question with her eyes.

30

Trevelle

"You're on in five, four, three, two . . ."

The music, a bass filled rendition of "Lift Your Burden" played while Trevelle touched hands before moving to the podium. Usually a few hundred were invited to sit in the very front and the editing spliced in the ten thousand strong from the old tape. Her audience was real this time. The crowd beamed with delight as the light closed in around her.

"Beautiful divas, stand up and give yourselves a round of applause. Stand up," Trevelle ordered with a wave of her hands. "Beautiful divas bound for glory and splendidness through Christ. Don't fight it, don't hide it. Turn to your neighbor and tell them, you are splendid and bound for glory."

The crowd of well-dressed women turned to one another, giving each the praise they deserved and craved.

"I spent many years of my life feeling unworthy. Didn't need a mirror. Everything was right up here," she said, pointing to her temple. "Seeds of self-hate and doubt planted by the devil himself. The devil may have planted those seeds, but guess what," she lowered her voice, "I was the one watered and fed 'em every day. No matter what seeds were planted you have a choice in weeding out the bad, tending to your garden, keeping the soil fertile and ripe, so new seeds can be planted." She stepped from behind the podium and did a hand-on-hip stroll to the edge of the stage. "Oh, you didn't hear me. I said, *new* seeds. The kind that grow bountiful and healthy, the kind that rise up and face the sunshine and the rain with equal revelry. The kind of seeds that grow with vigilance and can protect themselves from danger. Ladies, I'm talking about your soul. Your spirit. Your very essence. God's seeds need to be planted in your garden.

"Oh . . . don't get me wrong. Once you have these precious seeds in your possession, you've got to protect and nurture. Say it with me, 'handle with care.' Like the side of the package carrying the exquisite Tiffany crystal vase. What's it say? 'handle with care.' Somebody tell me what you get when you don't handle with care. You turn your back and leave the garden to tend to itself you get rats, snakes, gophers, weeds, and worms. Did I leave anything out?"

Trevelle scanned the audience, looking for the one person she could bring up on the stage to give a testimonial and share their fear and pain. She needed one person she could heal with a touch of her hand.

That's when she saw her sitting in the very front row. The young woman, a spitting image of Trevelle twenty years ago. She tried to take her eyes off her and get on with the business at hand. She needed someone wrought with pain, overcome by the daily grunt of work and no play. This young woman showed no signs of wear or tear. Spit-shined and polished, she wouldn't be sympathetic enough for her audience.

Yet she couldn't help herself. "Darling, what's your name?" Trevelle asked sympathetically.

"Keisha Hawkins."

"Bless you, Keisha. Come up here and let me talk to you for a minute."

The young woman wasted no time getting to her feet. They fell into an embrace and Trevelle for a moment forgot she was hosting an audience of thousands, tape rolling, her makeup probably smudged. Something about her, something she couldn't put her finger on. "Dear God," Trevelle whispered. "Bless this child, give her strength to walk in your light and to know your good grace. Now tell me, sweetheart, what's weighing on your heart tonight?"

Keisha looked down, preoccupied with the fact she was standing in front of thousands of onlookers in the audience. Trevelle gripped her hands. "Don't be afraid. We're all here under the same name of God. He is our only judge and he will never forsake you."

A tear fell down Keisha's cheek. "Sometimes I feel all alone in this world. It seems to be an uncontrollable weight on my heart. Don't get me wrong. My mother loves me very much, but I can't shake this sense of abandonment. I don't know who my biological parents are. I've never met them or anyone in their family."

Trevelle's own heart suddenly felt heavy with burden. She wondered briefly if the girl was a plant by her producer. The perfect sad story was sometimes hard to find. Looking into the eyes of the young woman Trevelle found herself tearing up. There was something eerily familiar, even beyond the outside appearance.

"You're not alone. Do you understand that . . . when he's in our heart and mind, you're never alone."

Keisha nodded, flushed with emotion. Her lip quivered while she held on dearly for some shred of control.

Trevelle felt a swell of nurturing, something she had no idea how to identify. Of course she'd cared and wanted to help, that was her pleasure. But this was different. The young woman would've been about the age of her own daughter had she not lost her. She pulled Keisha in against her chest and held on. "You are loved." The surge of the young woman's heart against her own made her lose all sense of herself. She wasn't standing on a stage with an audience at her beck and call. She wasn't planning her next sentence or move.

The two of them were standing alone in the universe. "You are loved," Trevelle whispered. Trevelle sobbed in hoarse whispers that were captured on the microphone clip on her chest. "Forgive me, Lord. Forgive me for my transgressions. Forgive me," she cried into the arms of Keisha, the stunned young woman who had no idea what was happening. She could only do her best to hold up Trevelle Doval who'd somehow made her the chosen one.

The audience responded, moving to their feet, clapping and yelling, "Thank you Jesus."

Trevelle slowly released Keisha, trying to get her faculties back, fighting hard to resume a grip on her actions. She stood on the stage with her arms stretched out as if to mimic Jesus' suffering on the cross, while an uncontrollable flow of tears drained down her face.

The producer uncharacteristically raised the lights and spoke into the tiny speaker in her ear. "Ms. Doval, are you all right? Signal."

Her answer was supposed to come in the form of two fingers raised high over her head, the signal they agreed on to let him know all was under control. But this time it wasn't an act. There was no moment to cue for commercial. Trevelle spun, arms outstretched and her white dolman sleeves sailing in the air like a boundless angel. Floating to her past.

His wife saw trouble the minute the young woman got out of the car. She hadn't expected such a pretty girl, tall and shapely with dark searching eyes. Eyes that begged to be rescued, what Kellogg did best, save damsels in distress. Even if said damsels sold themselves for ten dollars on corners, snorted coke, and carried a switchblade in their pocketbook.

She didn't look like a homeless girl who had no one to take her in, no grandmother, no aunt or family friends, which could only mean one thing. She was too much to handle, too much trouble for those that knew her well.

"This is my wife, Lydia." She was pretty with jet black hair and olive-toned skin. Kellogg had good taste. They made a cute couple.

The two shook hands at first, then awkwardly hugged. "Thanks for letting me stay. I promise to stay out of your way."

"No, I'd rather you be present and accounted for. With two boys under the age of six, help is what I need." Lydia smiled but her heart was already aching.

Trevelle was immediately enrolled in a small Christian school where she flourished and inhaled information like cool water in a dry desert. After school she did her homework like a model citizen then took the boys off their mother's hands so she could have some time to herself. The boys took to Trevelle like sand at a beach. They fell into the lull of her voice and behaved like little gentlemen. If she said take a nap, they laid down as still as possible, whether they were sleepy or not. If she said pick up your toys, they picked up what they could find and scoured the house looking for more. Didn't matter though. She could feel Lydia watching her even if she wasn't in the room. She knew it was only a matter of time before the honeymoon was over.

Meanwhile, Kellogg reminded his small congregation that there were homeless children who needed a family. She sat in church, hoping and praying no one volunteered. For months the praying did wonders. No one wanted to step forward, until one Sunday when Trevelle must've forgot to send out her usual plea, an older couple with sloped backs and gray hair stood up with their hands clasped into one another's bosom, as if it was the biggest undertaking of their life.

"We'd be happy to take on a child," the man spoke for both of them.

"No, please," she'd begged, after waiting up for Kellogg all night to come home from his twelve-hour shift. She even made the nutritional snack packs for him to hand out to the less fortunate girls still on the street. Sometimes she threw in a few M&M's 'cause she remembered it tasted better and made all the other bland dry stuff go down easier.

"We've already talked about this, Velle." He kept his voice low and steady while they sat in the twilight of the living room. The house was narrow with one floor below and one on top, where his wife and two boys lay sleeping.

"Everything's going so good. Haven't I did everything I promised? I go to school. I cook. I help with the boys."

"Shh, keep your voice down."

"What did I do wrong?" She begged for an answer, following him, then cutting him off when he tried to go the other way. "Why don't you want me here?"

His silence seemed indefinite. The wear and exhaustion of always being awake even when he was supposed to be sleeping showed as dark half moons underneath his sad eyes.

"Tell me," she tried to whisper but it came out high pitched with fear. She stepped closer and leaned into his face. "I know why."

"Stop it. Just stop it," he said, agitated. "This isn't right."

She moved closer only a breath away. "I can't help it, either. I know what you're thinking and it's okay." She pushed up against him. She kissed his lips lightly and felt the tremor. Passion? Fear? Desire and need? She knew it was all those things. "I won't tell. I swear. Just once."

With those words, he gently ran a hand across the softness of her cheek, then the other before taking her face into his grasp. Kissing him felt like heaven, her feet no longer touched the ground, floating forever on a warm cloud. His thick soft hands ran down her backside then up, taking with them her cotton nightgown. His hands caressed the tautness of her round bottom before sliding fully around her waist.

All the while he never moved his mouth away from hers. They were in a concise heated rhythm, the girth of his full body pressed solid to her firm teenaged breasts and solid hips, leaving very little room to do what she had to do. Work fast. She didn't want to lose him.

She unzipped Kellogg's pants. She worked with skill, taking the huge fullness of him in her grip, massaging the smooth ridges of skin. Here was the throbbing heart of a man in the palm of her hands, she decided, pressing him inside of her. He held her tight, filling every crevice and corner of her mind and body. All of her consumed and taken over by the love she felt for Kellogg.

She wrapped her legs around him and let herself be carried to the couch. He could have carried her to the end of the world and dropped her off. That's the way she felt, falling with no landing. An infinite flight where there was no sound around her, no memories of the past or fear of the future. They continued the long slow kiss in the way of great lovers. Every stroke with him deep inside of her made her love him even more. For taking care of her, for knowing she could be a better person. For believing. Having him all to herself was what she dreamed about. The excitement of finally having his thickness pulsing inside of her made her want to bust.

The swell of him inside of her soon deflated after he climaxed, panting exertion in her ear but still careful with his exhales, monitoring his inhales, not wanting to wake his wife. Velle waited for the empty feeling she was so used to, but it never came. Instead warmth swooned over her entire body, blanketing her from head to toe then coming to a dizzying crescendo. He was no longer inside of her and still just the scent of him, the closeness, the safety and love pulsed rhythmically like the beat of her heart. She didn't understand it. What was happening? Her breath left her body in spasms followed by sporadic jerks she couldn't control. He put a gentle hand over her mouth to stifle the deep uncontrollable moan.

"It's okay, baby." He held her tight while the waves of ecstasy settled and passed.

The first time she'd ever experienced an orgasm was in Kellogg's arms but it wasn't the last. They made love the next night and the next. All talk of her leaving faded quietly. But the guilt was loud and considerably visible for anyone who dared look.

"I know what's going on," Lydia said to Kellogg while they thought they were alone in the kitchen. His wife watched and waited for Kellogg's reaction. It was a test, he was being tested for his reaction. If not for the fact that Velle was supposed to have already left for school, she would have stepped in and rescued Kellogg. *It's a trap, don't answer her. She doesn't know anything.*

Instead she watched his head fall into his hands, admitting his sins. He wanted to be saved. He wanted to be free and didn't know how to get away. This was his chance. "I'll call the Clendons and see if they can still take her."

Lydia did what any wife with two small boys and a good life would do, she slapped him hard across the face then let him cry against her stomach and hoped and prayed it never happened again. Those thick arms wrapped around her waist would forever be missed. By midafternoon Trevelle's clothes were packed. What little she owned fit into one nylon bag used for laundry. She kissed the boys good-bye and hugged Lydia. What broke her heart was that Lydia hugged her back. "You're going to be all right. God has a plan," she whispered. "His plan is bigger than us."

31

Best Intentions

For the first time in days Delma was alert and feeling good. Thank goodness for having her phone number changed. She'd slept like a baby and was ready to take on the day.

She sat at her desk and read over the custody adviser's report for the Fisher-Parson custody case. Delma felt sorry for the mother, having lost her baby. No wonder she was fighting so hard.

She skipped to the biological father's summary and couldn't help but feel contempt for the man. Any other time she would've commended an absentee father for stepping back into the fold. Isn't that what she preached daily, that men should stop running from their responsibilities and take care of the children they'd fathered? Any other time, if he hadn't been married to Trevelle Doval, she would've given him a gold star. But he was and that wasn't Delma's fault. The man should be more choosey in picking a mate. She pulled out her pen and jotted down a few thoughts.

Abandonment. Three years. No contact. She circled the biological mother's name and added a smiley face. "One for the good team," she said.

Things were actually looking up. That is until Hudson entered carrying a bigger stack than the one already on her desk and plopped it to the floor.

"More?"

"You knew we were one stack short." He leaned over and straightened a few files that strayed from the uniform line. "Any more calls?"

"Nope, not since I had the number changed. Missed one," Delma said, pointing. At the corner of her desk a white envelope stuck out.

Hudson picked it up, instinctively grabbing the letter opener. He flipped it over to see nothing but white space. "No address." They gave each other the same knowing look. He ripped it open and pulled out the single sheet of paper. He read it, then slowly handed it to Delma.

"Oh, come on." Delma's fist hit, rattling the cup of pens. "I'm sick of this mess. Whoever wants a piece of me is gonna have a lot to chew, 'cause I'm not going down easy." She shook the paper with the typed message and read, *Give her back. It's time.*

Hudson let out a breath of defeat. "We've got to put an end to this. Now I'm pissed."

"I'm telling you it can't be anyone else but Trevelle Doval. This whole pretense of fighting for custody of her husband's child has been a setup."

Hudson put his fingers to his lips. "You know what, let's go get some coffee."

"Oh . . . right. Coffee."

As they were walking shoulder to shoulder out of the building, Delma saw Judge Lewis smiling and coming toward them. He waved to get her to stop then took his time getting up the steps.

"How you doing?" she said with as much enthusiasm as she could muster.

"I'm having a special dinner next week. I want you to come. In fact, you're required to come," he said, as if he were speaking in code.

Delma reached out and grabbed his arms to steady herself. "Are you saying what I think you're saying?"

"I'll have the invitation delivered this afternoon." He winked before heading off.

Delma did her best not to jump up and down like a giddy child. "Hudson, did you hear that . . . a special dinner. Did you hear that or was I hearing things?"

He leaned in close so she'd have no misunderstanding of his code word, "Coffee."

"Right," she said, still unable to contain her joy. She was going to the show.

◯◯

Delma and Hudson talked the small walking distance to the deli on the corner. He opened the door for her and she stepped inside, lively and full of energy.

"It's finally going to happen. I'm going to be free."

"I think you should hold off on your joy and celebration until we get to the bottom of this."

"Why are you so busy trying to talk me into being a coward? Just 'cause I let you kiss these lips doesn't mean you have a right to start telling me what to do."

He checked his watch as if she were boring him.

"Got a date?"

"As a matter of fact we do . . . fifteen minutes, court."

Delma gathered her purse and coffee that she'd barely tasted. There was a line of customers blocking the door. Hudson led the way like a seeing-eye dog. Delma gave his shoulder a shake, then pointed up to the television.

"Could you turn that up?" Delma strained to listen over the revving of the blender and pushy lawyer types.

It wasn't front-page news, nor was it anything unusual. The wild-haired woman being manhandled by the police. The little girl being rescued while sprays of glass littered the street. The little girl and the mother being reunited, hugging. The bittersweet embrace was captured perfectly like a picture for the front-page war story.

As a matter of fact, any other time Delma wouldn't have taken notice at all, not even a second glance. Nothing new about the black faces on the news. Nothing new about the police setting up arsenals in the middle of the day. Sadly to say, Delma was completely desensitized to the constant barrage of violence.

It was the close-up of the silky-lashed little girl frightened by the camera that stopped Delma cold. The child was the picture of innocence caught in the middle of a battlefield. Those wide and gleaming doe eyes were filled with confusion. The clip played again showing the car roll at a slow crawl. A cop trotting alongside of the moving vehicle and reaching inside to grab the precious child before the driverless car crashed into the side of a police car.

Funny how a second in time can change everything, destroy the best intentions. Was it asking too much for people to do what they were supposed to do? A simple plan. She would do her part. All they had to do was stay the course, act civil.

The cashier took a minute to reach for the remote and turned up the volume.

". . . her husband inside the building while SWAT planned its strategy. The wife suddenly decided to rescue her husband herself. Her child was in the car, unrestrained, while she tried to drive past the officers. Needless to say, this woman will face charges of vehicle recklessness not to mention endangerment of the child. The gunman was taken to Grady Memorial Hospital with critical wounds. The good news, the woman's husband was rescued and unharmed. Back to you, Lucy."

This was bad, very bad. Delma shook her head. She'd had every intention of doing the right thing by that girl. People would be watching, paying attention to her every move, her every judgment. She couldn't very well award custody to Venus Johnston now. It wouldn't look good on her record.

When they made it outside the deli, lightning bolted in the sky. Delma looked up to witness the gray clouds closing ranks. She closed her eyes and let the water land in heavy clumps on her face. She smiled, then fell into a healthy round of laughter. She wasn't going to let anything or anyone rain on her parade.

32

Venus

Georgina Michaels, normally cool under fire, paced back and forth. "Of all the possible things that could go wrong, and you do this?" She was furious and downright indignant. "How am I supposed to fix this? How in the world am I supposed to spin this broken wheel? We're finished, this is the final nail. It's out of my hands."

Jake kept his head down. But of course it was me who'd done the damage. Jake reached out and took my hand. He gave it a squeeze telling me he would've done the same thing.

"I panicked. I just panicked. I stopped before I got anywhere near the building and no one got hurt."

"You risked your daughter's life. This is the final blow."

"Stop it," Jake said coming to the rescue. "That's enough." He gave Georgina a hard glare.

"I apologize." Georgina spoke directly to me, but her tone was still full of anger. "Maybe there's hope," she said with fake optimism. Georgina gathered her bags that she never seemed to open. "Jake, can you see me out?"

Their private conversations were becoming a mainstay. I went to check on Mya. I relished the afternoon quiet when she took her nap. I peeked in on her. The sunlight filled her room. Calmness and peace blanketed her soft cheeks.

When I came back downstairs, Jake was still gone. I peeked out the front window and saw he and Georgina at her car. She paced the same way she had inside only this time she went short distances from one end of the bumper to the other. Jake was back in shame mode with his head down. I slipped on my shoes and was going straight out there to tell her enough. We get it. I get it. Next subject.

I opened the door with all intentions of stating my case one last time then realized I could hear their every word. I pushed the door back to a slight opening and listened.

"Sometimes you can't leave it up to one man's opinion, or in this case one woman's."

"You just said to stay out of trouble," Jake questioned.

"I'll handle it," Georgina said. "And yes, I mean it. Stay out of trouble. Obviously you two are like moths to a flame. I suggest you hole yourselves up in this house till this thing is over." She opened her car door and got inside. Jake waited until she was gone before heading back to the house.

I ran to the couch, took my position, and pretended I wasn't worried about the conversation I'd just overheard.

Whatever Georgina was planning couldn't be legal or ethical. I sensed danger and desperation. Maybe it was time to throw in the towel before something bad happened. Either way, I knew it was all up to me to fix everything that was broken.

33

Trevelle

Her head hurt. Throbbing, pulsing pain rushed to the front of her face when she tried to sit up.

"Look who's awake." The uplifting voice belonged to Nita, her long-time housekeeper. She was busy at the edge of the bed straightening her sheets and covers. "You thirsty? Can I get you something to drink?"

"Thank you." She was finally able to speak, but her throat was parched. Nita had worked for Trevelle for several years and they never became friends as the definition would require, but Trevelle knew she was trustworthy and that's all that mattered.

The door to her room creaked open slowly. Airic peeked his head inside before fully entering. A soft smile crept on his lips. "You're awake."

"Her throat's a little raw. Don't ask her any big questions that need big answers. I'm going to run and get her some juice. Be right back."

Airic wasted no time getting to her side and placing a kiss on her forehead. He squeezed her hand. "The young lady is still here. She's waiting downstairs. Do you want to see her? Otherwise I'll have a car drive her to her hotel."

"No. I want to see her." Trevelle grabbed his arm and pulled herself up higher on the pillows and waited a moment for her head to stop spinning. Her head had hit the corner of the podium when

she'd collapsed. The doctor said she'd been lucky there was no con-
cussion, though the vertigo would take its own sweet time going
away. She took a few calming breaths and closed her eyes. Still the
spinning.

Moments later the door opened and the woman she'd held on
to for dear life was at her side once again.

"I'm glad you're okay," she said.

Trevelle patted the edge of the king-size bed. The sprawling
bedroom was the size of an entire apartment but Trevelle wanted
her close. "Sit."

"I feel responsible . . ." She paused, sitting gently on the edge of
the bed. "I don't know what happened, but for some reason I feel
like I caused it."

"No, absolutely not. That was God's work. We can never be selfish or vain enough to believe we have that kind of control. Only
God has that kind of power." Trevelle reached out and took her
hand. "Tell me more about yourself." Trevelle tried to sound light
and without fear, though the shouting voice in her head screamed a
warning, *Let her go.* Satan was tricky. But she had been to hell and
back and learned the greatest armor was to face fear or confusion
head on.

She paused, brushing the straight bangs away from her eyes.
"I've been blessed in so many ways. I really feel awful for saying the
things I did. Ms. Doval, is there any way you can edit me out of your
taping? I don't want my mother to see, to hear me say those terrible
things . . . about feeling lost, alone. She's been my hero, my whole
life. I love her too much to ever want to hurt her . . . talking about
being adopted. It's just something we never talk about."

"Oh . . . yes, of course." Trevelle couldn't believe her own sus-
ceptibility to this young woman's needs. Especially after the producer had whispered how amazing the show was as she was being
carted out in an ambulance. "Amazing performance," he'd said.

Trevelle reached out and squeezed her hand. "I will make sure
that tape never sees the light of day."

"Thank you, so much."

"There's a connection between us. I would hate to let you leave and not make sure you were okay after what you shared with me. I want to be there for you, help you in any way I can," Trevelle offered.

Keisha squeezed Trevelle's hand. "Are you sure you're okay?"

"Yes. I'm fine."

Trevelle's heart filled with warmth and compassion. Trevelle extended her arms. They hugged. This time she wasn't afraid of the overwhelming emotion. The connection she didn't need to understand, only accept what felt like a comfortable trusting place.

"I promise you'll never feel that emptiness again. God is the master of filling in the void. I'm going to help you get to know Him. He is the master of divine wholeness. He will fill your spirit and be your guide. Someone introduced me to God and my life changed. I'm going to do the same for you."

"Well, I live in Atlanta, so I guess we can call, e-mail." She hunched her shoulders.

"Just so happens I spend a lot of time in Atlanta." Trevelle smiled warmly.

Keisha pulled out her business card and scribbled her address along with her home number. "Everything else is on the front."

Trevelle flipped it over and read her name out loud. "Keisha Hawkins. Well, my sweet, you've got a new friend, Trevelle Doval. So wonderful to know you."

"When do you think you'll be coming to Atlanta?" Keisha asked.

"Actually in the next couple of days, God willing, if my head can stop spinning long enough. My husband and I are in the process of adopting, well, I'll be adopting. The sweet child is his from a previous relationship. The case is taking place in Atlanta where the child currently lives with her mother, an unholy woman with no soul."

Airic entered the room just as Trevelle was about to elaborate. Good thing. She didn't want to come off as callous after just offering to help the young woman find salvation. But even the slightest thought of Venus and her shallow shortsightedness fueled something close to rage.

"You doing all right, sweetheart?"

"We're fine. Keisha lives in Atlanta. I told her we'd be spending time there during the court case."

Keisha interjected. "That's so wonderful. My mom's a family court judge there, Delma Hawkins. I'd be happy to put in a good word."

"Your mother," Trevelle sputtered. "Is Hawkins? Your mother is Judge Delma Hawkins?" Trevelle swallowed the dry ball in her throat. *How could that wretched woman have raised such a warm and loving daughter?*

Keisha nodded. "You already know of her?"

Trevelle blinked. "Yes, well, yes, she's the judge handling our case."

Nita arrived carrying a tray with two glasses and a pitcher of frosty juice on ice. All in the nick of time. "Here you go, nice cool glass of juice. Brought you one, too, sweetie." She handed each of them a tall crystal goblet full of ice and sparkling liquid. Trevelle drank and drank, not stopping until hers was all gone.

"Whew, you're parched, Lady T." Nita poured more from the decanter. "Plenty where that came from."

Trevelle fanned herself with the fabric of her silk pajamas. "Is it hot in here, or just me?"

"I'll let you get some rest." Keisha leaned forward and planted an unexpected kiss on Trevelle's cheek. "My flight doesn't leave until the morning. I'm going to head back to my hotel."

"No, are you sure? You're welcome to stay here," Trevelle sincerely offered.

"It's been such a long day. We both need to decompress. Thank you for the offer though."

"I'll drive you." Airic leaned toward Trevelle. "I have to leave anyway." He noticed the perspiration spilling off her brow as if she'd just ran a ten-K race and decided to kiss her on the nose instead. "Are you going to be all right?"

She fanned herself. "What do you mean? Where are you going?"

"To Atlanta . . ." He tried to sound nonchalant. "Remember, second Sunday of the month."

"Well, I would think you'd have a change of plans. I fainted, a blackout, for God's sake. You're rushing off to . . ." She remembered her guest and changed her tone. "Please reconsider."

Airic blinked a questioning stare. "I'd have to wait two more weeks. How would it look if I don't show up at all?"

Trevelle suddenly felt another blast of heat shrouding her body. "Go then. Don't let me stop you."

Airic stood back, not sure what to make of her public display. Normally she made sure to appear the good wife when others were around.

"Changing of the guard. Menopause," Nita clarified. "It's okay." She tried to comfort him.

Trevelle wanted to make her own clarification and tell Nita to shut up and mind her business. Logically she shouldn't be going through menopause, but she was indeed experiencing the same symptoms. Her uterus and both fallopian tubes had been removed when she was only thirty-two years old, a time when she should've been thinking about marriage and planning a family. Instead she'd suffered from fibroid tumors and a threat of cervical cancer, all because her body had been ravaged by sexually transmitted diseases at such a young age.

She hadn't told Airic about the constant need for hormonal medication, the siege of emotions and helplessness that sometimes brought her to her knees if she skipped just one dose. He was her husband, her helpmate, and the keeper of their castle. But one thing she knew about men, they didn't want to know the dirty details. A wife had a duty to present herself in the best light, facing tribulation with class and dignity.

"I'm fine, go, please. Keisha, I will be in touch." She fluttered her synthetic lashes. When the door closed those same eyes darted sharply in Nita's direction. "Do me a favor and don't take it upon yourself to discuss my biology with my husband or anyone else for that matter."

"I didn't mean—"

"Whatever." Trevelle waved a dismissive hand before Nita ranted on with her apologies. "Just don't let it happen again."

34

Venus

Round two, I was thinking when the doorbell rang. Airic was right on time.

"Is she ready?"

"Are you going to ask me that question every time you come here?" I shook my head and recharged. "Actually, she's going to be a minute. She's dressing her doll . . . trying to make it presentable for *Miss Trell,*" I said with exaggerated niceness. "Would you like to come in and wait?"

"No. I should wait in the car." He turned to walk away. I searched ahead of him to see if Trevelle was waiting in the car. I had a feeling I'd seen the last of her for a while. I'd left a lasting impression after the ice-cream shop debacle.

"Airic . . . please. Come inside. It's too hot out there."

He came inside. He was nervous. I still knew all of his facial expressions. Anxiety wasn't a particularly good look on him. The crease lines in his forehead went straight across in threes like tribal markings. His dark eyeballs went into a wide spacey glare. He paused before taking a seat on the couch.

"Jake isn't here. My mom went back to California. It's just us chickens," I said to ease his mind. "Be right back." I went to the kitchen and poured him a glass of southern hospitality. I'd asked Jake to leave so I could talk to Airic alone.

"Here you go."

He took the glass but didn't sip.

"It's okay. I swear." I put up both hands. Still he only stared at the glass and placed it on the coffee table. I picked up the iced tea and took the first sip. "See, I'm still alive." I handed it back to him. He put it on the glass table untouched.

"Airic, we need to talk."

"I don't have enough time to fit in a conversation and a visit with my daughter," he said ruefully. "Three hours, remember." He tapped his watch.

"It won't take long. I just want to say that I don't like what's happening here any more than you. I don't want our lives determined by a court, a judge, when it's us who need to decide what's right for Mya."

He leaned forward. "It's a little too late for that, don't you think?"

"No. I don't. We're the ones involved. If we come to an agreement, this whole thing can be put to rest."

"Are you saying this because of your latest run-in with police officers? Literally, running *down* police officers." He almost sneered. "I'd rather let the court handle it. At this point it's out of my hands."

"Airic . . . we're her parents."

"Oh . . . I'm her parent now. Before you were determined to make me disappear."

"You made yourself disappear," I said. "How was I supposed to feel? Three years, that's her whole life. And you wanted me to bounce with excitement that suddenly you want to be present and accounted for?"

"The past is the past. I'm here now. And not a minute too soon. Look at you, the way you're conducting yourself. You're still the immature person you were when we were together. You haven't changed. You proved that driving through a police barricade. You think everyone's supposed to bow down and follow your lead. Well this is your wake-up call. You have no control over me and how I want to spend the rest of my time on this earth, with *my* daughter."

"I don't want to control how you spend your time. We can agree to equal time. I'm willing to do that."

"Mighty big of you, Venus. Please, go get Mya."

"Okay." I stood up. "You're right. And I'm sorry. I know I hurt you in the past. I never did apologize for the way we ended things. I'm sorry for making you feel like you weren't needed in her life or mine. Just know that I love her with all my heart and she's my only concern. So you're dead wrong when you say I don't care about anyone else but me. You're very wrong."

I heard the *clink* of the ice against glass as I was going up the stairs. He'd drank the tea. I was grateful to have gained even a little of his trust.

"Mya, sweetie," I called while opening the door. She was on the floor still struggling with her doll, surrounded by all the cast-off clothing she'd tried and retried on her doll. I kneeled on the floor with her.

She threw the doll down, frustrated. "She's not pretty."

"She's beautiful. She doesn't need a fancy dress, sweetie. She's beautiful just like you." I picked up the little mocha-skinned doll to give her a kiss and saw her fluffy curls were pulled back and held straight with about fifty staples. "Mya, where'd you get . . ." I reached past her and found the stapler. "Where'd you get this?"

"Daddeee's office," she said with a pout and arms folded over her chest. "She's still not pretty."

"Honey . . . listen. I know you're worried about how Mommy acted before. I promise, no one is going to fight over your hair or clothes. You're perfect just as you are. So is Bunny, except she probably has a headache from having her head stapled, don't you think?" Besides, I wanted to tell her, Cruella Doval wasn't here today. There would be no one making judgments about her appearance.

Mya nodded up and down.

"Let's take the staples out, comb her hair, and get her dressed and she'll be ready to go."

◎◎

Airic was still in the same spot, elbows resting on his knees. He turned and saw me holding Mya's hand and stood up. "Hey Mya, guess where we're going," he said as though he'd rehearsed. "To see *Shrek*." He clapped his hands as if it were going to be the biggest fun in the whole world.

"Okay," she said with far less enthusiasm. I'd told her the night before Aric was coming. I explained that sometimes children were lucky enough to have fairy godfathers who popped in once in a while and wanted to sprinkle pixie dust and make life wonderful. Maybe in the form of gifts and fun visits to theme parks. I explained that a fairy godfather wasn't expected to stick around very long and came specifically to make sure she was happy and well cared for. She'd acted unfazed and completely uninterested. "Does a fairy godfather make you eat spinach?" She'd scrunched up her face.

"No, they let you eat whatever you want just to make you smile," I'd said.

Her eyes had widened like she'd discovered the only real reason to even be discussing such matters. "And I get presents?" she asked to make sure the deal was sealed.

I nodded.

"You promise you won't be sad if I go with him?" she'd asked.

"I promise," I lied. "I'll be here to give you a big hug when you get back." I had told the truth.

◎◎

He took hold of Mya's hand. I followed them out. I stared hard at his car rental to make sure Cruella wasn't ducking low in the backseat. I waved and blew kisses to Mya. She waved and blew kisses back.

35

Trevelle

From the moment she laid eyes on Keisha there was something that drew Trevelle's attention. There was an uncanny familiarity in her eyes. Somewhere inside, she saw herself when she was a young woman. In her eyes an unspeakable loneliness dangerously open to anyone who might be able to fill the void.

She wished there was something she could do to ease her heavy heart. Nothing she could do but pray and keep her in her thoughts. She would not abandon the young woman regardless that she was the daughter of the evil judge. There was only so much she could do. Until it hit her, exactly what she could do: find Keisha's birth parents. She knew exactly who to call to get the job done.

"Eddie, how you doing, baby?" Trevelle leaned her elbows on her large mahogany desk and cupped her hand lightly over the phone so she wouldn't have to talk much louder. "I have an important job. Shouldn't take you long." Trevelle smiled into the phone.

"So who is it this time?" Eddie asked, without the slightest hint of malice. He was stating the obvious. She was still his best paying customer. She gave the important details, name, approximate age, city, and state. Eddie Ray didn't need much more in the way of information. If he hadn't spent the first half of his life in the penal system, he could've worked for the CIA, FBI, or some other alphabet-toting crew. Prison is where Trevelle met him, when she devoted hours of ministry to the inmates of a Maryland correctional center. Community service was a requirement of her theology curriculum. She'd tried the women's prison first and found it too painful. They reminded her of the road she'd traveled and what her life would've been had she not taken a major detour. Sullen. Angry. Hateful. Most pathetic was their stubbornness, their outright refusal to hear anything Trevelle had to say even if it would help save their lives.

Of course the men's facility was no cakewalk. But she'd take their foul mouth catcalling over having her life being threatened by some hormonally unstable female any day of the week. Inside the concrete walls of the medium security correctional facility she held a ministry session twice a week. It went from eight men gathered in a paltry circle to over a hundred, and needing more space. Eddie Ray was one of the original members, sitting quietly with his Bible in hand, wearing the white prison-issue jumpsuit, his thick gut stretching the buttons to their limit.

His crime of identity theft made him a borderline genius at the time. Back then it wasn't so easy to seize an entire person's lifestyle with a push of a button. Working at a bank gave him carte blanche to check on people's status and accounts regularly but the idea never entered his mind until an elderly woman came to the bank and delivered her ex-husband's death certificate, requesting his account assets be turned over to her. He'd sent the ex-Mrs. O'Donnell packing that day, telling her she'd need more than a death certificate, she'd in fact need a court order. Ex-wives weren't entitled beneficiaries, he'd told her, all true. Meanwhile Eddie busied himself taking on the deceased old man's accounts, certificates, and bonds, adding up to a healthy six-figure bounty. Why stop there? Over the course of a few months he applied for credit cards, bought a new XJ Jaguar, a house in the prestigious Prince George County, and lived fat and happy until the ex-Mrs. O'Donnell showed up once again, judgment in hand to receive what was now duly hers. The accounts were empty. The debts were high. Mrs. O'Donnell wasted no time reporting the strange occurrence. Her ex-husband was a miser and a cheat. If she knew nothing else about him, she knew he'd squirreled away every dime that wasn't used for food or shelter. The investigation led straight to Eddie Ray's expensive, custom front door. Seven years incarcerated with two years of parole.

Trevelle had touched his soul, he'd told her. He needed Jesus in his life. He needed to be forgiven for his sins. Right there in the prison was where Trevelle conducted her first baptism. A couple of the inmates pushed together two wash buckets filled with clean warm water while Eddie wore a bedsheet with the holes cut out for head and arms, Trevelle washed Eddie Ray of his sins, sprinkling him gently with holy water she'd prayed over the night before. When Eddie got out, she was the first person he called, ready to be her devoted servant.

"So they'll be no problem," Trevelle whispered into the phone, "this judge being a public official?"

"Oh, you know times have changed since I first started out. Technology may have gotten more sophisticated, but it's also gotten real sloppy. I can break into any system these days."

"Good. I want to know everything about this woman. But most importantly, about the adoption of her child, Keisha Hawkins."

"No time like God's time." He chuckled then paused. His tone changed. "I won't let you down." Trevelle Doval did nothing unnecessarily. He would go forth as commissioned, a soldier at her side, bringing back the golden jewel of power called "information."

36

Hells Bells

The sound of the electronic bell sent a jolt to her heart. She flicked off the bathroom light and followed the ringing sound to the new phone she'd bought. She approached the contraption like it was a giant bug and couldn't figure out whether to kill it or let it live. She leaned in, daring to read the caller ID and saw her daughter's name. *Thank God.*

"Hey, there girly." Delma's attempt at sounding light and happy came out high-pitched and on edge.

"Mom," Keisha in turn sounded frantic. "I'm still in Washington, D.C., at the woman's conference. I've been so busy, so much going on here, I forgot to call and tell you I was staying for an extra day. Pearl needs food and water, Mom."

"Okay, sweetie. No problem." Delma was concerned. "Is everything all right? Why are you staying another night?"

A small catch in her throat, then she spoke. "I met someone. We ended up talking a lot longer and I missed my flight."

Delma knew this day was coming when her daughter fell headlong into some man. She knew this day would come no matter how much Keisha claimed her need for independence. "Who is he?"

"No, not a guy. It's a woman."

Delma inhaled her shock. "Well, okay."

"Mom, no, not like that. Something happened while I was at the conference. You've heard of Trevelle Doval, you know, the famous female evangelist?"

Delma could do nothing, say nothing but, "Ahuh."

"Mom, it was intense. She called me to the stage and she was whispering a prayer for me and all of a sudden she fell out, I mean, she seriously went into these convulsions, spinning and shouting, and then she stopped, stared me dead in the eye and kept saying, *Please don't leave me.* She kept saying it. I even went to the hospital with her because she wouldn't let go of my hand . . ." She paused for a brief breath. "The weird thing is, I felt it, too. Like some kind of transference. Like I felt this warm surge of energy. I don't know . . ." Her voice trailed off. "I don't know, it's just weird, Mom. So I just wanted to stay another day, one more, to make sure she was all right. For whatever reason, I feel responsible."

By this time, Delma couldn't hear the part where her daughter reminded her to feed Pearl. Delma's head was spinning in some kind of warp-speed craziness, where all she could do was sit still, numb and light-headed all at the same time. Everything around her was quiet. She still held the phone close against her ear. Instead of Keisha's voice, she heard Shep's voice mean and low, *You ain't gon have your daughter forever.* The words slowed and echoed like she was underwater.

"You had me scared to death, woman."

Delma ignored Hudson. She continued to stare into the ceiling, hoping to bore straight up to heaven, a personal call to whoever was minding the store these days, and doing a lousy job of it. Wires were getting crossed. Communication channeled to deaf ears. She hadn't asked for much in this lifetime. But what she'd asked for had suddenly been derailed.

No other way to explain the sad, pitiful set of events now in motion. Keisha and Trevelle Doval in the same room, let alone talking to one another. It just wasn't happening.

"Keisha's on her way," Hudson said, before leaving a warm kiss on her forehead.

She hadn't authorized any lip slobber. Besides, she had to focus her energy on what was important, getting out of the gurney she was lying on. She'd suffered a mild anxiety attack. Mild? Her limbs had frozen, her brain had gone blank, and that was *mild*? She wouldn't be lying there unable to slap this man breathing down her neck if everything were mild. She squirmed uncomfortably until Hudson released his soft grip. A look of concern frowned the edges of his mouth. His brows knitted together with the heartbreaking conclusion. "Well I can see you're back to normal."

"Hudson, I've got no time to be laying up in this emergency room. I need to get out of here." Delma was full of determination but made little effort to rise. What was the point? Her body felt like it weighed a thousand pounds. Useless. She was tired. A tube was still attached to her hand, distributing necessary fluids.

"You need to relax."

"I can't relax. My life is about to crumble beneath my feet. You don't understand."

The emergency area had all the necessary equipment but it was no place to be if you'd planned a full and long life. The doctor came in and pulled the curtain closed behind him. "Delma, you're fine. You do have high blood pressure but even that's much better than when you were admitted." He pulled up a stool. "You're going to have to change your diet, get some exercise, and hopefully take some time off work."

"Why would I need to take time off work? Work is not the problem. Can I go now?"

"Absolutely. Let me have the nurse finish some paperwork, get your prescriptions, and a wheelchair and we'll have you out in a quickie."

A *quickie* turned out to be three hours later. It took everything Delma had not to go find the damn wheelchair herself but then what would be the point? Hudson wasn't any help. Rules were the name of his game. He followed rules to the letter, even after she'd begged him to just get her on her feet and out the door.

He drove slowly, which maddened Delma even more. Finally he

turned to ask, "Are you going to tell me what sent you over the edge? No one could've called, the phone number was changed."

"Keisha met Trevelle Doval face to face. She had a personal moment with her at some women's convention," she blurted. "Then the woman invited Keisha back to her house. Now I've heard of coincidences, but this is ridiculous. Someone's hard at work trying to make my life miserable and I don't have a clue as to who it could be." She faced Hudson dead on.

"What . . . are you insinuating? Are we going there again? Woman, I'd jump off a building for you—well not a high building, more like two floors up, but you got to be kidding."

"I'm sorry, I know. I'm losing it here."

"Sounds to me like your fear is channeling a lot of energy."

"Oh," she mocked, "maybe the phone calls aren't even real. Maybe I wrote that note myself. Maybe I'm imagining everything. You're not even real." She poked him in the side. "Please, don't even start with me. All those dream-it-and-it-will-come books you've been reading. I don't want to hear it. There is someone out there terrorizing me. They've put this entire thing in motion starting the day Trevelle Doval turned up in my courtroom."

"Even if that's the case, you're giving this thing energy. Fear is like rocket fuel. You give it energy, it'll take many forms."

"Oh, thank you great philosopher Hudson. Just let me out of this car." They'd already pulled up to Delma's house. Convenient, because she was getting out whether it was the right address or not.

۞

Somebody's got a secret.

She jumped, startled awake by the voice so familiar having constantly played in her head.

"Anybody there?" she called out. For the first time in her life she was afraid to be alone in the dark. She pulled the covers over her head and did her best to find strength to get through the night.

37

Trevelle

"You're being manipulated," Trevelle warned. "Every time you return, you're not sure if full custody is the answer," she mocked. "Enough. This time I'm going with you."

"Absolutely not." Airic shook his head. Though he'd made claims he didn't enjoy going without Trevelle, here he was unequivocally telling her she wasn't invited. "Look, we're on civil terms. I'm getting along with Venus. The visits are going smoothly."

"So I would disrupt your perfect little family time, is that what you're telling me?" Trevelle stood over him while he laced his leather Johnston & Murphys. He'd complained about having to fly all the way to Atlanta to only spend a few hours with his child. Yet, he needed to spend the entire weekend. He'd claimed he only spent a few minutes picking up his child and hardly spoke a word to his baby mama, yet his attention to detail clearly said otherwise. He wore his close-knit sweater that showed off the hard-earned rib of muscle around his abdomen. He was a good-looking older man by any woman's standards. She watched him closely, taking in his sharp clean features. Gray hairs budded from his neatly trimmed mustache and framed his perfectly arched lips. To add fuel to an already hazardous situation, he'd doused himself with the smooth and tantalizing scent of Armani cologne. Trevelle had a sudden urge to make love to him right then and there; that would straighten him out, she was sure of it. But why should she be reduced to having to throw herself on her knees to be chosen over the likes of that insignificant woman?

After watching him rummage around for his car keys she decided to stop giving him the silent treatment. "Here they are." She'd had them balled in her palm the entire time.

She placed both her hands on his chest and slid them slowly across to take ahold of his shoulders. "I have to tell you one final time, I should be going with you. The more time you spend alone with her and Mya, the more you're being tricked and connived."

"I'm not being tricked by anyone or anything. In fact, it's me who's up ahead. My visits with Mya are the most rewarding experience . . ." He paused, rethinking how he should put it. "Instead of three hours like the judge said, she allows me the full day. I'd rather try to work something out between us then wait another four weeks and go through all the fighting."

Trevelle rolled her eyes. "We had her exactly where we wanted her and you're falling for this pretense of her being fair?" Trevelle took back the car keys as hostages. "Listen to me, please."

"I've been listening to you and all you've done is tell me how idiotic I am."

"If you were listening," she purred, "you would have heard me say what you were doing was idiotic. That's entirely different. For the sake of what we've been working for, you're accepting crumbs when you deserve the entire loaf of bread, sweetheart. That's all I'm trying to say."

He scoffed. "I'm lucky to have what time I can get with Mya."

Trevelle slapped her hand into her palm. "You see, there it is. Venus has got you eating out of her hand. Feeding you this incredible guilt trip."

"Isn't that the business we're in? Guilt." He snatched the keys back, this time slipping them into his pocket. "Repent, confess, make a new life. That's exactly what I'm doing, righting wrongs. I want a relationship with *my* child." He shot his eyes to the left, then the right, anywhere but in Trevelle's direction.

"*My child?*" Trevelle lowered her voice to almost a whisper, yet it could fill the sound of an auditorium. "You hadn't seen her since the day she was born. That child?"

"My child. And I'm proud to say it and I'll keep saying it." Airic's pale cheeks turned a soft crimson, letting her know he'd reached his boiling point. "My child."

"If it wasn't for me, you would've kept your deaf, dumb, and blind status forever. You wouldn't have any type of relationship with that little girl. I did the hard work by pushing you to stand up and be a man, to acknowledge your rights as her father."

He clapped his hands in a mock applause. "Thank you. Is that what you want to hear? You're right as usual. Without your enthusiasm and constant prodding, I probably wouldn't have this opportunity. But the fact still remains, Mya is my daughter. I'm going to stand up and be the man you've begged me to be and take responsibility for my child and decide what's in her best interest. And right now, that's what I'm doing." He headed to the door.

He turned suddenly toward her. "Sometimes I swear with all you've been through, I don't know how you can be so callous." The door slammed. She picked up the Ming vase filled with a fresh bouquet and heaved it; it only landed with a *thud*.

She was grateful it hadn't broken. She only wished she were as strong. She was shattered on the inside and owed the honor to every man who'd ever poked, pushed, prodded his manhood inside her tender walls. Each time they'd torn away a piece of her, leaving her small and degraded. She'd kept her distance from men in the past, avoiding relationships by refusing to acknowledge the glances of appreciation from various suitors. Not giving into their phony admiration and respect. Absolutely sure they were after one thing and one thing only. Letting Airic into her life had been divine intervention. God had finally called her out from behind the wall she'd built high and wide. She'd trusted Airic, she'd trusted God. He wouldn't have sent her someone who wasn't going to treat her with kindness and respect, not after all she'd been through. She wouldn't give up on him.

She needed to figure out how to put things back the way they were . . . 'before Venus. She wished she'd never pushed him into finding his daughter in the first place.

A wife has a duty to make things right.

⊚⊚

Lydia had barely raised an eyebrow and Kellogg was putting Trevelle out like a stray cat. Trevelle could only wish to have that kind of power over her husband. The kind that would make him do anything for the sake of their marriage, even leave his unborn baby on the street the way Kellogg had left her.

Even after she'd whispered the news, "I'm having your baby," Kellogg did nothing. She could understand how he didn't believe her. Seemed like nothing more than a desperate plea for help. But she wasn't lying. And truly not all that desperate. Cain had taken her back into his flock and treated her surprisingly better than when she'd run off. She'd heard how Kellogg had threatened him. If Cain laid a hand on her, that hand would be removed one finger at a time. Cain took heed, making it a point to ask, "I'm treating you good, right?" just to make sure there was no misunderstanding. "Yeah," she'd answer back. "Real good."

What more could Kellogg have done to save her? She refused to stay with the family who'd taken her in. He couldn't take her back to his home. All the shelters and halfway houses were full. So she was back on the streets and every time Kellogg passed her without stopping it broke her heart. The hardest part was him not believing her.

"I swear I'm not lying. You're the only person I was with that whole time I was staying with you. This baby was in me before you kicked me out, I swear."

Those words stung as she knew they would. Kellogg dealt with the guilt of having betrayed Lydia every day. The guilt of not being able to fix the hurt he'd caused. The guilt of not being able to fix here.

She felt the tears welling up inside. "I thought you'd want to love this baby, too, just like your boys," her voice squeaked. She was tired and hungry all the time now. "You're the best father I've ever seen. Please, Kellogg, I wouldn't lie to you. You have to believe me." The whole time she was begging, Kellogg stared straight ahead. The softness of him seemed to have tightened up, turning hard and bitter.

"Until you get off these streets, I don't want to hear nothing you have to say," he said, still not facing her to show he wasn't giving in.

"Where am I supposed to go, huh? Wait for Mr. Clendon to come creeping into my bed after Mrs. Clendon falls asleep? Well, I wasn't gonna give it away for free. I may as well work these damn streets if I'ma have his old ass crawling on top of me."

Kellogg slammed the steering wheel with his heavy palm then pointed a finger. "You should've told me instead of running around like some wild . . ."

"What, say it? Some wild bitch in heat? I've heard it all. You think you can hurt my feelings . . . huh, I don't have any feelings left. Leave then. I don't care."

To her utter shock, the car sputtered into gear and took off. Kellogg didn't look back. She was five months along. Her long lithe frame made it easy to hide the bulge. Her plan for the next four was to eat as little as possible so the baby could grow but she wouldn't. She hadn't snorted, swallowed, injected, or smoked anything to dull her misery. She took her daily dose of hell straight on, eyes wide open. She'd planned to take herself to one of those shelters after she couldn't hide the pregnancy anymore. They'd never turn a pregnant girl away days from giving birth.

Meanwhile, she was charging more and keeping the extra for herself . . . and her baby. She'd actually planned on keeping the small person growing inside her. She couldn't wait to hold him or her and hoped and prayed that some of Kellogg's goodness would make their child a better person. Someone with a big heart and a strong mind, like Kellogg. Even with him turning his back on her, she loved him still. Couldn't stop loving him even when she'd tried, cursing him and his wife and happy little children to hell. She couldn't stop loving him because he was true, honest, and loyal. Even if it was Lydia he was loyal to.

Two months later she packed up her toothbrush, two pairs of clean panties, and a tattered T-shirt with S.A.F.E. logo on the front and started her way out the door of Cain's nasty abode, determined to never return.

Only she never made it out the door.

"What the hell is this?" Cain stood blocking the entrance. It was three in the morning. He usually didn't come back til dawn. "I been driving around all night looking for yo' ass and you up in here?" He backed her inside with a shove.

"I'm on the rag. I had to come and get something to stop it up."

"Yeah, that's not what I hear." He slapped her arm draped across her belly. "Big as a damn house. You think can't nobody see that shit?"

Her head fell, shoulders slumped. More so out of relief. "I'm keeping my baby. I'm not doing this anymore. I—"

"I, I, what? No 'I' in 'team,' ain't you heard that, shugga? Word is super cop don't want nothing to do with you. Yo' ass is mine. You come and go when I say so. What you gon do with a baby? Raise it up to suck dick like you?"

"I—"

Her last thought left her mind with the slap that came hard and fast across her face. The throng of pain came late and slow. He'd struck her four or five times before her knees buckled and she realized he had no plans on stopping. On the ground she used her hands to try and protect what was most important: her stomach, her and Kellogg's baby. The punches found their way landing painfully. Every blow she knew the baby felt as she did.

"My baby, you're killing my baby."

"No baby, you hear me? You think I didn't know? He kicked her for final measure. Only thing she was grateful for was the kick to her head. She would gladly die before seeing her baby come into the world under Cain's rule.

38

Venus

Too easy, why hadn't I thought of this before? This was my overconfident self doing the talking as I sat facing Airic, eating slimy uncooked fish like it was yesterday. Also like yesterday, I was forced to partake for the sake of the relationship. How things changed yet stayed the same. Sushi was not my favorite food but it was his. And since I had to coax him into the meeting under the guise of defeat, I at least had to offer up a sacrificial meal. I chewed the last bite and swallowed without a hint of displeasure. With every bite I dreamed of chugging down gallons of water. I concentrated on looking pretty while chewing, hoping I wasn't making a *Fear Factor* face.

"Delicious," I said, while sneaking a peek at my watch. Airic and I had been sitting for the last hour and had yet to discuss Mya. I'd left her at the preschool and knew I only had four hours to make a miracle happen. Jake was tucked away at a sound studio to finish the recording he'd been working on before the shooting at Sugar Hill Studios. He promised he would be safe in an undisclosed location. No gun-wielding attackers. No hostages. No police. I wished I could make the same promise, that I was safe and doing the right thing. But I knew sneaking off to meet with Airic alone was a betrayal of the worst kind. If Jake found out, there was no telling what he'd do.

"Next time, give me some fried chicken and waffles," I finally said once the gagging sensation left my throat.

"I can't remember the last time I had fried chicken," Airic said as if it were akin to skydiving.

"Oh my goodness, are you telling me you're a vegetarian? I mean besides fish, of course."

"Yes, and it's the best thing I ever did. Completely cut out meat, eggs, and poultry. No cheese, no butter. I feel like a twenty-year-old." He slapped at his flat stomach. "Look at this."

"Impressive. Not that you were ever on the heavy side," I said.

"You're looking pretty good yourself these days."

"Thank you. Not easy being home all day with Mya. I end up eating double, whatever she won't finish and mine."

"So what's our next move?" he asked, wiping his mouth with the white linen napkin. The restaurant had a contemporary design, smoke-gray walls and tinted windows. The concrete floors were gray as well with a slight sheen. If not for the expensive pendant lighting hanging over every tiny gray table, it would be a dead ringer for the inside of a prison . . . a very contemporary prison.

I dropped my gaze and played with the edge of the plate. "Well, we definitely have some healing to do. It would only make sense that we take everything slow, for Mya's sake, so we don't fall back into the fighting. She's the important one here," I said.

"I agree," he said.

"I'm fine with visitation. I think it's been going well." I took a large deep breath. My stomach bucked and tossed the raw fish while I thought of other small talk. A serious toil and trouble was taking effect. I reached over and tilted the last drop of water from my glass and looked around for help. The waiter rushed over and poured. I drank some more. I thought about what I'd truly come to ask and said it. "Airic, I think it's time we took this out of the court's hands, don't you?" I squinted while I said the last few words; the growing gas bubble was now pushing against my already labored heart and lungs.

"Yes," he said quietly, then again more eager to be heard, "Yes I do. It never should have gone this far. In light of what I'd learned about Jake and his criminal association, all I wanted to do was step in out of duty. After seeing Mya, I can see she's happy and well taken care of."

"Well, thank you." I adjusted in my seat to try and move the gas from one side of my stomach to the other.

"Are you all right?" he asked.

"I'm fine."

"In retrospect I should've been the bigger man and ignored the way you and Jake snuck around behind my back."

I let out a long and much needed belch. Silent as it was, there was no denying my relief. "Oh . . . excuse me. I'm sorry about that . . ." I waved the scent of sushi and horseradish sauce out of the air.

"Thank you. I can't tell you how long I've wanted to hear your apology."

"Wait . . . I was talking about—"

"Venus, you know me, I put up a good front but my feelings were hurt. In fact I was devastated. You falling in love with someone else while we were together tore me up inside. Worse, you lying about it for so long, pretending he wasn't the reason." He calmly reached across the table and touched my hand. "I'm glad you've finally taken responsibility for your actions. It shows a lot of maturity on your part."

"Thank you," I said, while swallowing my pride and a few choice expletives.

He straightened his shoulders. "I plan to be a full part of our daughter's life. I'm not talking about visitation, Venus. I think the whole idea of seeing a child one day out of the week is a poor excuse and a cop-out. I want to be involved in every aspect of her life. I propose fifty-fifty physical custody. Trevelle and I will be buying a house in the area, that way Mya won't have to change schools or make any adjustments."

Before he could continue on with his grand plan, the waitress stepped between us. "Can I get you two anything else?"

"No, just the bill please," Airic said, while pulling out his wallet.

"What do you say we go find some fresh sorbet?" He gave his stomach a pat. "I still have room for dessert."

Surely anyone could understand desperate times called for desperate measures. Would it kill me to sit across from him and listen, laugh, and occasionally agree with his inaccurate retelling of our past? He had big plans. So did I. Determination and creativity were my strong suit. It was time I used them.

39

Sons and Daughters

Delma surveyed the beautiful grounds of Judge Lewis's home and wondered how much more a senior judge earned. The home was classic on the outside with huge columns posted at the entrance and wide plantation shutters flanking each of the multitude of windows—but on the inside everything shouted *I was bought just yesterday.*

Judge Lewis spotted her and moved quickly in her direction. "You made it." He appeared to look for someone else, over her shoulder, before leaning in for a cheek kiss.

"Well, of course." Delma pressed her cheek against his for a good old-fashioned southern welcome. The south had invented air kisses, contrary to the vain belief of the Hollywood rich.

"You're the only one who can put some life into this party." Judge Lewis wore a white open-collar shirt tucked into his belted tan slacks. The sun was warm and the breeze carried the distinct sweet smell of jasmine. Delma was glad she'd gone shopping and found the gauzy summer dress she was wearing. Something told her the day would be light and beautiful just like this. Hudson had remained stubborn and refused to be an accomplice to her brown-nosing.

"Delma, you're here," Judge Lewis's wife called out with a sweet syrupy goodness. She smiled wide and opened her arms wider. Her jet-black hair was cut blunt at her elegant neckline. "You look wonderful. Look at you, better than ever." If anyone else had given her the compliment she probably wouldn't have believed them. But Mrs. Lewis was genuine and chic with minimal effort. She wore a peach floral sundress and pearl earrings. Her skin was remarkably flawless for a woman in her sixties.

Delma appreciated the compliment because she felt better about herself than she had in a long time. "I'm feeling on top of the world. I had a run-in with Mr. High Blood Pressure and I've been eating healthier," Delma told her. "Trust me, it's not easy giving up your favorite foods, but if your life is on the line, the choice gets real clear."

She surveyed the rest of the party, seeking out who could be her potential competition. She breathed a sigh of relief to see only current board and committee members. All of them were already content in their privileged positions. Delma was the only one who needed a leg up.

Judge Lewis scooped his arm around her. "Come with me, I want to take you around to say hello to everyone."

Delma grew more confident with each hand she shook. She felt like she was on her way. A serious campaign trail.

"So how's Keisha doing?" Judge Lewis asked, once they were a small distance away from the crowd. He shoved his hands in his pockets and stood facing Delma with more concern than she guessed necessary.

"She's fine," she answered in a higher octave than she'd planned. The question took her by gentle surprise. Well, they were colleagues. He was perfectly expected to ask about Keisha, yet the question pivoted and bounced across her temples like a blinding warning signal.

"I haven't seen her in a while. Not since she graduated from college. Wow, that's got to be almost eight years." He stared out at the acreage that surrounded his grand estate, as if he were making a wild guess.

No guessing, Delma was thinking. He'd done the math. There was that instinct only a mother had when it came to her children, when someone was snooping in business where they didn't belong, or assuming what they had no business assuming. "Yes, eight years. She's doing well." She quieted the inner voice of Hudson telling her she was being paranoid.

"I should've told you specifically she was welcome. I should've invited her with a formal invitation. You know you're both always welcome here in my home."

"Yes, thank you," Delma said, growing suddenly weary in the warm sun. She lifted a hand to shield her eyes before looking in the direction of the house. "I'm going to head inside and see if I can be of help."

"Nonsense, you're our guest. So Keisha's at the entertainment law firm, right?" He focused on the clouds, as if he were searching the sky for answers. "What's the name . . . the Peabody Group," he said at the same time as Delma.

"Now that she has her fabulous career, it's about time she settle down, huh?" Judge Lewis smiled. His skin had warmed to an amber hue. The sun, perhaps. But Delma sensed it was something else. Nervousness. "You know all three of my boys are self-proclaimed bachelors." He continued, "I tell you, there's nothing worse than the prospect of these offspring not settling down and extending the family."

"Oh, yes, I know exactly what you mean." Delma took a deep breath. Relieved. It was all about commonalities. "Keisha loves her job and being independent. I'm certainly proud of her but then in the back of my mind, all I hope is that she settles down with a good man." Delma laughed at herself. "Isn't that silly. All this time I raised her to be self-reliant and now I want her to be somebody's wife."

Judge Lewis nodded. "Exactly. All we want is for our children to be safe and happy. All that prodding for a good education and good career falls by the wayside when you see them floating around without the commitment of a relationship. That's the true thing that will sustain you, whether it be between husband or wife, or mother and son, or even father and daughter." He quieted suddenly.

"Hey," Delma said quickly, "daughters are a lot of work. Don't think you missed out on the party."

"We always wanted a girl, a daughter," he mused. "But the boys were a joy. As men, they're a whole 'nother set of problems. Thomas is doing well teaching. Says he loves it. Clarence is running for Congress, did you hear about that?"

"I did," Delma said, hoping she sounded convincing. She'd been so lost in her own narrow world she knew very little about anything else. "And how about your youngest?"

"Kellogg . . . he's the jack of all trades, master of none. This year he's a sports agent. Befuddles me how the one named after me can turn out to be my complete opposite." Judge Lewis gave a quiet nervous laugh.

"Really. Keisha's group has a sports management team. Maybe he should give her a call."

"I was thinking the very same thing," he said. "I'll call her first thing Monday."

They headed back inside. She did her best to ignore the cloaked feeling along her arms and up her neck. Groped without hands, teased and bullied without words. She couldn't figure out why the uneasiness. After all, she was getting the recommendation from Judge Lewis. She was getting the better of him, yet she couldn't explain why she felt taken, used, and intruded upon.

He gave her arm a little pat. "Time to let everyone know who I think deserves a place on the big bench," he said with a wry smile. "Then before you know it, you could be on your way to chief justice."

Delma couldn't shake the feeling. What part of her soul had she just given up? And how big was the price?

40

Jake

Jake learned his lesson about ignoring the obvious. *What the hell is she so happy about?*

Watching his wife bounce around, exuding confidence and un-limited optimism set off an alarm in his head. Considering she had just been given a hundred hours of community service for reckless driving. Considering the fact any day now the court would probably award Airic full parental rights. Lastly, considering the fact she hadn't said two words to him directly in the past week, he knew there was something going on.

She came into the bedroom having spent a good hour in the bath-room. "Oh, I didn't know you were still here." She sat at the edge of the bed and opened a box of shoes she'd just bought. She slipped on the high-heel sandals, then stood up and pulled the jean skirt down to settle over her hips. The soft blousy top that fell halfway off her shoulder was too revealing, even in the summertime.

"Where're you going?"

"Shopping. I told you."

"Doing a lot of shopping lately, aren't you?"

"Making up for lost time." She did a mild model's turn. "Do you like these shoes? I got them for half price."

He could think of all sorts of things he could do with her in those heels and the skirt. Ideally, bent over backward, him directly behind. He shook his head. "I like the skirt, but it's kinda short, don't you think?"

"No. It's perfect. In fact, this one is tame considering what's on the rack these days."

"I know what's on the rack these days. I ran a clothing company, remember?"

"Yes, I remember," she said as if saddened by the reminder he'd lost his company. "I'll be back around nine."

"Nine?"

Her small but toned breasts had the nerve to jiggle underneath her blouse. *No bra?* He focused on her face, her full shapely lips. No, safer to look at her eyes, with smoky liner and perfectly arched brows. *Stop it.* Her cheekbones, high and defined with a touch of blush. "You plan to shop till nine o'clock? Sounds like you're putting in work."

"You said you were going to stay home with Mya. So I figured I could take as long as I wanted. The stores close at nine." She leaned near him for a kiss. Her scent, the fresh white tea oil she used on her body and hair infused his senses. He closed his eyes and pulled her close. She hugged him lightly. He inhaled anyway and held her there until she let go first.

"Which mall are you going to?" he asked, following her to the edge of the stairs.

"Umm, I hadn't decided yet. I'll call you when I get there."

"Venus," he said, not sure of what he'd had in mind to say. Her china doll eyes stared up at him. She stood with one toned leg propped on the stair and the other smooth and straight on the landing. "I love you, baby."

"I love you, too," she said. He had no choice but to believe her.

41

Venus

"That was a good movie. Denzel hasn't impressed me in a long while." Airic lifted his arm and put it around my shoulder as we walked out of the theater. I gently lifted it back and removed it, placing his arm by his side.

"Not a good idea," I said.

"Right." He nodded. He looked around and over his shoulder. "Forgot your husband was recently on *America's Most Wanted.*"

"Not funny."

He snickered at his own joke. "You know I'm kidding. Look, we're forty miles away from your home, here in Gwinnett. Unless he has a tracking device on your car, I think you're safe." He paused for a moment. "Does he . . . ?"

"No. Please." I gave it a moment's thought. "Of course not."

"Good, 'cause I'm enjoying our time together." He stopped in front of a restaurant with loud jazz playing out the open door. "Want to check it out?" The down and dirty rhythm of guitar, drums, and a touch of saxophone reminded me of a Tennessee Williams scene.

"Sure. But the odds of them serving anything without bacon or ribs are slim to none."

"That's okay. We'll have a glass of wine, listen to some music, then find another place for dinner."

The darkness played into the blues setting. The darker the better.

Even if I didn't know a soul past the Mason-Dixon line, I couldn't trust being seen with Airic.

"So, do you and Trevelle go out much?" I said over the music.

He leaned in close as if he didn't hear me, too close, brushing his cheek against mine.

"I said, you and Trevelle . . . go out . . . together?"

"She wouldn't be caught dead in a place like this." He smiled, then brought my hand to his lips and lingered.

The wine arrived along with a basket of rolls. I grabbed a roll and took a giant bite and chewed as if it were my last dying meal. I was taking my life in my hands after all. If Jake found out Airic and I were sitting around in dark theaters and jazz bars I could kiss my butt good-bye. Look for me buried with my ancestors in the backyard.

"I wish you didn't have to go back tonight," Airic said, eyeing my crossed legs spilling out of my jean skirt.

"I have a curfew," I said.

"You're a grown woman and you have a curfew. Nice."

"I do." I gave his arm a pat. "Your phone is ringing." He looked down to see the blue light blinking on his hip. I spun around in the bar chair to face the musicians, grateful for the break. I knew it could only be his wife and he'd have to go outside to answer the phone. But to my astonishment, he remained in his seat. He leaned his chin over my shoulder and breathed in my ear. "Since you have a curfew, we should leave and go someplace quiet." He finished off his proposition with a kiss on my neck. He spun my bar chair around so I was facing him. He put his hands on my thighs and pushed up to the hemline. "You never dressed like this when we were together."

My hands covered his. I leaned into his face and did the unthinkable. Our lips touched. His mouth opened slightly. My lips parted and I knew his tongue was approaching. "Change is good, don't you think?" I said, pulling away.

"Change is necessary." He cradled the back of my head with his hand. This time I couldn't get away. He engulfed my face with

his wet mouth and tongue kissed me like a teenaged boy in the back
of a Buick who wasn't going to take no for an answer.

I stayed still, waiting for the out of body experience to lapse, my
hands positioned in the air as if I were conducting an orchestra, and
my legs crossed as if I still had a shred of dignity left. He held on to
handfuls of my hair and pressed his cheek against mine. "Please,
let's go somewhere. Alone," he panted, warm breath against my
skin, "please."

42

Trevelle

Even after Trevelle had left several messages Airic hadn't called her back. She was furious. After it was her idea, her hard work and effort that brought him and his daughter together, he had the audacity to treat her like gum on the bottom of his shoe. Trevelle would not stand by and watch his little visits turn him into the rescuing prince while she was portrayed as the evil stepmother.

Her frustrations were interrupted by the knock at her bedroom door. She'd already shooed her housekeeper, Nita, away several times. The woman was getting more and more impossible. There were six other rooms she could be dusting and cleaning. Five other toilets she could be washing. Didn't stop her from hovering around Trevelle's door like an alley cat.

Trevelle swung the door open revved up to say something appropriately rude to make Nita understand she did not want to be interrupted again. Instead she found Airic standing before her like a wounded soldier back from battle. His warm expression said he was sorry before she had a chance to do any reprimanding. Airic came inside and sat quietly, taking off his tie.

"What happened? I was worried sick about you."

"I was in an area that had no reception." Airic looked Trevelle directly in the eye with a bit too much effort.

"Well, how was your visit?" Trevelle asked.

"Good. Mya's an angel. Sweet girl."

"Where'd you go? You and Mya?"

"A movie."

"Another movie, nice. What'd you see?"

"Ahh, the one with the animals. A cartoon. Then we went to the aquarium." He stood up and stretched. "I just wanted to stop in and tell you that I was home, but I'm exhausted. I think I'll go lay down, maybe catch a nap before the charity dinner tonight."

"That's probably a good idea," she said. "You look tired."

"All right, I'm detecting a little hostility. What?" he said.

"Nothing. I didn't say a word. Just can't figure out why you couldn't return one of my calls."

"I was in an underground aquarium. I think it's a little difficult to get reception when you're surrounded by concrete and steel."

"Please, don't make silly excuses," Trevelle said, unable to maintain calm any longer. "You blatantly avoided my calls."

"Because I was visiting my child. My time is limited as it is."

"It would've taken you two minutes out of your time with your precious child," she shouted.

"And I'm sick of you giving me a hard time," Airic shouted. "I wanted a minute of peace. Is that too much to ask?"

"Leave. I want you out of here. Out of my house."

"Your house?" he questioned.

"My house," she spat. "My house. My world. I let you in. I trusted you and you have the nerve to turn your back on me." She paced back and forth. "The minute you put someone before me, you showed me what kind of man you truly are."

He let his head fall in his hands. "I'm sorry. I'm sorry for making you feel that way. But now is not the time. We've got to stick together if we want to welcome Mya into a spiritually healthy family."

Trevelle did her best not to choke on the laugh caught in her throat. "Stick together? I told you from the beginning we should stay united. I begged you. And what did you do, fly solo to Atlanta all big and bad, not once or twice, three times. *My child*," she huffed to mimic him, *"not yours."* She paced and then stopped with her finger in his face. "I swore as God is my witness I would never allow myself to be hurt by any man. You have disrespected me and I will not allow it."

Airic gently reached out to her with the need to be forgiven.

"Let go of me," she uttered weakly into the well of his neck. Her resolve sank. She didn't want him to let go, not really. She wished things could go back to the way they were when it was just the two of them. She wished she hadn't prodded him into accepting responsibility for the child he'd fathered. If time could go back, all she'd wish for was to be loved by him the way a husband is supposed to love a wife.

"I will never hurt you again. I love you. Do you understand that? I promise," he whispered. "I don't want anyone but you. You understand? No one is more important in my life than you." He guided her chin closer, tracing her bottom lip with his thumb.

Trevelle felt the familiar confusion, the combination of anger and lust when someone was treating her badly, but at the same time confusing her senses, making her feel so good. She needed Airic. She needed his touch and his love. She swore after many years of counseling and soul-searching she'd never fall into another vicious cycle of abuse. She had to be clear not to fall back into an unhealthy relationship.

"Ouch. Damn that hurt. What'd you do that for?" Airic staggered back, holding his groin area and bending over. "I said I was sorry and it wouldn't happen again. What do you want from me?"

"Funny, this is the third time I heard those words, but it seems that your frequent flyer miles keep adding up." He should've known by now, once she'd made up her mind it would be easier stopping a charging rhino than changing her way of thinking.

"I'm going to give you a minute to think more reasonably. You let me know when you come to your senses." Airic ducked, as one of Trevelle's Gucci pumps turned into a projectile as he exited Trevelle's bedroom.

"Get out." She slammed the door behind him. *Now what?* She paced back and forth. It was she who'd encouraged Airic to go after

Mya. She who drew the first sword and began this little war. Now that the sword had been turned on her, she didn't know how to stop the damage from being done.

☉☉

Eddie Ray arrived at her front door holding the large sealed envelope. Trevelle had forgotten all about their meeting, even after he'd called to confirm only two days before.

"We had a meeting, three o'clock," Eddie Ray said, his huge frame blocking the bright sunlight from the entrance. He sensed his presence was a surprise.

She took the envelope with lackluster interest, motioning for him to come inside. "What is this?" She closed the door after peeking outside to make sure Airic was nowhere around. He followed her into her office.

"Delma Hawkins, the judge. You don't remember asking me to investigate her?"

"Oh, yes. I've had so much on my mind." She showed him to the leather couch.

"Getting info on a judge is like running up a hill backwards. But I found some very interesting puzzle pieces that don't add up," Eddie Ray said, reminding Trevelle again of why he was there.

Trevelle took the contents and splayed them on her desk. She read the first line, "Judge Delma Hawkins," in bold black type at the top of the file. Trevelle combed over each uninteresting detail; born in Odessa, Texas. Graduated from Midlane High school in 1972. College at the University of Maryland. Law school at Columbus University. Clerk for the juvenile division of the Atlanta district attorney's office.

Trevelle's eyes ran over the mundane details until she landed on adoption papers filed in Atlanta on June 20, 1978, for Keisha Marie Hawkins. There was a second set of papers underneath. A birth certificate along with biological parents' consent to adoption. Trevelle read the names carefully: Eugena Thompson and Kevin Smith.

She flipped the papers on both sides to blank sheets. "What's so interesting about this? I need to know where they are, Eugena Thompson, Kevin Smith. No contact information, nothing?"

Eddie Ray leaned in and picked up the birth certificate. "First of all, this is phony. There was no birth on record at this hospital that matched the date, the names, or any part of it. In fact, Eugena Thompson seems to not exist at all. There's plenty of Kevin Smiths but like I said it doesn't matter because the birth certificate isn't real."

Trevelle paced with a knitted brow. "How can it be fake? Keisha exists. She was born somewhere."

"She was born somewhere, but not in this hospital to these two people. The judge claimed her minor niece was the mother of the child and had signed over her parental rights. Notarized and everything, real official looking, but like I said, no Eugena Thompson was in that hospital, let alone giving birth to a little girl."

"So you're trying to tell me Judge Delma Hawkins either bought a child or stole one. If the birth certificate isn't legal, neither is the adoption."

Eddie Ray hunched his shoulders. "What is it you're after? Maybe I can corner a better angle."

"I . . ." Being at a loss for words was hardly Trevelle's MO. "I . . . guess I was trying to find the girl's biological parents so she'd feel some closure."

"You said the young woman herself is a lawyer, I imagine she's already delved into the proper channels, done a proper search. She probably knows exactly what I've just told you. Those two people don't exist. I could definitely see how that would leave one feeling a bit empty inside, knowing her adoptive mother lied to her," he said.

"Right. Exactly. She probably knows her mother has lied but doesn't want to confront her for fear of ruining their relationship." Trevelle tapped a finger on her cheek. "Doesn't mean someone else can't bring up the truth . . . for her. Possibly impress upon the judge to confess, tell the child the truth for closure's sake."

"Don't look at me." Eddie Ray was on his feet, adjusting his snug sports coat. "I don't deal with judges or anybody else who can have my ass back in a cell. I can't be involved."

Trevelle took in a deep long breath. "If a woman wants something done right, she knows she has to do it herself. All I need is one of those secret mics with a miniature tape recorder, something like that."

Eddie Ray smirked. "You know taping someone without their knowledge is unlawful. We're talking about a judge here. You're too pretty to be in jail." He stepped closer to Trevelle.

She put up her hand. "Don't try to disrespect me or my husband under this roof." They'd had a physical history, one she didn't like to recall. He certainly was far from the desirable hunk of man he was a decade ago. "Just get me the equipment." She strode around to the other side of her desk and pulled out her checkbook. She snatched off the payment. "The best equipment. I don't want a single word lost in translation."

"So in the midst of all this, you're trying to help someone else. I'm impressed." Eddie approved of the amount written on the check. "All for the good."

Trevelle hadn't bothered walking him out. He knew the way. Trevelle folded the life of Delma Hawkins closed. Eddie Ray was right, *for the good*. Finding the truth about Keisha's biological parents would be a wonderful deed.

But there was something else she wanted more. It was time to see what this information was worth to Judge Delma Hawkins.

43

Venus

Mya and I had spent the morning at the park. The past few days, I'd found myself heading there even when I had every intention of going somewhere else, like the grocery store or the bank. Regardless of my destination, all roads led to the very spot where I'd first met Alverene and Ralph. Mya certainly didn't mind. She came to expect a park visit. Most of the time they weren't there. But this time they were. I held Ralph and fed him a bottle of juice while Alverene knitted and Mya played with the other kids.

I was getting attached. It was the perfect distraction from the mess I'd made with Airic. He was due back for another "visit" and the thought made me sick to my stomach.

I wasn't expecting Jake to be home when I got there, let alone having a sit-down with Georgina in the center of the living room. Mya ran straight into Jake's arms. He hugged and kissed her grinning face. "Hey, baby, what'd you do today?" He brushed a pat of sand off her butt. "Someone's been at the park, huh?"

"How ya doing, Georgina?" I leaned toward her to give a hand shake. She surprised me reaching up putting her long slender arms around my shoulders for a sincere hug.

"You're glowing. Either you're happier than I've ever seen or you've been out getting some sun," she said in a measured tone.

"Yeah, I got some sun," I said. No denying it. My skin felt warm and tingly. My usual caramel-toned skin was three shades darker. But what she sensed was the joy that came of Ralph's hands wrapped around my fingers. The weight of his thick feet pushing against my thighs. The sight of him, the touch and smell of baby scent lingering on my clothes and sealed in my nostrils. He'd grown so big over the last month. Holding him was as close to heaven as I thought I was ever going to get.

Jake busied himself taking off Mya's shoes and socks. "Did you use sunscreen?" he asked abruptly. He brought my attention to the line distinctly marking where her skin was a deep bronze from the ankle up.

"Ah, no. We hadn't really planned the park visit. But that's what I wanted to tell you—"

"You have to use sunscreen. Dark skin is just as susceptible to sun damage as white skin, you know that."

"She's fine. Listen, I have to talk to you."

"You've got to pay more attention to doing things right," he said.

Georgina did her best to act unfazed. She kept her expression solemn. I on the other hand was no longer on my high. In fact I was headed for a crash landing. "Jake," I said, without caring that Georgina was sitting in the room, "what do you think of adoption? A baby boy. He's seven months old."

"What?" he asked incredulously as if he hadn't heard everything I'd just said.

Georgina's mouth was open in shock. She glanced in Jake's direction then back to me.

"I know . . . crazy, huh? The same age JJ would've been." I licked my lips from the dry reception I'd just received. "I think it'd be great. We've got this huge big house and a hole in our souls that you could park the Titanic in. Doesn't it just make sense? He's such a good baby. Right now he's in foster care."

"I think I'll go and let you two talk."

"No, listen. Stay, Georgina. You being here is perfect. She should hear this, too." I still had enough gumption to attempt a smile. "He's seven months old. His name is Ralph." I smiled bigger. The name still evoked visions of Ralph Cramden in my head, *Bang, zoom, to the moon, Alice,* which couldn't be further from his angelic face and big brown searching eyes. "You should see him, he's so sweet. He has asthma, too." As if that were a selling point. "I know you're going to fall in love with him."

Then to Georgina, "You could handle the adoption. We've already given you all our money anyway. What's another legal item on the tally sheet going to cost us?"

Jake frowned, shaking his head. "All right, enough."

"Let me say something," Georgina interjected, "and then I'm going to leave so you two can discuss this privately. Adoption is difficult enough. There are a lot of rules and red tape that make it extremely complicated, which is why so many people go out of the country to adopt. I'm not saying you couldn't qualify, but I want you to know it's a tough system . . . especially when it comes to the investigative clearance. We still haven't dealt with the reckless endangerment charge and the—"

I held up my hand. "I get it."

Jake almost seemed relieved. He took in a short burst of air. "Well, all righty then." He stood up to walk Georgina out.

Georgina touched my bare shoulder as she readied to leave. "We'll figure something out. Let's get through this first." What she meant was, *Let's concentrate on keeping the child we already have. Forget about replacing the one who was gone.*

If it were possible I would forget in an instant, erase the memory just so it wouldn't hurt anymore. If it were that easy, I would. But it just wasn't the case.

44

Line Two

"How was the party?" Hudson asked without making eye contact. She hadn't mentioned anything about her pending doom, cryptic calls, or anonymous notes. She was all business and planned to keep it that way.

"It was very nice."

He folded his arms over his chest like a jilted lover. "Just nice?"

"I said 'very nice,' get it right." She looked up from her desk. "Hudson, try to put your professional hat on and stop all this nonsense. We've got work to do."

"Right. Here you go, all set for your signature." Hudson plopped the stack at the foot of her desk.

"Thank you."

"Let me know if you need anything," he said barely audibly before slipping out the door.

She cautiously peeked at the stack to make sure no blank envelopes fell out. No threatening packaging whatsoever. Just her usual. She did notice the file directly on top. She picked it up to see exactly what she knew was coming. An addendum to the complaint by Airic Fisher regarding Venus Johnston. The reckless endangerment charge was added to the tally sheet of criminal offenses. Minor as her misdemeanor charges were, it was a matter of record. She couldn't very well side with the young woman with her new post on the line. In a way Delma was grateful to her for making the decision easy. Up to that point she'd wrestled with ambivalence.

Welcome to your chance at motherhood, Trevelle Doval.

Her phone beeped. Delma picked up the receiver. "Yes."

"Judge Hawkins, you have a call on line one."

"Oh Hudson, stop. Please."

"Why, whatever are you referring to, your judgeship?"

Exasperated, she asked, "Who's on the line?"

"Ms. Trevelle Doval, should I put her through?"

Delma wasn't prepared for this. She swallowed hard. "No. Absolutely not. I've already held the personal contact meeting with her husband. I'm not about to talk to her. I can't."

"Judge Hawkins, I have already informed her of this detail. She says it's regarding your daughter, Keisha."

"Excuse me? She wants to talk about Keisha?" Delma spun in her chair.

Hudson didn't respond. He stayed on the line in silence, waiting for instruction from his honorable lady.

Delma had already put the phone down, marched out of her chambers and up the hall to where Hudson sat in his cubicle leaning back in his chair with his eyes closed. Delma reached over and snatched the phone out of his hand, startling him. She put the receiver close to her bosom, eliminating the possibility of sound travel. "You got about three seconds to take control of this situation or your ass is going to be looking for a job."

"Ms. Doval, you were not ordered to meet with Judge Hawkins in this case and any further contact could jeopardize your husband's custody matter and the outcome." Hudson cut his eyes toward Delma. "Yes, I see. I'll let her know. Thank you and have a nice day." He hung up and had the sincere look of fear in his eyes. "She says she has some very interesting documents concerning an adoption in 1978. She says this issue will not reflect well on a judge's reputation if these papers were to get out."

"It's been her all along." Delma put her hands to her face,

somewhat relieved, but still worried. "She's been responsible for the calls, the note. So she knows about Keisha."

"Shh," Hudson corrected. "Coffee?" His eyes darted quickly to the door. "Let's go."

"We can't go anywhere. We've got a case in ten minutes," she whispered for no reason.

He pulled out his legal pad and started writing. *Sounds like she did some serious digging and found Keisha's adoption papers, that's the secret, mystery solved.* Hudson pointed a warning finger at Delma, then wrote, *She knows nothing about who Keisha really is. You are not to meet with her. She doesn't know anything and you're not going to tell her. That's where it ends.*

Delma took the pen. *I have to meet with her. I'm telling you, it's been her all along.* She shook her head. She scribbled fast, *I don't have a choice. If I don't my whole life could end, I could go to jail for forging documents, Hudson. Court documents.*

"All right, but I'm going to be right there by your side," he said, taking her hand. "You're not going without me."

45

Trevelle

Trevelle liked the idea of cleaning house, taking care of business with one wide sweep of her elegant hand. She sipped on the hot tea and surveyed the small bistro for anyone who could witness or identify the two women. Besides herself and the sweet doe-eyed hostess, only one other customer, an older gentleman wearing a hat and hearing aid with all his attention focused on his newspaper, were present.

The café was conveniently a block away from the courthouse. No excuse for Judge Hawkins. Trevelle had flown in early and rented a car. She'd already been sitting for nearly two hours, OD'ing on green tea and packages of artificial sweetener. She wanted to get the meeting over with. Besides blackmailing a local judge she had other pressing business to attend to. Namely the whereabouts of her husband, who claimed to be at a fund-raiser on behalf of the Doval ministries. She had ways of checking. Especially since an overnight stay was part of his trip.

Two minutes and counting. Trevelle nervously twisted the heavy gold links of her diamond watch. She went over her plan to take her mind off the seconds ticking by. She repeated the threat in her head: *Fraud and forgery by a member of the justice would lead to a heavy price, loss of your judgeship, loss of your reputation, and far more grave, a possibility of prison time.*

The door of the bistro swung open. The woman looked like

she'd been caught in a windstorm. She approached reeking of madness and elevated anger. It was game time.

Trevelle stood. "So glad you could make it."

"Wouldn't have missed this day for all the money in the world," the judge retorted with surprising confidence. She slung her overstuffed bag across the back of the chair and plopped herself down. "Well now, how you enjoying our fair city? Little humid, but fall makes up for it. Sometimes you have to suffer to get to the good stuff, right?"

For a brief moment Trevelle felt confusion, she might even say fear if not for the fact that she'd banished the emotion from her terminology. *Fear no man or woman,* she repeated to herself. "Judge Hawkins, this isn't a social call. I have two words for you, *forged documents.*"

"I have two words for you, bitch please."

Trevelle sat down, not so easily thwarted. "Your vulgarity is expected. Anyone who would lie to their own child about something as important as this, is capable of anything." The copies of adoption papers and birth certificates appeared on the table. Trevelle pushed them toward her nemesis.

"I don't know how you got your hands on sealed records, and I'm not really interested in what you're selling. I came here with my own message. Stay away from my daughter. She doesn't need to hear a single word from the likes of you about where she came from, or didn't come from." The judge leaned closer, so there'd be no misunderstanding, "People in glass houses should never throw stones and accusations, you hear what I'm saying? I know who you are, and where you come from."

"Of course you know, the world knows and I made sure of that. But the only one who matters is my God, cherished and all knowing." Finally, Trevelle felt her strength. There was silence between them, only it didn't last long.

"You may have been forgiven by God, but he's not the one presiding over your case, now is he?"

"You or no man can be my judge. God presides over all things." Trevelle was hardly short of words, but she wanted to get to the point. Her past was not the issue at hand. No indeed, it was Ms. Delma Hawkins who was on trial here. "You forged documents, that much is clear. The question is why? Did you steal Keisha, buy her off the street? All I know is the ruse is up. Keisha deserves to know who her parents are, her real parents. You've lied to her long enough."

"What kind of business is it of yours?" The judge raised her voice. "Let me tell you something, I am that child's mother. I have been her mother since the day she was born . . . since the day I found—"

The older gentleman started having a coughing fit, slamming the table with his hand for assistance. The young hostess rushed to his side with a glass of water.

The judge quieted and took a moment to gain her composure. "This conversation has come to a close. I have no reason to be afraid of you. I did nothing wrong. Besides, you care too much about Keisha to make false accusations against her mother." A curt smile appeared. "Or is that just another one of your acts?"

Trevelle slammed her fist on the table. "That's where you're wrong. Right now the only thing I care about is putting my family back together. You're going to make it happen. I promise you one thing, if you don't, your so-called sealed adoption will be on the desk of one of my very good friends who works in the United States justice department. I'm sure a judge who goes around forging documents would be of great interest. And who knows what else they might find."

"I knew you weren't concerned about Keisha. Selfish. But that's fine with me. You know what, fine. You want to have a crack at motherhood, I'll give you your shot. You didn't have to show yourself like this because I had planned to award Mr. Fisher with full parental rights and fifty-fifty physical custody."

"But you're wrong." Trevelle couldn't help but smile. "As a matter of fact, I want you to make sure Airic doesn't receive custody . . . not even visitation."

"Excuse me?" Judge Delma's face twisted and frowned. "What in the world are you talking about? You don't want him to have contact with his child?"

"I'm glad we're clear." Trevelle breathed easy, feeling victorious even if she'd only gotten half of what she was asking for. In the world of negotiations it was better than leaving empty-handed. Keisha would have to find her real parents on her own. She'd done everything she could and now on to the next item on the agenda.

"I have no grounds for stopping this biological father from seeing his child unless he's caused some bodily harm to that child. And even then he'd get supervised visits. You're asking me to shut him completely out of this little girl's life . . . and your reasoning for this insanity—"

"None of your business why. All I know is that you're going to do what I say. Why are you finding this so difficult? I know you hate me . . . for whatever reason. I've seen the way you've looked at me and my husband. Seems I'm only asking you to do what you wanted to do from the beginning."

"That's not true. I pride myself on being as fair and impartial as I possibly can."

"Oh please." Trevelle laughed with sarcasm. "Impartial? All I'm here to do is make sure you don't suddenly find your moral compass. Do exactly what you'd planned to do. If you don't, you'll find yourself in a very awkward situation on the other side of that bench you sit so high and mighty on. Not to mention the shame and heartache you'll bring on Keisha herself."

Delma Hawkins leaned forward, eyes wide with serious intent. "Don't mention my child again, do you understand? She has nothing to do with any of this."

"Keisha is a grown woman, not a child."

"'That 'grown woman' will always be my child, I don't care if she's seventy and I'm a hundred and ten. You can stop pretending to care about her to get to me."

Trevelle wanted to correct her and say loud and clear how much she cared, but thought better of stepping over the indelibly drawn line. They faced one another with deep intense glares. A standstill with both parties' hands on the trigger.

"Fine. Done," Trevelle breathed out with an exasperated sigh. "I'll stay away from Keisha."

Satisfaction rose in the judge's voice. "Okay then, we have a deal. I wish I could say it's been a pleasure. But I can't." She stood up and snatched her purse and turned to leave. "After next week's court date, I hope I never see you again. I might even get the cable cut off just so I don't accidentally land on your late-night angel façade."

Trevelle stood up as well. "Wait a minute. I want you to know, I sincerely care about Keisha." She held up her finger to cut off the woman before she went on a tirade. "She's troubled. She knows you've lied to her, but she respects you too much to bring it to the open. Forget about me and whatever you may have against me and do what's right for your daughter."

A flash of compassion crossed the judge's face, then just as quickly turned cold with hatred. "Like I said, *my child*. Don't even think of crossing me."

Trevelle watched her leave and felt a light wave of relief.

46

All the King's Men

Delma waited in the car around the block for Hudson to meet her. She felt like laying on the horn out of frustration. "C'mon, man." She rocked impatiently behind the steering wheel. She saw him turn the corner then pick up to a nice trot. With his powder-dusted hair making him look like a seventy-year-old man, someone would've been shocked to see him running.

He jumped into the passenger side. Delma sped off.

"Did you hear that crazy woman? She's insane." Delma swerved to pass a car in front of her, refusing to slow down. "Out of her mind," she sang out. "In all my days I've never come across crazy like that."

"First of all, pull over so I can drive."

She came to a stop and they quickly played musical seats.

Once seat belts were buckled, Hudson stepped on the gas and wasn't doing that much better. "I heard every word, that's why I went into a choking fit. You were about to spill the beans. Lord knows things are weird enough."

"Understatement. All of a sudden she doesn't want her husband to have custody, not even visitation. That's one vindictive chick. Poor man has no idea he's married to the devil incarnate. She's dangerous, just like you said. What if she really tries to report me? Oh Lord, I'm going to prison. I'm going to lose everything, my reputation, my life, my daughter."

"Stop it, now. You did good. You didn't admit to anything. Seems to me she'd have a tough time trying to explain blackmailing a judge in the first place." He pulled the tiny plastic piece out of his ear. "Besides, we've got a tape, too. You didn't implicate yourself in the slightest."

"But if I do what she says, it'll be an admission of guilt." Delma wrung her nervous hands together in her lap.

"Calm down. Breathe. I need you to relax, Delma."

"I'm fine. I'm okay." She turned the air-conditioning up, letting it spray her face. "I'm half-relieved. Strike that, I'm relieved she knows nothing about my child's biological mother or father," she said with pristine calm. "Finally, my life is back on track. Whew, I thought I was going to have a heart attack in there." She let out a nervous giggle.

Hudson reached out and laid his hand on top of hers. His eyes shot a look of concern and honest caring. "Don't even play like that. I'm not done with you yet. I plan to spend the rest of my life with you, a long life." He squeezed her hand.

Delma didn't know how to respond. She turned her face toward the window and focused on what was important. Getting through the next few days. Presenting a believable finding as to why Airic Fisher couldn't have custody, let alone visitation. This was the last and final hurdle she'd have to jump and then she'd have her life back.

47

Venus

I was back at the park. Mya was in the play area and I stood off to the side, a safe distance away so I could hear my mother on the other end of my cell phone without kids screaming with playful joy in the background. I'd spent the last twenty minutes assuring both my parents I didn't need them to come out and do any hand holding.

"I'm sure. However this turns out, Jake and I need to deal with it together." My focus was on Mya, where she played on the slide.

There was an awkward pause. The phone moved and adjusted before my father's soft husky voice came on. "Hey precious, everything is going to work out, you here? No matter what the outcome, you've got everything to be thankful for. You make sure Jake understands that. You've got your health. You've got your whole lives ahead of you."

"Dad, I know. I'm okay, really. I was just explaining to Mom that it's going to be a hard adjust . . ." I trailed off, not wanting to give any hints of what was really going on. How the tension between us was thick enough to slice. "You're right, we have each other."

I'd expected the letter from Airic by now with the terms we'd agreed to. But it hadn't come. I felt duped and embarrassed for trusting him. Maybe if I'd gone through with my part of the bargain. At the last minute I couldn't go through with it. He said he understood, but still no letter from his lawyer. Instead, I was left counting down to our final court date, feeling helpless and bitter.

"Precious, your mom and I don't mind flying out. In fact, we'd give anything to be there." My father's love reached through the phone and wrapped warm arms around me. *Go ahead and let it out, precious.*

"Dad, really, I'm fine."

He handed the phone back to my mother while trying to whisper, "She's not doing good." My mother was back in force on the phone. "All you need to know in your heart is that you've done all you can do."

Well, that was a definite understatement. I'd pretty much done everything possible—to ruin my chances, not the other way around. I couldn't tell her how I'd ran through a police barricade, received a hundred hours of community service as punishment, or how Child Protective Services had sent a warning letter . . . thank goodness they were undermanned.

"I'll be praying for you," my mother said. "If you need us, me and your dad will be on the first thing flying."

"Thanks, Mom. Tell Dad I love him. I'll talk to you guys soon." I swiped at my eyes to keep my vision clear to see Mya. She was standing at the top of the slide, holding up the line. She spun around and signaled for the other kids to give her space like she was a band leader. I headed toward Mya to try and quell the chaos. "Mya, sweetie, let the other kids go if you're not ready."

"They have to back up, Mommy."

"Sweetie, if they back up too much someone's going to fall off the edge. Just slide down. Come on, I'll catch you."

She shook her head and pinned her eyebrows closer together. "They're in my way, Mommy." I thought back to what Airic had said about me . . . *selfish, immature.* "Mya, move out of the way or slide. Those are your choices. Now," I emphasized with a deepening of my voice.

"Daddeee," Mya yelled and waved. I followed her line of vision to Jake. He wore a breezy white shirt with his sleeves folded back.

His slim denim jeans were courtesy of his JP Wear line and reminded me of when we were happy.

She slid to her butt and pushed off. She came shooting down with her legs straight for propelling ease, landing on her feet and into Jake's arms. How he'd managed to leap in front of me when I'd just been staring at him was beyond me. Lately my mind had been in slow motion and false starts.

"What're you doing here?"

"Saw the note," he said. He'd been to the barber. His head was freshly shaven. Only hair left on his head was his dark and lovely eyebrows, lashes, and trimmed mustache. He held Mya for a minute before putting her down. "Go play and be good. I saw you up there bossing everybody around." After she got a few feet away he said, "That's my baby, don't let them little boys try to push you around." He grinned, with his hands in his pockets, then started to look around.

I gave him a one cheek frown. "He's not here today," I said, knowing it was his next question. "He's not always here." My disappointment was evident. Jake and I hadn't broached the subject of Ralph and adoption again, putting it in the stack of other unmentionables.

All the benches in the shade were taken. "Sit here," he said. "I'll push." I squinted around with hesitation before sitting on the sunwarmed swing. "You think it'll hold me?"

"I'm sure it'll hold you." He gave me a soft push. I sailed softly forward then back. On the second push I closed my eyes, feeling the weightless surge of movement. Pretty soon I didn't feel Jake's push. I was pumping my legs back and forth.

"Look," Mya's voice called up, "Mommy's flying."

I wasn't worried about the sturdiness of the swing anymore. Mya was right, I could fly. My head flung back, legs extended, light as air without worry or fret. The smile plastered across my face was nothing short of a miracle. I swooshed across, feeling like a superhero, taking a second to open my eyes. I was unlimited and all powerful just like the blue sky, bountiful green trees, and the hint of heaven peeking through. I was more courageous than the fear calling my name. I needed to be present and accounted for and I wasn't going to run and hide.

It wasn't until Jake grabbed me, snatching me out of midair that I realized he and Mya had actually been calling my name.

He held me tight. "I thought you were headed straight up and out of here."

"You were flying, Mommy," Mya squealed. "Did you get scared?"

"Nope, I was loving every minute of it," I said. "Okay, your turn," I said to Jake.

"Now you know I'm not about to fit all this man into that swing."

"Sit," I ordered. I was just over five feet, so it was going to be a job, but I mustered every bit of strength and pulled back and gave him a running start. I moved out of the way before he came crashing into me. I jumped in front to see the biggest smile I'd seen out of him since I could remember. All white teeth surrounded by perfect tawny lips. I lifted my arms. "Go baby, go."

He laughed. I smiled. "Who's flying now?"

There was hope and I had to at least try one last plan of attack.

48

When Truth Knocks

After tossing and turning half the night Delma found herself gazing into the white light of the television. She had basic cable, which added up to five or so English-speaking channels with infomercials, the rest Spanish and Asian, also infomercials, selling products with the same enthusiasm.

Before long she was sleeping soundly, or so she thought until the deep and throaty voice sang out, "God's love is divine and infinite. God's love has no judgment or conditions. All that is required is that you accept him as the father and the Holy Ghost."

"Say it with me, say his name. Dear God, I come before you heavenly father, humbled by your love . . . ready to give of myself completely. No more secrets, dear heavenly father. No more fears because with secrets and lies come the greatest fear of all, to be found out, to be discovered a fake, a fraud.

"You have watched me deal with this pain and guilt. I come to you open and honest about my past. A baby, dear Lord. An innocent child died one night nearly thirty years ago and I have blamed myself every waking day. She was born without a breath in her body."

Delma's eyes flew open. She sat straight up to face the television and Trevelle Doval, dressed in a glowing white robe with her arms opened wide like an angel, looked straight into the camera as it zoomed in. "I was only fourteen years old when I gave birth to a

baby girl in the back of an alley. I have prayed the memory away of
that cold lonely night. I held that secret for many, many years.

"My baby's in heaven right now smiling down upon me because
she knows . . . she knows God's love heals all wounds. So I ask of
you, each and every person watching me tonight, is there a secret
weighing on your heart? Is there something you wish you could
turn to your husband, your mother, or your child and say . . . I have
a secret I want to share? You have to trust in God and know that he
will protect you and guide you. Your burden is his burden if you
give it over to him. You don't have to carry it alone."

Delma picked up the phone and dialed Keisha's number. She
didn't pay attention to the glowing clock that said 2:00 A.M. How
many times would she be led to the door of truth only to run the
other way?

"Mommy," the groggy voice on the other end answered. "What's
happening, are you all right? It's two o'clock in the morning."

"I was up, couldn't sleep. I was watching that woman, Trevelle
Doval."

She paused. "Yes, Mom let me explain."

Delma was taken aback. "Explain what?"

"I was hoping you'd never see that. She told me they would edit
the tape."

"I have no idea what you're talking about, Keisha. What tape?"

Keisha sighed with relief. "Oh, well, no . . . I thought you were
talking about the show. I was taped with Ms. Doval when she collapsed, and I thought . . . how embarrassing it was to have her fall in
my arms." She paused again. "Maybe I should let you tell me why
you called. Are you all right, is everything all right?"

They both let out collective breaths echoing of *thank God* that
neither knew what the other was talking about.

"No . . . no . . . I'm fine."

"You're not fine. You wouldn't be calling me in the middle of
the night if you were fine," Keisha said, full of compassion.

"I love you, that's all." Delma sniffed back the onslaught of emotion. "I'm lucky to have you as a daughter, as my best friend."

"Mom, you're not lucky, you're blessed, that's what Trevelle says. There's no such thing as luck. We're blessed to have each other," Keisha said quietly, settled with the notion of loneliness as the reason for Delma's mini-breakdown.

"Keish . . ." She paused, afraid she was making a big mistake. She stopped and looked at the television once more. Trevelle Doval was the spitting image of Keisha. How could both of them not see it? Maybe it wasn't meant to be known. Wouldn't God *bless* Trevelle Doval with the knowledge that she was talking to her very own daughter if she was meant to know? "Don't end up like me, Keish. Find yourself somebody to love, to marry."

"All I've ever needed was you, Mommy."

"Go back to sleep. I'm sorry I woke you." She hung up the phone and continued to watch Trevelle Doval. She set the TV on mute and simply kept staring. The world was a crazy mixed-up place, yet all things seemed to work in a systematic order. Full circle. Trevelle Doval befriending her own child some thirty years later. There was no explanation, no rhyme or reason.

The address on the bottom of the screen kept popping up for donations. The Doval Ministry Foundation. She sat up in her bed and continued to watch and wonder. Would Keisha still want to be friends with the great Trevelle Doval if she knew what happened that night? Or would she cut off her own nose out of spite?

Delma sighed before pressing the power button. The black screen was a relief. She scooted down under her covers up to her nose. Maybe it was all a bad dream. Soon, Trevelle Doval would disappear from whence she came, never to be seen or heard from again.

49

Venus

Jake was standing outside of the shower when I pushed the glass door open. I jumped, seeing him there, not sure if he was real or an illusion.

"Hi," I said, blinking past the steam. I stepped out even though he was doing a good job of blocking my way. "What're you doing?"

"I think the question is yours to answer. You wanna tell me what's going on?" He held up the credit card statement. "Every time I ask you where you're going, you say shopping. I look here to see what kind of damage I'm in for and you know what, you must be getting some serious bargains 'cause we're all clear."

"Like that's my only credit card," I said, wrapping the towel around me.

He folded his arms across his chest. "Stop playing games. Tell me what's going on. So what, you're spending all this time with that baby . . . you think I'm going to be mad about that?"

"No, well yes, sometimes I'm at the park. Okay, you got me. Ralph and I are planning a clandestine rendezvous at Babies 'R' Us."

"Stop it. Okay. I know when you're lying. I know when you're trying to hide some shit."

"You're right. I already admit it. I've been spending time with Alverene and the baby. You saw for yourself, I spend a lot of time at the park."

He snapped the paper statement with a finger flick. "Gas in Gwinnett. That's over an hour away."

"Sometimes, I just drive. I get in the car and I keep going. What's so hard to understand?"

He stood silent for a few moments, not sure of what more he could say. "I get scared." He laced his fingers over his head and searched the ground for something that wasn't there. "I get scared when you walk out that door, that you're not coming back. You want to adopt this little boy, fine. Let's do it. Whatever it'll take to keep you safe, 'cause you're scaring me."

"I swear, I'm fine." I tried to assure him. But the underlying reason behind his fear went deeper than not knowing where I was spending my time or with whom. He was referring to the day he found me sprawled across the king-size bed unable to respond. I could hear him calling my name. I heard his voice past the crowded buzzing in my head. I smelled the beach on his skin after his run. I couldn't tell him I was all right. My lips wouldn't move. But I heard him, frantic, more so by the second. "Awww, shit, babe. What'd you do?"

He said the spilled red wine at the bedside was the only reason he panicked. He knew there had to be something wrong for me to allow the white carpet to get soaked unabated. When I wouldn't wake up, he called 911.

There's no law against trying to get some sleep by any means necessary. Unless of course your toddler is left alone to wander the halls, to watch TV, get bored, then get up and walk out the front door. Jake said the lifeguard found her at the foot of the shore, building a sand castle. He tried to make me feel better by admitting he'd probably ran right past her himself. But he was the kind of man who'd notice a child too close to the water, whether it was his or someone else's. He was always aware of danger. When it came to me, he had a sixth sense directly linked to my hazardous logic.

"Sometimes I just want to be alone." I hunched my shoulders. "Besides, there's nothing either of us can do but wait."

He searched the ceiling the same way he'd searched the floor. Then he willed his eyes to look at me with the regrettable truth. We were powerless to change what was about to happen. The fact that we might have to hand Mya over to Airic and Trevelle, and possibly be the ones picking her up on Sundays for visits, became an ugly reality that we both had to face. And all we could do was wait.

◎◎

I couldn't tell Jake of my dastardly plan. It made little sense even to me but I wasn't about to talk myself out of taking a chance. I had to try.

It was a purple-hued sky, nearly dusk before Airic pulled up beside me in his rented Jaguar. He looked nervous and hurried. The window rolled down. "I'm sorry I was late."

I got out of my car and made sure it was locked before going to his passenger side.

"You look beautiful," Airic said. Though I hardly felt it. In my attempt to dress down, I ended up in a white tank and jeans that felt a couple of sizes too small. He reached over and squeezed my thigh. "Sorry I'm late. Just call me Bond, James Bond. I had to double back a couple of times for safety."

"Trevelle knows something?" I asked. "I don't understand."

"She's made accusations. I couldn't take a chance. She might've had me followed."

"What the . . ." I put my hand over my mouth to keep from spilling the laughter. "You've got to be kidding."

He stared straight ahead as if he'd already said too much. "She's capable, trust me." He started the car. "Let's just have a good time, shall we?"

"Right." I put my seat belt on and adjusted my sunglasses, feeling like the other woman for once in my life. It didn't feel good. I couldn't wait for the whole charade to end. We ended up at the same jazz bar as the week before. I made sure to get gas in Atlanta this time, in case someone was checking.

"So what do you tell her?" I sipped on the ice water.

"Same as the last two times, I was here to see Mya." He paused, thinking I'd correct him. He hadn't seen Mya at all. Hadn't even asked about her.

"That also happens to be in Atlanta," I added. "So why was she suspicious if you're just visiting your daughter?" I asked with impartiality. "Have you done this sort of thing before . . . said you were one place but gone another?"

"Haven't we all?" he said.

I had an entirely new perception of Airic Fisher. When we were together, he made it absolutely clear he wasn't a gaming man. He didn't have the time or the energy to chase skirts. He wanted a stable, strong relationship where both parties understood their role. If I was a betting woman, I would've said he and Trevelle were meant for each other, yet here he was, leaning into my shoulder, his knee brushing against mine, whispering words that would haunt me for all of my days.

"We have unfinished business," he said. "Why don't we get out of here?" He stood up, slightly off balance. The single sleeping pill I'd dropped in his drink was taking effect. "I'm going to the restroom. Then we can get on the road. I made reservations at the Guerlain hotel."

"Take your time," I said. I raised a hand to get the bar guy to come my way. He seemed disgusted by my thirst for only water. Now it was time for a heavy hitter. "Dirty martini," I said. "Fast and in a hurry, if you get my meaning."

"Coming up." He seemed pleased by my choice.

"Somebody's lookin to get dirty," the man's voice sang over my shoulder. He was dressed in an awkward-fitting suit, too big, too wide, too blue. "Hey Miz Sexy, let me get that for you. And one for me, too," he called out to the bartender. His eyes were seriously bloodshot. His dark skin was riddled with hair bumps along his neck and cheeks.

"No thank you, really. I have it covered." I'd spent enough nights out on the town to know not to be rude. A polite "no thank you" usually did the trick.

"Pretty lady," he said, smelling like distilled vinegar, "I won't take no for an answer. You too pretty to be sitting here all by yourself." He opened his wallet. "Recognize that guy?" It was a picture of a boxer with his dukes up, wearing a fancy champion belt.

"No, can't say I do."

Both martinis were placed in front of me. He leaned over, grabbed his and finished it off in one, two, three gulps. "Your turn," he said, far too close.

Airic returned not a second too soon. He tried to scoot into the chair now being occupied by our new friend.

"Hey man, I'm talking to the lady."

Airic calmly faced him. "I'm sorry, did I interrupt something?" He looked to me for the answer.

"No . . . I'm finished. We should go." I probably should've mentioned Mr. Blue Suit was an ex-boxer.

"We'll go when we're ready," Airic said. "I'd appreciate it if you backed out of our space."

"You'd appreciate it if I backed out of your space?" Mr. Blue Suit wasn't budging.

"Move along." Airic put his hand out and moved between us.

I was up on my feet. I waved to the bartender. "Check."

"Nah, pretty lady. I got this."

"You don't have anything. I can pay my own tab." Airic pulled out his wallet and tossed a couple of twenties on the marble bar. "Come on," he grumbled. "It stinks in here. Like someone's all washed up."

What'd he say that for?

Mr. Blue Suit spun Airic around and got in two punches before either one of us knew what hit him. Airic dropped to the ground with a *thud*. He threw up his hands and danced around. "I am the greatest, I am . . . the greatest," he sang. A few patrons clapped with slurred cheers and whistles.

The manager rushed over. He leaned over Airic, who was completely dazed. "Sir, are you all right? Do you need an ambulance?"

"No . . . please no, just ice," I said, not wanting anything to end up in a police report. I couldn't chance it. "We're leaving." I pulled Airic by his arm and shoulder. "Come on, you have to get up." He only moaned, his eyes opened then closed again.

"Now talk pretty for me." Mr. Blue Suit was still riding on the steam of his knockout.

"All right, that's enough. I want you out of here. This is the last time I'm putting up with this." The manager pulled the cell phone off his belt. "Out or I'm calling the police."

"I'm leaving. Whatever."

I helped Airic to his feet. The ice pack didn't come fast enough. His left eye had swollen and the discoloration had already started underneath. "Just hold it there," I told him as I did my best to steady his lanky frame. We got outside without incident.

"I could sue him for everything he's got," Airic slurred through his swollen lip. "He should be in jail."

"Not today," I said, unlocking the car. The last thing I needed was another run-in with officers of the law. I helped him into the passenger side. I ran around to the other side. "You knew who that guy was?" I asked. "And you had the nerve to provoke him?"

"It's a free world. I can say what I please." He leaned back and closed his one good eye. The ice pack covered the entire other side.

I was about to start the car, then stopped. I grabbed my purse and pulled out the folded paper. I'd planned to wait until he was in a drug-induced stupor. But being punched silly by a crazed ex-champion boxer would have to do.

"Airic, I need you to sign this . . . I need you to agree to . . ." Suddenly my mouth was dry and my throat nearly closed. I fought it back. "Airic, you have to sign this."

"What . . . sign what?" He held the ice, covering half his face. I figured he wouldn't be able to see it anyway.

"It's just a release that Mya needs for preschool. It . . . well . . .

you're her parent, too, so I need your permission." I held my breath, "Please. I just need you to sign, here." I put the pen in his hand and positioned it over the paper.

"I'm not signing something without reading it first," he mumbled under the ice.

"Just sign it. It's a parental release form, field trips, that kind of thing. That's what it's for." I tapped the pen. "Airic, please."

He moved the ice pack off his face and held the paper steady to get a look with his one good eye. "What the hell is this? What're you trying to pull? Are you kidding?" He folded the sheet and ripped it in half and threw the pieces in my lap. "Why would I sign a relinquishment of parental rights? Did you really believe I would sign this?"

"You explain to me how you're supposed to be visiting with your daughter and all you can focus on is getting a piece of my ass? You don't care about her . . . you never have!" I yelled. "You're incapable. Yes. Absolutely. I thought you'd sign it."

"In exchange for me being able to sleep with you?" He shook his head. "You're giving yourself a whole lot of credit."

"How about in exchange for a million dollars of your wife's money? That's right. I did the math. Three and a half years of child support that you conveniently forgot to pay right along with every medical bill, preschool tuition, and day care. Don't even try it," I said, furious, my finger in his face. "I read you from day one. Your only goal has been revenge. Getting back at Jake and me for hurting your precious ego. And you thought why not . . . why not pretend to be the innocent father caught between a pushy wife and a bitter ex?"

"You've put a lot of thought into this," he slurred. "But you're wrong."

"Which part, you wanting a relationship with your daughter who you haven't even mentioned, not *once*. You haven't asked to see her. You never once asked to talk about who she is, her likes, her dislikes. You'd rather spend your time with me, rehashing the past."

"You're making a fool of yourself, you know that, don't you?"

"Well you see, that's the difference between you and me. I'd make a fool out of myself for the people I love. I wouldn't stay away and not see my child for three years out of spite or embarrassment. I'd give my life for the people I love."

"I hear you already tried that. Didn't work out too well," he said with enough venom to make me see what I was really up against. So I tried another approach.

"Airic, I know you. I know how you feel. Your ego was hurt. All you've wanted this entire time is to try and get back your pride, the dignity you lost when I chose Jake over you. Don't you see that? You think it'll stop you from being angry. I know that feeling, I've lived it. But you can't ever put things back the way they were. When you make room in your heart by letting go, you leave room for something better."

He shook his head, then let out a strange sound. I thought he was crying. I thought I'd finally broken through, but instead he was laughing. Hard, hysterical laughter that made him wince in pain from the swelling on his face. Then he'd start again, laughing so hard he was losing his breath. "The truth is," he inhaled and exhaled slowly to get hold of himself, "I knew with everything stacked against you and your fake gangsta husband, there was a solid chance I could get custody of Mya. Then it occurred to me, I could get two for the price of one. A family set. I wouldn't mind having you back. It would be a shame to separate the child from her mother, barbaric even." He smiled. "So you see, I was doing you a favor. But I never wanted *you*."

Unable to take being near him any longer, I got out of the car. Before I slammed the door I leaned in. "I didn't even know it was possible to hate you more than I already did."

He put the ice back on his swollen eye. "Is this where I'm supposed to get scared? After you've exhausted all the possible avenues to make me go away, now your husband will put a hit on me like he did his accountant?" He laughed again.

"Good-bye, Airic."

"I'll at least let you have visitation," he said. "That's more than you were going to give me."

I reached inside and snatched the car keys out the ignition. Even after all he'd said and done I didn't want him crashing from the pill I'd slipped into his drink. I hurled them into the pocket of tall grass and trees a good fifty feet away. I walked back into the jazz bar and called a taxi to take me to my car.

50

Trevelle

She could only hope it wasn't too late to salvage her and Airic's relationship. The court date was approaching in less than twenty-four hours, and soon this entire can of worms she'd opened would be back in its nesting place. No more Mya. No more Venus. She allowed him his one last visit.

She heard his keys at the door and moved quietly to the chaise near the open patio. She positioned herself like she'd been taking a nap. He entered the house and closed the door with extreme care.

"You're back," she said, stretching and gently yawning.

He acted startled. "I didn't see you."

"So how's Mya?" she said, getting up and coming toward him. She stopped midway, not sure if she was seeing things. "What happened to you?" She took a few steps closer. Airic turned his head, avoiding her. "Oh, my . . . what in the world? Look at you." She summoned the compassion to rub his shoulder. "What happened? You were fighting with her husband. He hit you?"

"No . . . it wasn't anything to do with Venus or her husband. This guy . . . I made an off-color comment about an ex-boxer's washed up career and he hit me."

"An ex-boxer? You were somewhere with your daughter and an ex-boxer comes out of nowhere and beats you to a pulp?"

"You know, it was probably the worst experience I've had in my life. And right now, I'm not in the mood to be grilled by you."

"Okay. Let me at least help you." She went to the edge of the circular stairs and called out, "Nita . . . can you come down, please?"

The housekeeper arrived at the top of the stairs. "You need something?"

"Mr. Fisher needs an ice pack for swelling. And can you check the medicine cabinet up there and get him some pain relievers?"

"Sure." Nita couldn't help but take a peek. Her face twisted and her jaw dropped seeing Airic's black-and-blue face.

"Thank you," Airic said to Trevelle. "I appreciate you understanding. And I swear, I'll explain everything. But right now I have to go somewhere and close my eyes."

"No problem, sweetheart," Trevelle said. She gently put both her hands on each side of his face. The day-old scent of smoke and alcohol assaulted her senses. He hadn't respected her enough to even shower. A picture painted a thousand words and his story was told. She didn't need him explaining anything. "Go rest," she said complacently, *'cause you're going to need it.*

She walked over to the chaise and picked up the phone. She dialed and didn't bother saying hello. "Everything set?" Her face was tight with determination. "You're sure, no mix-ups. I can't leave this in the hands of the judge." She smiled with assurance. "Perfect. The wonders of what money can buy. Thank you, Eddie, I'll put you in my prayers."

She could relax now. Her white leather-bound Bible was never more than a reach away. The pages practically opened themselves. She read Psalm 35 out loud. "'Plead my cause, O Lord, with them that strive with me: fight against them that fight against me. Take hold of shield and sword, and stand up for my help. Draw out also the spear and stop the way against them that persecute me. I am thy salvation. My soul shall be joyful in the Lord, it shall rejoice in his salvation.'" She closed the book and rested her head, knowing all would be right again soon.

51

Venus

I'd tossed and turned all night thinking about my failed and final meeting with Airic. *Now your husband will put a hit on me like he did his accountant.* I couldn't figure out if Airic was really afraid or just doing a little mudslinging. Either way, it hit right between the eyes.

Jake and I had decided to never speak about Byron Steeple, though it was always between us. We'd made a silent pact to never broach the subject in open air. BYRON STEEPLE, BEATEN TO DEATH, a huge headline stapled across both our foreheads. By never talking about it we'd hoped it would go away. But it never disappeared. Always imprinted on our minds and spirits no matter how far we tried to run. The night Jake told me everything, I was prepared to accept the fact that maybe I didn't know my husband as well as I thought I did. Turns out that part was true.

After Jake found out Byron Steeple was siphoning off millions of dollars, he set out to prove it. He hired an auditing team to investigate, find out how the money was being taken and where it was stashed. They came up empty. Byron had cleaned his trail spotless, all the while denying everything. To add insult to injury he leaked the information that JP Wear was near bankruptcy, ripe for the picking by anyone who wanted a piece.

Conveniently, Fenny Maxwell, a woman exec for one of his biggest department store buyers, made an offer to buy JP Wear for half its worth. Jake immediately suspected foul play. She threatened to pull the plug on millions of dollars' worth of orders if he didn't comply. He had no choice. Sell, and quick, or JP Wear would be left in financial ruin. It didn't take long to add up the connection between Fenny Maxwell and Byron Steeple. Their secret alliance sent Jake into a tailspin. He wanted retribution, if not with the return of his money, then maybe with blood.

He wasn't sure what he was going to do the night he followed the thief to his brand-new Bentley, compliments of the embezzled funds from Jake's company. He followed him for what seemed like forever, an endless maze through traffic and streets until landing in the West Hollywood nightclub district. Byron pulled over, rolled his window down, and flagged bills for attention. The street boys flocked to his car, vying for the job Byron was willing to pay for.

He'd trusted Byron as the money man from day one. When Jake's company made its first million Byron was right there crossing the *i*'s and dotting the *t*'s. He knew how to make the cash flow work, turning it over with the right investments. The day Byron sat Jake down and asked to be a partner he almost thought it was a joke. "Doesn't have to be a huge split, just like thirty percent," he proposed. "I've busted my ass for this business, went the first year on slave wages just to help a brotha out. I'm just thinking it's time for just rewards."

"You're paid. You want more money, that's cool. But I'm not giving you part of my company, man. I've worked too hard to start giving away what I've built."

"A lot of us have worked *too hard*."

"No doubt. And I appreciate everything you've done." Jake noticed the beads of sweat across Byron's forehead. "Look, man, I know coming to me this way wasn't easy. Let me give it some thought. You know, just give me some time to think it over and I'll get back with you." They shook hands that day . . . two years later and Jake never got back with him. He never broached the subject and neither had Byron. Their arrangement stayed intact. Byron was the money man and that's all Jake cared about. Until that night, Jake knew nothing of the man's personal life.

"Shut up and get ya ass out of the car." Those were the words Jake heard coming from a short distance away as he watched from the street. Two men, one on each side. He thought he was seeing things when he caught a glimpse of a gun.

"What the hell are you doing? Get your hands off me." Byron tried to roll up his window but one reached inside and hit him hard across the back of his head. "Say another word and I'll blow your head off," he yelled.

Byron tried to struggle. Even with passersby looking on, they struck him again, then shoved him over to the passenger side of the car, then the other trotted back to a dated Mercedes parked across the street.

The Bentley moved fast into the street and sped off with the Mercedes close behind. For a split second Jake sat still, shocked. Had he just witnessed a carjacking? Then without reason, he started his car and hurried to follow. What was his plan, to save Byron Steeple's life? He didn't know. All he knew was the man was being kidnapped in plain sight and no one had offered a shred of help or concern, including himself. He pulled out his cell phone and steered with one hand while the other prepared to dial 911. All he needed was a license number. And then he remembered who he was dealing with, the LAPD. The Los Angeles Police Department and black men were like oil and water, and did not mix. No matter how innocent, he'd get drawn in and somehow assumed guilty. Whether it was this crime or one that happened a year ago, he'd become a suspect and he wasn't about to sacrifice his own life to save Byron's.

All Jake could do was follow, slowing when they slowed, speeding when they did until finally reaching Byron's long driveway. That's when he knew it was more than a carjacking. Far more personal.

Jake parked on the street just far enough away not to be seen and got out and stepped lightly through the densely landscaped path. On the other side, the Bentley idled but inside Jake saw bodies moving. He pushed himself behind the tall shrubs and waited, scared to death. He cursed himself for being stupid enough to be so close. What had he planned to do? he kept asking himself. He also kept telling himself to *Go back, turn around, and run.*

But he couldn't. He stood crouched in the brush, in shock by what he was seeing and hearing.

The car windows were down. He heard voices, whimpering, and sobbing, then a few moments of moaning and grunting. Jake knew what was going on, but thought, no. He wasn't witnessing a man being sexually assaulted. "Bring him in the house, man. I want him on some of those fine sheets he got in there."

"Naw, the accountant likes it raw and dirty," the assailant said in between grunts. "Ain't that how you like it, baby?" Byron tried to struggle in the backseat of his car, determined not to go in the house.

Jake watched in horror, he felt the clamp on his chest, the asthma taking hold. He stood holding his breath, afraid his next inhale would be a loud wheezing. He needed to go back to the car, get a crowbar. Just start swinging. He couldn't stand there holding what little breath he had left. *God, help me.* He pulled out his cell phone. He stared at it briefly, realizing the dialing might make beep tones. Why couldn't someone invent a phone that didn't sing every tune, or *bleep* every touch of the key?

Byron started to yell something but before he could get two syllables out the sound of a fist landing against flesh and bone shut him up temporarily.

"Where's the appreciation? At least I used a little ChapStick."

"How . . . considerate of you," Byron said weakly.

"Hey, you mess around with the bull, you gonna get the horns."

"I've got money . . . in my safe. I'll give it to you, please."

"We know, man. What'd you think, this was a social call?"

"Then let me go inside and get it."

"Naw, naw. Then you come out blasting with that little twenty-two you got in there for sissies."

"How'd you know . . ." This gave the conversation new meaning

for Byron. He must've thought he knew who'd sent the men. "No . . .
he wouldn't do this to me. You did something to him . . . you threatened him. I'll kill you." He mustered enough strength to try and fight
again. The sound of slapping and hard thuds calmed him.

"Somebody's gon call the police up here. Let's go, man."

"Right," the main one said. "Okay, here's the thing, you give me
the combination. I go inside and handle business and then we're on
our way."

"Kiss my ass!" Byron spat.

The sound again and again. Hitting, thick serious connections.
By this time Jake was bordering on collapse. *Just give 'em the combination.*

Byron had stolen from Jake and now someone was stealing
from him. Made sense. They weren't going to kill him. He could relax and wait them out. He'd call 911 from Byron's phone for the
paramedics as soon as the goons cleared out. But then something
ridiculous happened.

"I rather die than give you shit," Byron said with a mouth full of
blood and spit. "You think I care, I don't care." The blows became
deftly concise. One, two, three, like beating a pillow, only it was now
Byron's swollen head.

"Play nice, and we go, simple as that."

"Mutha—" Before Byron could get the rest out, he went silent.

"Aw, man, now what. He's out cold."

"Get the water hose."

The one who never got his turn started toward the garden patch
near the entry. He was only a foot or so away from Jake while he un-
coiled the hose. He walked back and shoved it through the open car
window. Byron came to. He still refused to cooperate, even after
they used the hose for more than soaking him down.

"He's done," the main guy said. "I didn't get paid enough to be
putting in overtime."

"We still don't have the money."

"We got paid, anything else was going to be a bonus."

Within minutes it was over, the two men drove in the Mercedes and Jake was still afraid to move. He forced himself to take a step, then another, approaching Byron's car. Jake went to open the door then thought twice. He used his jacket cuff and covered his hand before touching the handle. Water flooded out where they'd left the hose on. "Byron . . . man, wake up. Can you hear me?" His face was ballooned and bleeding.

A mild moan was music to Jake's ears. Byron's closed eyes moved from side to side behind his lids.

"It's Jake, man. Come on, try to sit up."

"You . . . ?" Byron's accusation was slurred. "You ain't shiiiit."

"What . . . no. I'm trying to help you, man." Jake pushed the Bluetooth symbol on the steering wheel of the Bentley, ready to dial 911.

"You know what they say, a fool and his money will soon part." Byron let out a ragged cough. "I just took it before you lost it anyway. You're never gonna see a dime of it."

All that could be heard was the laughter coming from the inside of the car. Jake could see his bloodied tongue and teeth gleaming with a smile. He yanked Byron out the car by his collar. "Fool, I'm trying to help you and you're still trying to play me."

"Don't hate the play—"

Jake let go of Byron, letting him slide to the wet ground, running water snaked around his limp body. "You probably got exactly what you deserved."

"And you got what you deserved," Byron said weakly.

Jake stood up and pressed 911 and listened to the operator ask, "What is your emergency?" The question came again as he stared at the man on the ground and felt nothing but contempt.

@\@

He said he could've saved Byron if he'd called for help sooner. I knew who Jake was and I didn't think he was capable of killing anyone. But I truly learned how big his heart was when he cried for hours, wishing he'd done something. Wishing he could turn time around. He'd been awash with guilt and heartbreak. He was convinced every bad thing culminated from that moment. We lost our son. A life for a life. Now we were going to lose Mya. When would the debt be paid?

52

The Chosen

The courthouse was ominously quiet. The usual storm of anger and bitterness had shifted and moved and Delma wondered where. Somehow feeling it was a trick, she walked cautiously through the halls waiting for danger to jump out and grab her.

So used to dealing with human misery on a daily basis, she felt confused by the calm. No solemn faces or arms folded over chests. No screaming children in the halls. No screaming adults for that matter.

Hudson greeted her as she came through the heavy oak doors. "Hey, lady."

"Is it a holiday I forgot about?"

"No. But I will agree it's quiet out there. Not one single argument taking place in the halls. I even moved straight through the security line. No one trying to get a single weapon through."

"What is it, a bomb scare or something? And why are we the only ones still left in the building?" She'd come in prepared for the chaos that would take place in the courtroom when she read her judgment over who would get Mya Fisher. But now the eerie calm threatened her disposition. "I'm serious . . . what's going on around here?"

"For one, it's the first day of fishing season. Calendars are empty. All except yours, of course. Today's the big day."

"You don't have to remind me, trust me. I'll be in my chambers."

"Oh no you don't." He followed fast behind her. "Let's see it."

She paced a few moments before opening her briefcase and pulling out the ruling she'd spent all night writing.

He eyeballed the piece of paper shaking in his nervous hands. Hudson read silently for a few minutes. "This is perfect."

"Oh stop patronizing me. Bottom line, I feel like I've made a deal with the devil, no matter how I've painted the decision."

"You have no choice. If someone's going to win, someone else is required to lose. You're doing what you have to do, and that's that." He headed for the door. "Forget about everything and focus on what you have to do." Hudson gingerly touched her chin before leaving her alone.

Delma knew he was right. "The best interest of the child," she repeated to herself, while trying to settle down. There was no other purpose to be discussed or initiated. In this case, it just happened it was her own child, Keisha, who she was thinking about. And the best interest for her was to never know who her biological mother was and to make sure Trevelle went away quietly once and for all.

By the time she had settled with herself, Hudson was knocking on her door again.

"It's time."

"I'll be there in a minute." She picked up the paper with her statement typed out. She read the first sentence out loud, "In the case of *Venus Johnston-Parson versus Airic P. Fisher* regarding minor child Mya Fisher, the court has entered a decision." Her voice cracked at the start of the next sentence. Delma balled up the paper, crushing it to its smallest form before throwing it in the trash. She walked to the wood-paneled wall and stared at seemingly nothing until she reached out, sliding aside a small circular disk. She pressed her face against the hole. There they were, both sets of parents. Poor Mya was somewhere else without a clue her life was about to be changed forever.

"Father Lord, Jesus, give me strength." Delma straightened her robe, picked up her gavel, and headed out to make what would be her third most regretful decision, the one that could end her career, her relationships, and all things as she knew them.

53

Venus

"All rise."

The scattered group stood up while the judge settled into her wooden throne. She adjusted the bifocals at the rim of her nose before gazing over her captive audience. "Good morning. How's everybody doing?"

No one answered back, as if it were a rhetorical question. Jake and I continued standing, waiting for the magic word to be seated. Airic stood next to his lawyer. The swelling on his face had gone down, but the dark ring was still visible where he'd been hit the hardest. I craned my head around looking for Trevelle and met the eyes of our attorney who stood unassumingly behind us, ready to intervene at any given moment but discreet enough to not be a distraction. She winked and smiled for assurance. Trevelle stood a short distance away. I smelled her before I saw her from the corner of my eye, the thick well of heavy-handed perfume. The well-placed makeup and extended lashes couldn't mask the exhaustion around her tired eyes.

The clerk stood up and read off the names while gesturing to the empty tables in front. "Airic Fisher and Venus Parson go ahead and take your seats."

Jake and I both moved, assuming the position. I felt like we'd been sitting in the same spot of judgment for months, since the first night Airic called and said those debilitating words, *I want to see Mya. She's my daughter.*

"This decision was not easy for me," the judge started out slowly. She turned her attention directly to Airic. "To some of us, three years isn't much time at all. Most of us don't even remember what we were doing three years ago because usually it's the same thing we always do, busy moving from day to day, week to week, month to month. Birthdays, Christmas, New Year's, days we take for granted, assuming they will just keep coming.

"But for a child, this particular child, three years is a lifetime. I sometimes find myself wondering when and how adults become blind to the gift of a sunrise, sunset, then sunrise again. When do we begin assuming tomorrow will come, so we lumber around with no urgency, no goal of resolution, only continuation of the same?

"I'm guilty, no different than the rest of the world. Living in the same daily grind and struggle with no resolution, then comes the day when we shout 'Hallelujah,' better late than never. Right here, right now there's gonna be a change." The judge smiled and shook her head. "And just as quickly our moment of inspiration evaporates and we're right back to the same.

"Tomorrow," she whispered. "There's always tomorrow. But sometimes, Mr. Fisher, we have to admit that we waited too long, gave it too much thought and not enough action. And tomorrow becomes too late."

The judge turned her attention to my direction. Jake squeezed my hand under the table. "Mrs. Johnston-Parson, have you told Mya what's going on? Does she understand who Mr. Fisher is?"

My words were caught in my throat. "No." The word came out broken and scratched. "I mean, I said he was someone important to her, like a fairy godfather, but . . . I never told her." I inhaled, searching for the right answer. "I planned to tell her. I'm going to tell her," I said.

"Mr. Fisher," the judge seemed satisfied and had turned her attention back to Airic, "if you were Mrs. Johnston-Parson, how would you explain *you* to this child? What words would you use exactly?"

"Ahh, well." He shot a pleading glance to his lawyer, who couldn't help him.

"Go on, Mr. Fisher, just look me in the eye and pretend I'm three years old and my name is Mya. I've had a wonderful life so far with my mommy and my daddy. Today we're sitting at the park just feeding the ducks and you turn to me and say . . ."

"Sweetie," he started, before being interrupted.

"Little louder, Mr. Fisher."

Airic swallowed hard and adjusted his tie as he scooted closer to the microphone. Louder as requested, "Sweetie. Sweetheart." He stopped then started again. "Mya . . . I have to explain something to you. You know there are lots of little girls in the world with two daddies." He wiped the moistness building around his temples. "You are one of the lucky ones who gets to have two daddies."

"Wow, two daddies, I am lucky." The judge leaned forward, drawing every eye of anticipation. "It's such a perfect world, and I understand everything at three years old, but could you explain why I have two daddies? Can anyone be my daddy? Maybe I can have three or four daddies? Why not?"

A snicker or two floated forward. Airic shifted uncomfortably before trying to answer.

"No. Of course everyone can't be your daddy, your father . . . you have to be the father by birth. Jake, your dad, who you think is your dad, didn't make you. I made you, me and your mommy."

"You mean out of flour and sugar like the gingerbread man . . . how did you make me?"

"No, well, sort of just different ingredients, an egg from the mommy and a sperm from the daddy . . . and that's how babys are made."

More chuckles in unison escaped the onlookers, although I had to admit he was doing pretty good. I hadn't been able to think of an easy way to tell Mya or I would have done it.

"Well, isn't that special," the judge retorted. "Mr. Fisher, a three-year-old will not understand about eggs and sperm."

Mr. Young stood up. "May I interject? A child may not understand everything right now. In a few years—"

"Sit down, Mr. Young. Do not interrupt me. I'll tell you this, Mr. Fisher, doesn't matter how old a child is, she will never understand how or why someone ignored them, refused to be in their life when they had the chance. Doesn't matter if they're two, twenty, or sixty-five, doesn't make a difference. The pain and consequence of feeling abandoned will always be there. I'd like to read the definition to you from the dictionary, Mr. Fisher. To abandon: 'to leave completely and finally. To give up control of. To relinquish. To banish.'"

"Excuse me, Judge Hawkins." Mr. Young stood up again. "This isn't a moral trial. We are addressing a father's rights. Doesn't matter if he stayed away three years or ten. He has a right to be a father to his child. He never signed away his parental rights." He cut his eyes in my direction. "Even though someone tried to coerce my client into doing so."

"Mr. Young, I'll let you know when I'm finished. I've only started with the verb. I've got the noun, the adjective, adverb. Hell, I'm just getting started. 'Abandoned,'" she roared. "'Forsaken or deserted. Utterly lacking in moral restraints.' Have you any idea how it feels to be abandoned, Mr. Fisher? To be left for dead. To have someone turn their back and walk away without a thought or hesitation?"

Judge Hawkins stood up and pointed seemingly at Airic until realizing the visual trail landed behind him where his wife sat. "Abandonment. Leaving a newborn child left for dead in the backseat of her pimp's car."

The deafening silence in the courtroom made time stand still. No one scratched, blinked, or breathed. The satisfied smirk on Trevelle's face quickly went blank with confusion.

The clerk approached the bench, whispering the judge's name. "Delma, take a recess." He turned toward the spellbound audience.

"Fifteen minute recess." His hand fumbled for the gavel, finally grabbing the handle and clumsily banging it on the wood base. "Adjourned. Recess."

"I don't need a recess."

The clerk spoke in panicked whispers. "Shh, Delma. Just ten minutes. Take a recess, please."

Everyone had the same confusion. The judge had lost her marbles. I leaned over and took in Trevelle staring straight ahead as if her mind had left her body.

54

Delma

"Order. Order in this courtroom. This is my courtroom and I'm not finished yet." A sigh of regret escaped her lips. "As much as I know you were wrong, Mr. Fisher, you have every right to be a father to your daughter. If there's one thing I've learned, you don't want her to grow up with that tiny little festering scar on her heart where she feels unworthy, unloved. Even after you've done everything right. Because that's what children feel, deep inside, when they know there's a parent out there who didn't try, who didn't step up to the plate. You deserve a second chance. Sometimes we all do." The judge's gavel hit the wood block again. "I'm entering a judgment for equal parental rights. As for physical custody, Mr. Fisher will have six months, and Mrs. Johnston, you will have six months."

The room went deathly silent.

"Judge." Hudson lifted a hand, waving a piece of paper.

"No, I'm fine. At this time I ask for all parents to stand."

"Judge Hawkins, this is urgent." Hudson shoved the paper in front of her eyes.

Delma blinked several times, not sure what she was looking at. "DNA Test Result," it read. She scanned down to see the parties' names. *What?*

Jake Parson 99% probability of biological parenthood.
Airic Fisher .03% probability of biological parenthood.

She read the results multiple times, scanning the page up and down waiting for the information to magically change. "What in the world is this?"

"The results to the DNA test just arrived, Judge Hawkins."

"I can see that, Hudson. Order in this courtroom," Delma demanded. "I'm sorry . . . it seems we have a problem." The paper shook in her hands. She looked at Hudson, who gave her a nod. *Read it*, he mouthed.

She read the results out loud. "Mr. Fisher, it appears you aren't the child's biological father."

"That's the most ridiculous thing I've heard. Judge, there's been a mistake. I am Mya's father. There's not a shred of doubt in my mind. There's been a mix-up." Airic pointed toward Jake. "That man is a criminal. He probably paid someone to change the results. This is ridiculous. Mya *is* my child."

"Mr. Fisher, at this time I have no choice but to enter this paternity test into the record. You have every right to pursue legal action." It took every ounce of energy in her body to stand, then she sank back down, feeling her knees buckle.

Hudson was fast at her side helping her to her feet. He leaned past her and spoke into the microphone. "Judge Hawkins will have to reschedule the rest of you."

There were a few moans of disappointment, mostly for the fireworks having ended.

"I'm fine." Delma pulled away from Hudson's grip and found herself staring at Trevelle Doval. She thought she'd see satisfaction on the woman's face. Instead she looked as if she'd seen a ghost. Trevelle's lips moved slightly. Delma followed her line of vision to Judge Lewis, standing in the center aisle. He hadn't been there the entire time, she was sure . . . at least she'd hoped. He stood watching the disorder with a disappointed expression. Delma shoved past Hudson, pushing through the door so hard it slammed against the wall.

❧

"They're not going to get away with this. Someone's going to jail for this." Airic was livid. His face turned red-hot as if he'd been scorched in the sun all day long.

"All we need to do is file for an immediate appeal. We'll have a new DNA test. Don't worry, we'll have this resolved in no time."

"It should be resolved now. My wife was right about you. You're an imbecile. There's no regulation of these tests?" he screeched. "You just let anyone conduct a DNA test, then have no control over how the results are reported?"

The lawyer was taken aback by Airic's uncharacteristically rude outburst. "Please, rest assured a new test will be ordered," Mr. Young said with mild contempt.

"Why should I have to start this process all over? What am I paying you for?"

"You've made a valid point, Mr. Fisher. If you're going to bark around insults and orders, you should have the decency to have paid in full. I have not received a check for services rendered."

"Move, get out of my way. Pay you for what . . . doing nothing?" He extended a hand to his wife who only sat still as if traumatized. He put his hand on her shoulder. "I'm sorry for all of this. I'm sorry you had to go through any of this."

"There was a man standing there, did you see him?" Trevelle said when she finally spoke. "Right there, he was right there."

Venus

I was still unable to move from the very spot I'd heard the judge say Mya was not Airic's child. Or, more to the point, Mya was Jake's child. I kept shaking my head waiting for the fog to clear, waiting for someone to tap me on the shoulder.

"Babe, come on. We'll work it all out later." Jake was talking close to my ear. Georgina was on the opposite side of me, giving my elbow a soft lift up.

"How . . . when . . . ?"

"Come on, upsy daisy." Georgina focused on the task at hand of helping me to my feet.

"You're not going to get away with this," Airic yelled from the other side of the room. The bailiff was lifting his arms to keep peace between us. Thank goodness. I had a feeling if Airic had come anywhere near Jake, he would make the ex-boxer's beatdown look mild in comparison.

"Sir, go, move along," the bailiff said to Airic.

We moved out in a small huddle with me in the center. I couldn't help myself from looking back, although it was Trevelle who'd caught my eye. She continued to stare forward like she was in a trance, completely oblivious to the breakdown of her husband.

"Why can't anyone hear me?" Airic shouted. "They fixed the results."

Raising Hell

"She did this, first-class evil." Delma paced, talking to Hudson. "How? How in the world did she get ahold of DNA records?"

"Maybe she didn't. What if the test is correct and the child really isn't his?"

Delma gave it a moment's thought before a knock at the door signaled the answer would have to wait.

"Judge, I can explain," Delma said. "I'm so sorry you had to witness that outburst. I've been under so much pressure." She'd seen Judge Lewis come into the courtroom during the melee. She'd tried to get herself under control, but the damage had already been done.

"Can I talk to you alone?" Judge Lewis gave a no-offense smile to Hudson.

"I'll be out here, if you need me." He left and closed the door.

Judge Lewis sat down and looked as if the bad news was even too much for him to bear.

"I understand," Delma started in. "Don't worry about what you have to say. I brought it on myself and I completely understand."

"You did such a fine job raising her," he said.

"Raising who?"

"I expected you would have told her by now." He closed his eyes and rubbed the exhaustion away with a thumb and forefinger. "What's it going to take?"

"I don't understand." Delma said. "I've had a full day if you get my meaning, judge. So I'd appreciate you telling me exactly what you came to say."

"I thought if I put her in your courtroom, you'd be grateful for the opportunity to tell her that her daughter was still alive. I thought there couldn't have been a better alignment of stars, and you still wouldn't tell her."

Delma plopped down in her chair, stunned. "It was you . . . all this time. The phone calls, the note. How did you know?"

"Something you said out there really touched me, Delma. When you said there'd always be a festering scar on a child's heart because there was a parent out there who didn't step up. You're right. And I know now what I have to do. What I should've done a long time ago." He pulled out a folded piece of paper, a letter thick enough to be a will and testament. "I wrote this a long time ago. I wanted to give it to you but there was never a time when I didn't fear it would end my career, my life, my marriage. Keisha is my child," he said without blinking his sad dark gray eyes.

"You were the john that got that girl pregnant?"

"I wasn't a *john*, I was a cop who cared about her with all my heart. I wasn't able to save her. I never saved any of those girls, they always went right back out there. But I knew Velle was different and I tried to help her. I got her off the streets and moved her into the house with my family. When she had to leave, she fell apart and ended up back out there, pregnant."

"You didn't know she was pregnant?"

"I knew, but I couldn't take her back in and she wouldn't stay at any of the shelters." He shook his head.

"How did you know it was me, that I had the baby?" Delma asked.

"Velle called me and told me she'd had the baby. She told me about Cain. I picked her up and she showed me the car, and where the baby would have been had it still been there." He looked up at Delma. "After I got Velle back to a safe place, I went to the hospital and asked questions and found out it was a lady from the district attorney's office who brought her in. All the receptionist could remember was *D* . . . period. I checked and found only one first initial of *D* in the whole office and it was you. They said you'd taken a leave of absence. My only goal at the time was to find out everything you knew. I didn't want Velle to go to jail for killing that punk. She'd already been through so much."

Delma's mouth was hung open. He read the question on her mind. "I saw you come out of your house holding her like she was the most precious possession of your lifetime, and I just knew. I knew it was Velle's baby. I couldn't tell her any different. I couldn't tell her the baby was still alive. I couldn't tell anyone anything. If I told on you, I'd be telling on her, and myself, a white cop getting an underage black girl pregnant. I couldn't take that chance."

"Does she know you're here? Do you two have a relationship?"

"She doesn't know . . . or maybe she does but I haven't talked to her since I took her to a relative's house some twenty-five years ago.

"Read this, and then give it to Keisha. I've had it for a long time and I've not changed a word of it, so it's straight from the heart." He held it out but Delma only stared at the letter. "Please," he said. "Take it."

"No." Delma surprised herself. "No." She shook her head. "How do I know you're really her father? She was a whore, any number of men could be her father. Now you want me to say to my child, *This man . . . that you've met at picnics and work functions is really your daddy?* All those times you sat in front of my child and talked to her like a pure stranger, you want me to go to her and say he's really your father? It would break her heart."

"Delma, why keep hiding the truth?"

"Because I don't know what the truth is." Delma found herself up on her feet.

"I do . . ." The voice came from the opened door. "I know the truth." Trevelle Doval stood, blinking hurt and astonishment. "All this time you were right here," she said to Judge Lewis. "Right here and you never once tried to contact me."

Hudson was standing behind Trevelle with an uh-oh face. "You want me to call security?"

"No," Delma said, defeated. "I think it's time we all talked."

☙❧

The night Trevelle gave birth, Cain had beat her within an inch of her life.

"Oh God, it's coming. I have to get to the hospital." Trevelle felt the fluid pop and spurt between her legs. The warm liquid soaked through her panties and skirt then pooled on the dirty carpet.

"Yeah, right, I'll take you to the hospital," Cain said. "Get yo' ass up."

The blood running from her nose and lips, the bruising on her forehead, her eye swollen closed, those were the last things Cain wanted a doctor to see. He dragged her to her feet, helped her down the apartment stairs and to his car. He pulled her into the backseat of the bronze Cadillac that had lost its shine a long time ago. Ripped seats and trash littered the floor.

He spread the dirty towels he kept in the backseat. "Don't get no blood on my shit."

It was still dark outside. Darker than every night that came before. Blackness shrouded her mind. The only way to deal with the convulsions of pain ripping through her body was to shut down and let the darkness take over.

He drove slowly, making too many turns to nowhere.

"Where're you taking me? You have to take me to the hospital," she panted, doing her best to breathe through the contractions. The baby was coming hard and fast and she knew something was wrong.

"Shut the hell up . . . you think I'm walking in there with you all tore up?"

"Then drop me off. Just drop me off, Cain. Nobody'll see. Please, I won't say a word."

He didn't answer. The slow pace had a dizzying effect. More

turns like a merry-go-round. Every time she felt close to passing out the pain snapped her back into alertness.

"Then to my mama's house, please, Cain."

"Yo' mamma don't want nothing to do with you." He cracked up with a wheezing cough at the end. He'd been sick for the last few months with a bad hacking cough. The bones of his shoulders protruded from his shirt like a wire hanger. "She shacked up with Crazy J," he said. "They both strung out on rock. Where you been, girl? Just all out of touch." He turned slightly to make sure she was listening. "She can suck a mean dick. Guess it runs in the family."

What happened next was beyond her control. She reached for whatever she could grasp, searching with only her hands. The hard circular glass bottle rolled from underneath the seat. She gripped it and came up swinging. She hit him hard across the side of his head. The car swerved. "What the fuc—" He tried to fight and protect himself from the blows and lost control of the car. Even at the slowed pace the car hit the corner STOP sign like a truck rolling over it, then landed into another car parked on the side of the street.

She swung again and again, the sound of thickness slamming against his skull, then the wet slap as blood coated the bottle. "Don't you ever talk about my mama. Ever!" she screamed. She kept on screaming long after she'd stopped swinging. The contractions came like a freight train pushing through her insides. She leaned back against the seat with her legs propped up and pushed.

No one could hear her on that dark street. No one came to help a fifteen-year-old girl giving birth to her baby in the backseat of the bronze Cadillac that once felt like smooth velvet underneath her skin but at that moment bit into her backside like a bed of nails.

She pushed the baby out with her last bit of strength then passed out from sheer exhaustion. When she'd awakened, the last thing she remembered was being angry enough to kill. A miraculous moment of victory fluttered across her eyes when she saw Cain leaning forward on the steering wheel, unconscious or dead, she wasn't sure. And then she remembered the other accomplishment.

Her baby. She wailed with shock and fright when she saw the tiny mess of a thing, rigid but warm. No movement. Not a breath. This wasn't her baby, not the one she'd planned to love and cuddle. This wasn't the child she'd planned to show Kellogg and say, *You see, she's yours and mine.* This wasn't her child, sickly and covered with blood.

What else was she to do?

Her legs felt like broken sticks. She could barely stand but managed to get out of the car. Blood still trailed from the gash above her forehead. They hadn't gone far. Cain never intended to take her to the hospital and had merely circled the block. She was delirious. She saw the headlights coming toward her and hoped with all her heart it was Kellogg. But it wasn't.

Delma wiped the moistness away from her eyes. "Poignant," she said, holding on to her stance. "I still have no proof he's the father."

"I don't care about that," Trevelle said. "One thing we know for sure is that I'm her mother. And I will not go away," she said. "You took my child."

"You left her to die," Delma said, holding her own. She felt like the wagons had circled but she wasn't backing down. "I raised her. I'm her mother. You think the two of you can just waltz in here making claims. I spent every day of my life caring for that child, sacrificing my entire life while you, the millionaire evangelist, and you, Mr. Local Chief Justice, focused on no one but yourselves."

"If I had known she was alive . . ."

"What'd you think, she got up and walked off?"

"She thought she died, Delma. Why is that so hard to understand?"

Delma didn't know how to answer that without sounding like a mere pitiful child, but she said it anyway, "Because I don't want to understand. What's done is done. We all have something to lose here if this story comes out. All of us." She glared at Trevelle. "There's no statute of limitation on murder." She then turned the same look of disgust on Judge Lewis. "There's no statute of limitation on covering up a murder, either. You may have disposed of Cain's body, but I saw him with my own eyes and the man was dead."

Judge Lewis shook his head. "Delma, I expected better of you."

"Sorry to disappoint. Now get out." Her voice trembling. "Get out of my sight, both of you."

◎◎

"Well, this is a fine mess." Delma used the tissue Hudson brought her and blew. "Can I have a do-over?" She sniffed back the tears.

"I'm proud of you."

"You are?"

Hudson bounced his head in appreciation. "You're seriously the no guts no glory kind of girl. But what I'm proud of most, is you having the courage to tell Keisha the truth."

"I'm not. I can't, Hudson. Keisha will hate me for lying to her all this time."

He turned his back and stared out the window. "What you said about a parent making a child feel abandoned. I've always felt that way about my father leaving my mother, leaving me. This thing inside, of feeling lost and unloved." Hudson turned to face her. "I'm fifty-two years old, and if my father walked in here right now and told me he loved me and he was sorry, it would mean the world to me. Wouldn't even matter how much time passed."

Delma was quick on her feet, this time it was her handing him the tissue. "It's in all of us. No amount of healing ever makes it go away. We simply have to put it in its place."

"You're going to do the right thing." Hudson patted her hand. "For Keisha . . . no matter what kind of disappointment she feels, she'll be better for it."

Delma rested her head on Hudson's back, where she'd hugged him from behind. "I love you, Hudson."

He twisted around. "Okay, you wanna say that to my face?"

57

Venus

The sun rose and cast a silvery glint off the bedroom walls. Waking up had never felt sweeter. I'd slept for what seemed like the first time in months. Jake must've felt it, too. He lay still, sleeping by my side. I rolled over and kissed him on his cheek and his eyes fluttered but stayed closed. I got out of bed and tiptoed to Mya's room. I went to her bedside where she slept. I stood over her and then kneeled to give her a kiss. She turned to face me, only it wasn't Mya, it was Airic. "Good morning, Mommy," he said, wearing a wild mangy wig and a bow.

I screamed and fell backward, caught in Jake's arms.

"Babe, wake up." Jake was shaking me. He looked panicked. "You were struggling like you were drowning."

I blinked in confusion and looked around the room. "Mya," I said, jumping out of bed and rushing down the hall. I approached the door and opened it slowly, my heart thudding through my chest. Her back was facing me and I crept one step at a time, trying to ignore the feeling of déjà vu. I leaned over her and saw her angelic face. She smelled of vanilla and little girl sweetness. I kissed her softly and pressed my face against hers.

"Everything all right?" Jake whispered behind me.

I nodded and put my finger to his lips. I waved for him to follow me out. I took his hand and led him to our bedroom. He wasn't quite awake so my dream was at least partly correct. One of us had gotten some solid sleep. I sat on the edge of the bed. He joined me, and we sat side by side. I ran a hand from his head to his cheek down the front of his bare chest. I kissed him lightly. "I can't live with it, Jake. I can't live with a lie."

"You think I had something to do with that DNA test." It wasn't a question. He was stating the simple truth. Frustration clouded his face. "When are you going to trust me again, if ever?"

"Back when I asked you what happened to Byron Steeple . . . you wouldn't tell me. All you did was put me off by saying I didn't want to know. By the time you gave me the truth, I'd already formed my own opinion."

"I was too ashamed to tell you . . . you don't know what I saw, what I witnessed."

"I understand, I do. This time, I don't want to guess or worry myself to death because I don't have the answer. Was it Georgina? Did she pay someone?"

He shook his head, and cut his eyes away from me. His dark lashes closed and rested. He leaned back and stretched his muscular arms over his head. "What difference will it make? Trying to change the information on paper will never change the truth. You know it and I know it." He pulled me toward him.

How tempting it was to fall into the strength of his arms and be done with the conversation. But I knew the only way I'd stop seeing Airic in my nightmares was to address the issue head-on. "Tell me the truth."

"I had nothing to do with it," he said. "That's all the truth I know."

I rose up. He thought I was walking away, doing my usual run-away-angry thing. Instead I stood up and climbed on top of him, straddling him with my knees positioned over his arms. I leaned over and kissed him, tongue, lips, and all. "Guess I'll just have to beat it out of you," I said, tasting his smooth chin.

"My answer will still be the same," he said. "But I sure would like you to try." He held me tight until I couldn't move a muscle. "Listen to me, babe. Listen."

I realized at that moment I had no choice. He had my undivided attention.

"All I've ever wanted was for you to trust me again. To have a little faith in me. I know you lost the baby because you didn't know what to believe. You weren't sure who you were married to and it was eating you up inside. Trust me when I tell you, I'd never hurt you like that again. I had nothing to do with the test results. If Georgina made it happen, she didn't let me in on the fun, and that's all I have to say. You understand?"

I nodded my head up and down.

"But I wouldn't mind getting started on making some new DNA, mixing a little of yours and mine," he said, sliding his hands down my back. He pressed his mouth against my collarbone and trailed to my shoulder. My head spun with delight and relief. I understood what love meant between a husband and a wife, the act of coming to the rescue, again and again. It was the tiny promises that tomorrow will be all right and the reassurance that no matter what, we had each other. We'd made it through another storm. It was time to pull the boards off the doors and windows and let the sunshine in. We made love in the big Georgia mansion for the second time, and, yes, I was counting.

I had faith, something I couldn't ever remember having a whole lot of before. I had a fresh outlook, one that included picking up Ralph twice a week and taking him to the park myself. Maybe I couldn't adopt him just yet, but when it was time, he was going to know exactly who to call Mommy. It took a few days but I finally called Airic. I told him he could see Mya whenever he liked. If he wanted to try again to sue for custody, that would be his choice, his fight, not mine. I knew my heart and mind were in the right place. If I'd learned anything at all over the last few months, you had to believe you deserved some peace and joy to get it, and I was definitely ready for mine.

58

To Err Is Human

"Mommy," Keisha called out, searching the house in a panic.

Delma sat on the edge of her bed still wearing nightclothes, though the sun had rose and set again. She stayed quiet, staring down at the box in her hands. She'd come to this point in her life by a full bursting circle of flames. It was time.

"There you are. You had me worried to death not answering the phone. Hudson said you were taking a much-needed day off." Keisha sat beside Delma and kissed her on the cheek. "I knew something was wrong. Since when do you take a day off voluntarily?"

Delma faced her daughter. "I have something to give you. But first I have to tell you about your mother, the one who brought you into this world."

Keisha looked relieved and sorrowful at the same time. "You'll always be first in my life, Mommy."

Delma hugged her fiercely and kissed her daughter's cheek. "You'll always be first in mine."

Kristi Fontamillas

TRISHA R. THOMAS is an NAACP Image Award for Outstanding Literary Work finalist. She's a Literary Lion Award honoree by the King County Library System Foundation and was voted Best New Writer by the Black Writers Alliance. Her debut novel, *Nappily Ever After,* is now a Netflix movie. *O, The Oprah Magazine* featured her novels in "Books That Matter" for delving into the self-esteem of young women of color and the insurmountable expectations they face starting at an early age. She lives in California with her family where she continues to write the Nappily series.